Love
BEYOND THE
Footlights

Love

BEYOND THE

Footlights

ELIZABETH SHARLAND

iUniverse, Inc.
Bloomington

LOVE BEYOND THE FOOTLIGHTS

iUniverse books may be ordered through booksellers or by contacting:

iUniverse
1663 Liberty Drive
Bloomington, IN 47403
www.iuniverse.com
1-800-Authors (1-800-288-4677)

ISBN: 978-1-4759-2312-4 (sc)
ISBN: 978-1-4759-2313-1 (hc)
ISBN: 978-1-4759-2314-8 (ebk)

First published in Great Britain in 2002 as 'The Best Actress' by Barbican Press.

Reprinted and revised in the USA.

iUniverse rev. date: 05/12/2012

In memory of Gerald . . . .

Preface

PART 1

THIS NOVEL IS ABOUT NICOLE, a young British actress, whose story unfolds about her career and the choices she has to make. Many people have asked me to write about my own career so I thought it might be of interest to write a preface to this book, as mine went in a totally different direction, beginning with my arrival in London. as a music and drama student.

My parents wanted me to become a professional pianist and it wasn't until I saw the Hollywood film about the life story of Frederic Chopin, that I realized that I too wanted the same thing. I hadn't been practising with much enthusiasm. The film 'Song to Remember' starred Cornel Wilde as Chopin and Merle Oberon as Aurore Dudevant, with the nom de plume of George Sand. Jose Iturbi, played the music for the film. It was after seeing that movie I was motivated to seriously seek out a concert career.

We lived in Hobart in Tasmania, a long way from London. My parents went on a trip to England and unbeknownst to me, they enrolled me in the Guildhall School of Music and Drama for the following year. When they told me I was over the moon, I applied and won a scholarship to study there for two years . . . both piano and drama. I had played leads in the local Repertory Company, and as the Guildhall wanted you to study a second subject I chose theatre.

Arriving in London was overwhelming. The history, the colors, the shops, the whole place was so exhilarating. I arrived with a girlfriend and we walked everywhere. We had three weeks before the classes started at the Guildhall, and my parents had mapped out a schedule for travelling around England by the Greenline buses, to include visiting relatives who were scattered across the country.

We journeyed to Devon and Cornwall, up to Wales, Chester, Scotland, back down through Stratford-upon-Avon, Norfolk, Suffolk, staying at youth hostels, full of hope and energy.

Laurence Olivier, Vivien Leigh, Ralph Richardson, Edith Evans, Noel Coward. were all acting in the West End, and we had seen them in movies that had found their way to Tasmania. 'Gone With the Wind' 'Brief Encounter' 'Henry V' and many others. They were famous throughout the world because of their films. And to be able to see them in the flesh onstage was a very exciting event. As drama students they were our whole world. We would sometimes sleep overnight on the pavement to get seats for their new plays in the West End. Or sit on the little folding chairs that were placed in rows along the outside of the theatres for the queues that formed everyday. We would sit in the 'gods' and take notes.

The excitement and enthusiasm were unforgettable. Theirs was a whole world, that was glamorous, mysterious and so far out of our reach. We looked at the luxurious sets and costumes as if they were straight out of Hollywood or Mayfair. In those days, there were many 'living room' comedies playing, including plays of Noel Coward, and we were used to seeing sophisticated drawing-room sets, with the drinks trolley, behind the white sofa, centre stage, coffee tables, with silver cigarette lighters, and crystal ashtrays, wall sconces, and maybe a chandelier.

The actresses wore beautiful clothes, their feet tucked around their ankles showing off expensive shoes.

We were totally in awe when they were drinking martinis and putting cigarettes in long cigarette holders. Then of course, we discovered the more classical theatre. Our first Richard 111 played by Olivier, or John Gielgud at the Old Vic. I'd cross over Waterloo Bridge, my feet hardly touching the ground. The stars we'd seen on the stage, were as exciting as the ones over head.

Many Australians have told their stories of arriving and surviving in England. Clive James's book, 'Falling Towards England' is a timeless classic, and Dame Edna, Barry Humphries has written the definitive book, about where he came from, a Melbourne suburb, and his first arrival in England. I devoured them all, and still admire their comic touch dealing with the constant irritations, disappointments, and the shock of experiencing the still present British 'class' system. It was the first time I had been called a 'colonial' and many times was confused by some rather spiteful, it seemed to me, remarks. I quickly tried to rid myself of my Australian accent. As Rex Harrison said,

'Your accent absolutely classifies you and dismisses you as a colonial.' Of course it still exists and includes not only, Australians, New Zealanders, but Americans also. But that is another whole story to be told.

Every day I walked down to the Guildhall marvelling on how lucky I was to have this opportunity, At the end of two years, I gave my recital for the Guildhall judges to decide if they would award me my Licentiateship, LGSM. I had already received my Associateship in Australia.

I played a Bach Prelude and Fugue, the 32 Variations by Beethoven, the Schumann Sonata in G minor, and a Chopin Mazurka. Also the Variations on a Nursery Theme by Dohnanyi for piano and orchestra, which I played with the school orchestra. (Amazingly enough I just found them all played on Utube yesterday)

My tutor, Dennis Dance, had been very patient because I didn't have a piano at that time, so I had to get to the Guildhall early every day, to grab a practice piano, which you couldn't reserve. First come first served.

Each day, after classes, I would try to see one of the plays on either at the Old Vic or in the West End, and also attend any lectures and readings that were taking place that evening. I went to hear Peter Ustinov speak, John Gielgud, and many other stars give poetry readings. I was too shy to go up to them afterwards. Then there were the marvellous concerts at the Royal Festival Hall and many other venues

I was totally in awe of the Australian pianist, then world famous, named Eileen Joyce. She was regarded as one of the finest pianist of her day. We were fascinated to read that she changed her evening gown, at intermission, to suit the music she was about to play. I remember her playing in a pale blue satin gown, for a Grieg Concerto before changing to a deep green velvet for the second half of the concert for the Rachmaninoff. How glamorous! She was born in Tasmania, and before I left Hobart an old friend gave me a letter of introduction to her, but I was too shy to go backstage to give it to her. However little did I know how much it would help later on.

London was incredibly beautiful. We would try to get to Green Park, or Regent's Park most weekends. The little window boxes filled with flowers everywhere, and the huge baskets of flowers hanging outside most of the pubs. The flower market a Covent Garden and the chestnut trees in bloom, along the Embankment were glorious. But there was so much practising to do, each day for our teachers, and learning lines for our drama teachers. Monologues and plays which we were working on for the end of year presentations.

I kept a diary which I still have, and I am truly astonished at my daily schedule. 'Down at the Guildhall at 8.am to find a piano.' To save money, I didn't take a bus, but walked from Southampton Row, down the Kingsway, along Fleet St, down to John Carpenter street where the Guildhall School was in those days. I did this sometimes twice a day, there and back. Back to the hostel for supper of perhaps, sausages and chips, it was pretty awful, then back down to the Guildhall for evening classes and rehearsals.

My parents had put me on a budget and had helped pay for the two year course. I had no money left over, so I looked around to see if I could find extra income. I was determined to stay in London as long as possible, so I tried to cut the budget and only spend half of it. I remember reading years later, that Michael Caine, when a drama student, had to decide if he wanted to buy a half a pack of cigarettes, and walk into the West End . . . miles it seems, or spend the money taking a bus. He too, was broke. I would buy one of those hard rolls with a slice of cheese in them, for lunch and used to take the sugar from the cafeteria and mix it with hot water for a drink. Cheaper than tea.

One friend, a drama student, was a part time usher at the open air theatre in Regent's Park, and she told me one day, she was leaving, so maybe I would like the job. It was a way of seeing the plays for free, and also getting paid.

I got the job, so my days were even more hectic, as even though I didn't have to be there everyday, matinees and two evenings were enough, I read that I would be down at Guildhall at 8 am, back for dinner at the hostel and to the piano a girl friend had at our hostel, then up to Regent's Park at night, then learn lines afterward.

One day I received an invitation to Buckingham Palace for Afternoon Tea. It came out of the blue. Then I realized that when I first arrived I had registered with the Agent General's office at Tasmania House, which used to be in the Strand, and each year they were given invites for visiting Tasmanians, and I was chosen as one of them. I had nothing to wear. A girlfriend came to the rescue with an appropriate dress, hat and shoes. Again my diary says I went to the Guidhall that day, for classes, then down to Buckingham Palace, then out to Regents Patk for the evening performances. I just can't imagine how I could get around London to do all this. It was chaotic. I must have changed clothes somewhere. I remember thinking how much easier it would be if I could only sleep at the Guildhall then I would be on the spot next day, to find a practice piano. I thought of sleeping in the ancient theatre prop room one day on one of the folded canvas backdrops, but I was scared to, because there may have been mice in there. Probably were, if not ghosts. It was such a huge building, it would be very scary to be there alone. But I bet someone did it.

My cousin from Hobart who was in London too, had received the invitation. I remember we had taken a taxi to the Palace. A taxi!! What extravagance!. However the traffic was so bad we got out half way up the Mall, and walked the rest of the way. My borrowed shoes were hurting like mad, and the soles seem to be on fire. The Palace was gorgeous inside, all red carpeted hallways, red plush curtains, and gold trim. We went through the Bow Room outside to the Garden. Down came the rain. Fortunately there were two large marquees, and people crushed together under them. There were bowls of strawberries and cream, tiny sandwiches, little cakes, and biscuits. The Queen and Prince Philip came out, under an umbrella, but the crush was so great we only saw them from afar. How kind of them to invite us. Evidently there are three of four of these parties every year and it certainly was a highlight to write home about. No one even thought of taking photographs. I think it was forbidden anyway.

The race continued. Each day walking early down to the Guildhall, I practiced my monologues out loud as I walked. I didn't care if passers-by thought I was a mental case. My drama teacher, John Holgate was extremely kind and if he heard traces of my Australian accent he didn't mention it. It is rather an Australian Voice, that you can never really eradicate. Reams have been written about it.

Rain in Regent's Park almost wiped out that season at the Open Air theatre. Sometimes I would be grateful for rainy days, it gave me more time to catch up on other work.

Then one day, another friend said she knew her cousin, who was an usher at the Old Vic Theatre was leaving, and would I be interested in working there full time. Would I? It sounded great. I went for an interview and was grilled by the Front of House Manager, who was quite formidable.

She reminded me of what Lilian Baylis, the founder of the Old Vic could have been like. She gave me the two matinees of the week. Wednesday and Saturdays. I reluctantly gave up my job at Regent's Park. The Old Vic was much easier to get to, and it was just a walk across Waterloo Bridge and up the Kingsway to get back to the hostel. An even better perk was that in those days, the front of house staff, served an Afternoon Tea tray for patrons. If you ordered before the show began, you could have a tray with teapot, milk jug, sugar, cup and saucer and a plate with biscuits and a piece of fruitcake on it. How happy I was when we had to collect them, if someone hadn't touched their fruitcake. The ushers were all mostly older women, who seemed well fed, or weren't always hungry, so it was a treat to finish up with a piece of fruitcake. So long as they didn't catch me. Food was very important in those days, and it kept me going.

At the end of my first year at the Guildhall, I remember watching my first production of Die Fledermaus in the school theatre. Beforehand there was a reception which included strawberries and cream, cream cakes and sandwiches and wine. I felt ecstatic, totally ecstatic, watching the operetta afterwards. The food and wine making it unforgettably enjoyable. I think of that evening, whenever I hear that music.

Working at the Old Vic was a new world. Richard Burton and Claire Bloom were playing the leads. I watched Burton play Hamlet over 50 times, and still remember all his stage moves, intonations and delivery of the famous monologues. Claire played Ophelia and I was very envious of her for doing so. He was magnetic and all eyes were on him whenever he was onstage. The front of house staff were allowed to eat in the tiny cafeteria backstage between the matinee and evening performances, and we would go there, hoping to meet members of the cast, which we did except the leads, who stayed in their dressing rooms or went out for the break. Michael Hordern came down, and John Neville, and many of the other members. Richard Burton usually went out with Claire Bloom.

Michael Benthall was the director that season, and when I was working in the Dress Circle after the lights had gone down, he would sometimes come in, and stand next to me at the back of the house, and watch the play. He would smile and nod his head. George Devine would do the same thing, and I would be thrilled that they at least acknowledged me. They seem to be in a different world . . . they were so close but oh so far from reach.

At the Guildhall, it was graduation time, after two years, it was time to make some decisions. It was made clear to me by my piano teacher, that unless I had the money, or a backer, to give a debut recital at the Wigmore Hall to obtain some good newspaper reviews, and be seen, then a concert career would not likely happen. I knew my parents didn't have that kind of money, and I would never ask them for it even if they did, and I knew no one who could sponsor me. He was sorry that I hadn't thought ahead about this. So was I. But all that practicing did pay off. I have enjoyed playing all through the years. In fact, it was because I played so well, that I met and fell in love with a man who was to become my husband for 54 years. That comes later.

Feeling really down and depressed I decided to send my letter of introduction to the pianist Eileen Joyce and to try and ask her advice. Was it to be a music career or a life in the theatre? I was surprised to receive a note a week or so later, inviting me to have tea with her in her studio in Chelsea. How wonderful I was going to have tea with one of the most famous concert pianists in the world. As I walked up to the front door on the appointed day, I felt very nervous and shy. She opened the door, and showed me in. She was alone, in a very large room, with a grand piano in the centre. We sat by the window and she served tea. Mercifully she didn't ask me to play. We talked about her career, and she seemed pleased I had been to so many of her concerts. Then she proceeded to tell me just what her life had been like. She said that she still practiced evry days for hours, because, like a ballet dancer, you have to stay in shape, your fingers have to stay flexible and supple. That even though she was regarded as one of the world's best, it was a terrible drudgery and was a life that was very very narrow. She said there is no time to enjoy the many other things in life, and it is a life full of sacrifices. She ended up by saying that if I could possibly find some other career, then to grab it with both hands. Maybe it was a bad day for her, maybe she was tired or discouraged, but I was very grateful that she had confided in me about her career. It was hard to believe, but then when you think about the discipline needed, I wondered if I had it, and I wondered if I was willing to give up so much of life to do what she had done. Besides I knew I didn't have that talent of being able to memorize easily. I knew some musicians who could do this easily. She also said that concert hall recitals were on their way out. The recording studios had taken over, and now you could hear the greatest pianists in your own home. No rustling of sweet wrappers, or chocolates, no coughing, no huge expense to buy seats.

Walking home after that afternoon was unforgettable. I knew that that particular dream the one I had for so long would not come true. I'd always be able to play the piano, but it was no longer a matter of a discussion with regards to a professional career unless I wanted to teach. I didn't want to teach.

Ten years of work, hours of practicing, the last frantic two years of training the whole Guildhall course were suddenly swept away, quite quickly. Almost like a death. It had gone. The dream was over. I felt devastated, but at the same time relieved. I hoped that I could survive in the theatre.

After the final term was finished, both music and drama, and we had presented our drama workshop for various agents and invited casting people we all graduated from the Guildhall. I joined many hundred of hopeful actors, writing letters, spending large sums of money on having photographs taken, résumes printed, buying stamps and envelopes and sending them off to all the theatre companies across England. Nothing happened. I waited to hear from any of them. Nothing. Week after week we would all buy "The Stage" the theatrical newspaper and comb the want ads looking for jobs. Nothing. I kept my job at the Old Vic and kept asking when they would be having auditions. There were none coming up in the near future. Then one day, after walking home in the pouring rain, I received a letter from a producer of the Felixstowe Repertory Company offering me a position of Assistant Stage Manager known in the business as an ASM and playing bit parts as cast. They wanted me to start next Monday! I couldn't believe it. Without even an interview? It sounded too good to be true. I phoned them, and spoke with Margaret, the director's wife, who said she would meet me at the station when she knew what time train I would be on, the following Sunday night. I could stay with them in the boarding house not far from the theatre. I couldn't believe my luck. I gave notice at the hostel and very reluctantly gave up the job at the Old Vic. As I walked down Waterloo Road, and looked back at the building, I said to myself that I had to leave it, to move on, that one day I hoped to be back there. It seemed my last hope of having any of my dreams come true and I was walking away from it. But I had a job and it was not as an usher.

Part Two

I was met at the train by both the producer and his wife. They were so kind carrying my suitcases, and driving me to the boarding house. In those days you were expected to take your own stage wardrobe with you when you went into Rep. Men had to have evening clothes, and suits, sports jackets, the lot, because the wardrobe department didn't usually supply them. So my two large cases were rather heavy with clothes of all sorts. My room was at the top of the stairs in a large house on a long tree-lined street a few blocks from the theatre. As we sat having a cup of tea, in the communal dining room, they interviewed me and had my photo and résumé on the table in front of them. Later on I asked them why they had chosen me out of all the dozens of applicants they must have had and they laughingly told me what had happened.

'We received over 200 applications, photos and résumés, we chose one of them and she accepted. She was to have started last week. We tore up the all the other photos and threw them out. There were far too many to return them all. Then last Wednesday she phoned and cancelled saying she had another better paying job, she was sorry but she wouldn't be joining us. We were really stuck, because the last girl was leaving on Saturday and we knew we had to have an ASM for this week's show. Then in the next mail, your photo and résumé arrived. I guess you had sent it out a week later than the others."

"Yes, and I thought it would be a waste of time because you would have already chosen someone, but I bought The Stage late that week.". Such is life. It didn't make me feel that my accomplishments had meant anything at all, just that it was a stroke of luck. Talent had nothing to do with it.

Each week the company presented a new play. We would have Mondays off, to learn lines for the new play. We then rehearsed from Tuesday onwards, during the day, then playing the current play in the evening. We'd help strike the set on Saturday night, so that the set designer could start on the new set on Sunday. Usually we'd send out for fish and chips after the curtain went down, to keep us fortified for clearing the stage of the furniture, and taking down the set if necessary.

This is not the time to go into the workings of a weekly Rep company. Any actor who has done it, never forgets those times. We had a built in audience. Mostly people who either walked or came by coach from far and wide, as our nearest competitor was the Ipswich Rep.

Each week I'd send off letters for auditions for more well known companies, and especially for companies nearer London. If necessary I'd take the train on a Monday, learning lines in the carriage for tomorrow's rehearsal and to attend an audition somewhere. Then one day a card came from the Old Vic announcing forthcoming auditions! I stared at the card and my heart pounded and I felt dizzy with excitement. Of course I had to have time off to get down to London.

The day came, I had to get up at 5 am in a freezing room, in the dark. We had been very late the night before, and I felt totally exhausted. I wondered was it all worth it. It was so dark and cold, it was difficult to get up the enthusiasm for what was ahead. I thought of all the effort Robert Helpmann must experienced to get ahead, and that spurred me on.

When I walked onstage at the Old Vic, the theatre was dark, except for a light on a desk, half way back in the stalls. I heard a voice speak to me. It was Michael Benthall and he recognized me.

'Hullo, how are you? Where have you been?"

I was so nervous, I really didn't know what to answer. Should I mention the Felixstowe Rep? I took a chance.

"I have been working in Rep."

Thanks goodness he didn't ask which one. Just in case he'd never heard of it.

He then said, "Why do you want to come back to London?"

I was floored. What kind of question was that? Every actor wants to be in London, every actor that I knew of, wanted to be with the Old Vic.

I lamely answered. "Because I want to act with the Old Vic." I was tempted to add, you must know that.

I did my two audition pieces, and he didn't stop me or interrupt.

"Thank you, thank you for coming. We'll be in touch." he said afterwards.

I walked to Waterloo Station in a daze. How did I do? What did he think? Who knows. I had no idea.

I passed about at least a hundred actors lined up outside the stage door, waiting their turn.

I caught the train back to Felixstowe.

In those days, the job of the ASM was to be the first person at the theatre each morning. To open up and put the kettle on for morning tea, in time for the other actor's arrival at 10.am. Turn the rehearsal lights on, the heat on if there was any, and generally clean up. You were also expected to sort out the mail that had been pushed through under the backstage door. One morning after putting on the kettle, I started to sort the mail, and there was a small buff colored envelope for me. Another bill I thought. I was wrong. It was a note from the Old Vic. From memory, it read something like the following . . . Dear Miss Sharland,. Thank you for coming for the auditions. We would like to offer you a place in the company for the Australian Tour with Katharine Hepburn and Robert Helpmann heading the company, playing as cast in three Shakespeare productions, for six months. The salary would be 20 pounds a week. (I was getting two pounds fifty at that time.) Please reply at your earliest convenience, so we can make the necessary arrangements . . . . or something like that. I caught my breath, and stared at the letter. I was in shock. My eyes blurred over with tears of joy, as I re read the note. It had the Old Vic letterhead on the top, so I knew it couldn't be a joke, but I was absolutely staggered. I sat down and the kettle boiled over. The director arrived alone, shortly afterwards and found me in tears.

He was concerned and said.

"Whatever is the matter?" I handed him the note.

Reading it, he began to smile, and then afterwards gave me a big hug.

"Congratulations darling. You deserve it."

Whether he really thought so I have no idea. But he was kind.

I felt such a fool. I had to leave the building before the others came and saw my red face. I felt they would laugh at me. I went for a long walk, waiting till they had finished their tea, had been told the news, and were into the rehearsal before I went back. I had an hour or so, to collect myself before the break. Everyone was happy for me and I said I hated to leave them all, which was only partly true.

I left two weeks later and went to London for the costume fittings and rehearsals. Our tour was to open in Sydney a few weeks later. We played in Sydney, Brisbane, Melbourne, Adelaide and Perth, but unfortunately not in Hobart. My mother came to the opening in Sydney.

During those six months I learnt so much about the profession. The different audiences, their reactions varying each night, the constant rehearsing for the understudies. I was understudying as well, and the whole routine, of keeping yourself fresh for each performance. The routine of each week and the arrival in each new city was soon began to pall,. the accomodations, the parties, the gossip, the constant contact with your fellow players beame second nature. People went crazy for Kate and Robert, they were photographed everywhere together. It was the first time is 25 years that Robert had returned to Australia during which time he had become famous as the ballet partner for Margot Fonteyn at Covent Garden and gone on to make the films, "The Red Shoes" and "The Tales of Hoffman." I would often stand beside him in the wings, and he would be doing exercises at the barre in costume as he waited for his entrance. He was in a world of his own. It was amazing to watch him and know how he had played the lead in all those most famous ballets, onstage at the Royal Opera House. He had worked with Sir Frederic Ashton and all the great dancers and choreographers in the world of ballet. Kate stayed mostly in her dressing room before her entrances as she always had the closest one to the stage.

During the six months of touring, I had plenty of time to observe my fellow actors and saw just how much they missed their families. They couldn't wait to get back home to England. At least two of them, had decided to leave the theatrical life, and take up a different career. I began to wonder if I had made the right decision too. It was the tediousness of repeating the same lines every night, night after night,and the fact that the creative process is all done actually in the rehearsal room. The final production stays the same, and you repeat that, whether it be for six weeks, or six months, over and over again. Here I was acting in one of the most famous theatre companies in the entire world, and I was becoming bored. I couldn't believe that it was happening. I supposed making films might be more creative, and at least the process didn't go on for so long.

But all this was going to change. At the end of the six months, after playing in Perth, we all boarded a ship to sail from Fremantle, back to London. In those days the voyage took 28 days.

I shared a cabin with the youngest actress in the company, and we were delighted to have a sea voyage that would take us to Colombo, Aden, Port Said, Naples, Marseilles Gibraltar and Southampton.

On board I met the Junior Doctor who was from Dublin. He looked incredibly handsome in his ship's uniform. He had just qualified as a doctor, he was working his way around the world, before leaving to study to be a psychiatrist in the States when he got back. There were dozens of pretty young Australian women on board and they were all looking for young men, preferably Officers to dance with in the evenings. I was playing Chopin in the passengers lounge one afternoon, and this doctor came through the room, and heard me. He stopped and came over to the piano. He smiled as I played and said that he played the same Waltz. It turned out he had won a Chopin competition at University, but he wasn't allowed to take my place at the piano. He was in uniform after all. I played more, and I think that is when the chemistry kicked in. We were inseparable after that, when he was not working. I think we would never have met if he hadn't heard me play. At least my music stood me in good stead in landing the most eligible bachelor on board!

He was off duty when we were in port, so he would take me ashore for drinks or dinner. By the time we arrived back in England, we had fallen in love and he asked me to marry him. I was head over heels in love. I just couldn't see how acting was more important than the career in medicine, saving lives and caring for the sick. I had to make a choice. Besides, maybe there would be acting work in America.

I made my decision and later on we were married. I went to the States with him. Now, after many years of marriage, I've just lost him. So I dedicate this story to him.

Chapter One

I COULDN'T BELIEVE MY LUCK. I had met Michael at a party at the
Cannes Film Festival two years previously and we hit it off immediately.
I found out he was from an old English aristocratic family who had a
huge country estate and he was worth millions. He produced movies as
a hobby and was presenting one at the Cannes Festival, which was well
received. When I arrived at the party, I looked across to see a very tall
elegant man who had the bluest eyes I've ever seen, soft blond hair and
strikingly handsome—like a young Peter O'Toole. When I asked the
person beside me who this man was, I was told he was the host. It was
one of those magical evenings you never forget and one which you will
probably comfort yourself with in your old age. Like the opening night
of a very successful play, when you are playing the lead, a new door opens
and your life suddenly brings unexpected happiness.

I still can't fathom out why he was attracted to me; after all, I was no
raving beauty. My height was only five-foot-five but I did try to make
most of what I'd been given. My blond hair was cut short in a bob and
people often said I looked like a young Bette Davis.

When I think back to our first meeting and all that has happened
since I still can't understand what happened. It was instant attraction.
I was in Cannes to promote my first film, which had been rather badly
received—not because it was a bad film but because it hadn't been
promoted properly. Years before I had been in Cannes with a journalist,
just fooling about sight-seeing at the Festival.

Now here I was in Cannes again and I had just won an Oscar for Best
Actress and I had just lost Michael.

How could I have been so stupid to leave Michael alone in London thinking I could go off and make movies in California without losing him? He actually meant more to me than my career although I didn't seem to understand this at the time. He was rich, very rich, handsome and available. When he was not producing films he wrote screenplays, and liked to call himself an investigative journalist too. He wore three different hats every day, and I adored him. I had always dreamed of winning an Oscar, ever since reading about the Academy Awards, and always keeping the dream alive through drama school, depression, boredom and bad weather.

People's smiles and congratulations seemed to turn into a kind of Fellini-type nightmare. I felt as if they were all smiling at my loss, at my shock and distress. If only they knew what I was really feeling.

It was total despair. I thought of all the clichés I'd heard in songs, but it was suddenly true. "I can't live without you," I thought to myself. "What is life without you?" Money and fame now suddenly didn't seem to matter any more.

Like some nominee at the Awards being asked to sit beside a dying father instead of accepting an Oscar. Hollywood seemed so unreal. Designers, PR firms, the media blowing it up out of all proportion until you begin to believe it all. I felt like an empty shell. I needed nourishment immediately. If I had stayed in the theatre there would have been far more of it. You never feel empty when playing Shakespeare to a live audience. It's almost a totally different acting world where the actor is giving part of his soul to his art and that hardly ever happens on screen.

I thought back to when I had finished my last film and tried to search for the moment when things had begun to go wrong. It was three months ago. I remember it vividly as I had just been nominated for the Award.

Arriving at Heathrow in the rain, I grabbed a taxi and went straight to our flat. He was not home but came in shortly afterwards with a bottle of champagne. We laughed, we hugged each other and ended up in bed before any champagne was touched.

"You will come to LA with me for the Awards ceremony, won't you, darling?" I asked him. He laughed "Of course I will, I wouldn't miss that shindig for anything." He got up, put on his robe, went to the kitchen to get more wine.

"If only I'd known, back in drama school, that this was going to happen," I said, lying back on the pillow.

"You wouldn't have worked so hard if you had known, so therefore it would never have happened." He put down his glass and kissed me on the cheek.

"All those freezing rehearsal rooms, those wet grey Sunday afternoons when you had to learn lines for the next session. You know, sometimes energy and enthusiasm are severely tested by the lack of creature comforts. I never felt warm when I was a student, and it was awful when you were supposed to be swept away by some emotion and your woolly underwear was making your skin itch."

"My poor Nicole, you should have been born in California." He laughed as he kicked off the quilt.

"I think Sunday afternoons spent alone in a provincial town must be some of the most depressing experiences ever. Manchester, for example. The only thing is to sleep through it."

"Darling, I know you're being nostalgic, it's the champagne, but let's have some happy nostalgia, shall we? How about since we've been living together? Sunday afternoons haven't been all bad, have they?"

"You're right, I apologise. They haven't even bothered me at all. It just shows you, if you are with the right person, time flies. I've been talking about me all the time, tell me what you've been doing."

"The story about that Mafia chap is going to be big. I submitted an article about him last week, but I don't know if they are going to print it or not."

"Won't it be dangerous if they do?"

"Not really, they won't print my name, I've asked them not to."

"Let's get away somewhere soon," I said, with a sudden premonition that something dreadful might happen to him. He was too well known in the Mafia world because he had been writing about the London gangsters and their stories for years. His screenplays were all about them.

"Where would you like to go?" he said, reaching for the champagne bottle again.

"When are we going to Capri? When are you going to show me that little place you have there? I'm so curious, it sounds so romantic. You never seem to use it now."

"Well, yes, we could go there."

"You always say that, but we never go. I know we've been too busy up till now, but it does sound divine. I can imagine a white sun-drenched stone cottage, covered with vivid coloured flowery vines, cobblestones, perfumed air with fabulous views of the Med and the glittering water far below."

"Yes, it is exactly like that, I suppose. When I got it I thought I'd stay there and work for years in the shadow of Graham Greene. The place is a haven, no telephones, no computers, only solitude, perfect for writing. You'll love it, I know."

"When can we go?"

"We'll wait till the Academy Awards are over, then we'll go before your next film offer comes up."

"It's a lovely thing to look forward to, but the question remains, why did you ever leave there anyway?"

"I was getting rock fever. You know what they say about living on an island. It's as simple as that. Now we both deserve a break."

"I bet Sunday afternoons aren't boring over there." I laughed, tipping out the final bit of champagne left in the bottle.

We were at some kind of pinnacle in our careers. I must write all this down in my journal. It was getting dark, so I got up to turn on some lights.

"Pity we don't have a fireplace. I feel I'd like a cosy fire and roasting chestnuts."

The phone rang shattering our love-nest peace. When Michael answered it, my antennae went wild. He was using a new tone of voice that I had never heard before. It was not my Michael speaking. First of all, it was all in monosyllables: "Yes—no—yes—yes—I'll see—yes . . ."

"What was that all about?" I asked.

He looked ashen. There was a beat before he spoke. "Oh, just some complication about my article. They want me to change a lot of it, damn them!"

I wanted to say that he didn't usually react in such a manner, but I decided not to dwell on the matter, his mood was definitely not inviting questions; nevertheless it worried me. Why such a reaction? I wanted to feel his arms around me again, so I wasn't going to continue questioning him.

Lying in bed after we had made love again, I turned on my side and watched him sleeping. I memorised his profile; for some reason I felt as if I was in danger. Was he being unfaithful to me? Was this the last time I would lie beside him looking at his face? Was it just the jetlag? Just an anxiety attack, making me imagine danger where there was none?

In the little time I had known him I had seen him lie to other people, I wondered whether, if he could lie to them, he could lie to me.

The next morning Steve called me with an offer I couldn't refuse. I had been tested for another film ages ago and finally they had decided on me for the role.

"But I just got back here, Steve."

"Well don't unpack your bags, sweetheart."

"I already have."

"Do you want the film or not?"

"Of course." I said, staring out the window at the rain. I had no time to ruminate about going or not going.

I was slightly hurt at Michael's reaction when I told him that Steve had got me another film.

"Darling, that's marvellous, when are you going?"

"They want me there by Monday. It looks like I'll be there up for the Academy Awards, as they're doing most of the shooting in LA."

I wanted to hear him say that he didn't want me to go, that he would miss me too much, that he had arranged for us to go to Capri. But he kept saying how brilliant I was to get another movie so quickly. He really was excited about my leaving.

⊷⊶

Two months later: I am here but Michael is not. It's the day of the Academy Awards. During the past few weeks working on the new film it had been extremely difficult to concentrate, as I had this premonition that something strange was going on back home. Michael was never home. Steve is on his way here to the theatre, he was the one who told me that Michael had missed his flight connection from New York. My cell phone has been switched off while I slept this afternoon, so I haven't yet spoken to him. When I got up for a shower, got dressed, Peggy phoned and told me the news.

"Darling, don't believe it. Michael didn't miss the plane connection, he's still here in London. I went round to your flat, the desk man let me have the key, as instructed by you. Sweetheart, he's gone! There was an envelope addressed to you on the hall table. As it wasn't sealed I opened it."

In a split second I knew exactly the shape and size of that envelope—it was one of his cream heavy bond ones from a set I had given him. What fate is in an envelope? From the old-fashioned ones bordered in black to announce a death, to a perfumed blue from a lover, or one with see-through cellophane, usually a bill, sometimes a stiff parchment one containing an invitation, to one covered with scribblings, music or a grocery list on the back, you remember the ones that changed your life, or rather the contents of them. For people who live abroad the blue air-letter will be deeply entrenched in their memories.

"He's met someone else, it seems. I guess he didn't want to talk to you."

"Oh please, he just left a message with Steve that he'd missed his connection."

"Maybe he was planning to go or maybe he wasn't planning it at all."

"No, Peggy, I can't believe it."

"He didn't even go to the airport. His note says that he moved in with someone else. All his things have gone too. I hate to have to tell you all this now, but honestly he won't be there."

I phoned Steve with the news and asked him to sit with me. I couldn't believe that Michael had lied to me.

It was time to get dressed even though it was so early. I was shaking with shock. What will everyone think? Total concentration was needed to stop my shaking. I took a shot of whisky, which helped, then a valium. The limo was due in thirty minutes. There was not time to waste, as I lifted out the jewellery I was expected to wear. Peggy should have been with me.

Keep concentrating, be alert. Just another small shot.

It's the Oscars! Los Angeles, stomach cramps, jagged nerves, "who can you trust?" paranoia.

I am here! The auditorium is full. The Academy Awards are about to begin, the crowd has all taken their seats and there is a charge of electricity in the air. The lights and cameras are on, it is only a matter of minutes. A well-known designer has given me a pale pink silk dress to wear.

Arriving at the Awards was truly unique, all the directors, actors, designers coming together, all being interviewed as they walked down the red carpet. I was appalled to see how young most of the actresses were, and they all looked like skeletons! Except for their busts. Where were all the mature actresses? There were hardly any I could see. Most of them were already seated, I expect they came early to avoid the huge seething masses pushing to get in. They knew the ropes. But the younger actresses looked weird; their gowns were lovely, but their hair looked as if they had just got out of bed. I can't stand my hair hanging over my eyes. It gives me a headache, even just a small strand, so how do these girls cope? Beats me.

I suddenly thought that I had misjudged everyone. Looking at all the actors crowding into the auditorium, seeing their expectation, their excitement, their glamour, I felt totally lost.

The role I had played, the role I had been nominated for, was about the loyalty and deep love of a woman for a man, a classic love story as powerful as *Romeo and Juliet*. Before beginning the film, I had researched all the great love stories in literature. I believed Michael felt the same kind of loyalty when writing the screenplay even though he hadn't been nominated. Now I felt as if I had been totally misguided. If you are a successful actor your work must come first, personal relationships come second; it was blindingly clear I was some kind of idiot ever to think anything else. No actor ever gives up a good part just because of a wife's or lover's well-being. They know that this is their life's work. I had believed in the role so deeply that it was a tremendous shock to think that I had been so swept away by a falsehood. It was a betrayal of everything I had put into the role. I felt like a twelve-year-old in an auditorium full of adults. Everyone else had grown up a long time ago. The passion that Juliet had felt for Romeo was in Shakespeare's day. After all, it had nothing to do with grown-ups. Ask any actor.

I am sitting in the aisle seat now, but it is not how I thought it would be. I can't focus—I can't enjoy it like I thought I would. Concentrate. Feel the emotion running through the body and relax. Relax, breathe. Why ruin what is to be a memorable night? Breathe, you idiot, or you are going to pass out. I can feel the cold sweat running down my back. My knuckles and neck ached with tension. My stomach churned.

The Oscar goes to Nicole Bennett! I never remembered how I got up to the stage. The lights blinded me. I remembered to thank everyone and got off the stage without falling down.

All during this horrendous captivity, back in my seat, I knew that the man I was desperately in love with was right at this very moment having sex, or making love (always more painful to imagine), to another woman. He was not here beside me. The moment I had dreamed of, the moment I wanted, was here, but he was not.

If someone had told me this fact two years ago, and said you can have one or the other, would I have known what to decide? An Oscar or Michael? Michael came into my life when I was at the bottom. He was the miracle everyone wants. He inspired and stimulated me, and not only was he fabulous in bed but my whole world lit up when we were together. He was a present, a gift from the gods, one which every female in the world should receive—just to know what it was like to have a man who knew what to do and how to do it. I'm not whole without him. I couldn't imagine going on without him. He made me laugh, he made me achieve things I never thought I could. He was exceptional. I could never understand how I was lucky enough to get him. But there I was. Why, when all great things happened to you in life, was there always something you had to pay? Or did you just have your own devil sitting on your shoulder doing it all for you?

The ceremony finally ended, people came up to me and the cameras were flashing. We surged as a crowd through the doors on to the parties.

First, there was a television interview. Some girl pushed a microphone into my face to ask me how I felt. Was I expecting to win? "Please tell us how you feel." Right; how do I feel? Shit. I was dumb-struck. Here we go, I thought, you have to look and sound brilliant.

"Brilliant, I can't believe it!" I heard myself saying. "But everyone was brilliant, weren't they?"

Several friends came over to congratulate me. The Oscar was getting slippery with sweat. What do I do with the darn thing? Steve came over with a glass of champagne. He was ecstatic, he gave me a hug.

"You were incandescent, darling! Here, let me take Oscar for you, go—enjoy yourself. I'll put it in a safe place."

"Yes, why don't you, in case we get separated, keep it till the morning."

Putting on my happy-face mask, I began circulating around the room. The noise was incredible. I knew that after the champagne I had to eat something or I'd get drunk immediately. The buffet was fabulous. I took a plate, helped myself to shrimp, smoked salmon, lobster and pasta. Everyone was pushing, so I went to the back of the room to sit on a little gilt chair. More photographers came up to me. Where was Steve? Maybe I should take my plate into the ladies' washroom for some peace.

My nerves were so strung up I needed more champagne—no problem, there it was. Bottles of it. Dumb broad! I began hating myself. This is your finest hour and you messed it up!

I wanted to send an e-mail to his brain. E-mail directly to between his ears at this minute. "Stop it! You loved me once, how can you do this?

You belong to me. You are me. You are all I want." I was going out of my senses with grief and anger. I was ready for any compromise and prepared for more degrading humiliations if only I could see him, but he was gone. He had made a fool of me, he had no pity, he had no kindness, he had no charity; I felt I would never overcome this passion, and I was disgusted with myself. I could kill him.

Commit murder? I thought of buying a gun. The rage boiled up inside me, I was still in shock. Phone him politely and ask him for a drink after dark at one of those huge hotels out by the airport. I'd suggest we'd meet in the rear parking lot, so our cars would be near each other. When he came up to me I'd shoot him, making sure no one was around beforehand. The noise of the planes taking off, flying directly overhead would drown out the gunshot. Then I'd get in the car and leave. Who would ever know who did it? Those parking lots are dark and deserted. The adrenaline and relief produced by such thoughts made me feel better. But then, if I shot him, I'd never see him again, with or without a woman on his arm. A world without Michael? No, I'll let him live.

I was coming down. I need more champagne. Suddenly it was two a.m. The party moved on. I was ushered into a stretch limousine with about ten people, it seemed, we all poured into another party. There were musicians who were great. I always take notice of them, they are rarely recognised for their playing. People ignore them, even though they don't know that most of the time it's their playing that keeps a party alive. The pianist was handsome; I sat beside him on the piano stool watching his fingers. How can he do that so effortlessly? Michael used to be annoyed with me, often saying, "Are you here with me or with the musicians?" We used to go to a restaurant in New York to listen to the big-band orchestras. Sixteen musicians playing 1920s' charts, from Hot Stomps to the Charleston. I couldn't keep still. The music was incredible.

I saw Steve on the other side of the room. He blew a kiss, waved goodbye, then pointed to his watch. Oh Yeah, I know it's late. Never mind, this is my evening, and besides, I want to blot out any feeling of grief. Michael was in London, the Awards wouldn't have been shown there, so I knew he wouldn't be watching. Probably never even taped it. I thought he just didn't want to know. That was the most shocking thing to me. How could I have been so mistaken about him? He had been so supportive. "Go for it!" he'd always say. "You can do it, you're the best."

I felt the room sway a bit, my eyesight was slightly blurred. Perhaps Steve was right, it was time to go. I have to be able to walk to the limo, after all.

Next morning I woke up to golden sunshine filling the room. Maybe I'd died and gone to heaven! I was in a rented apartment not far from the Beverley Hills Hotel. Not that luxurious but it had pretty yellow curtains and carpets which made the place cheery. Two big geranium pots on the patio and a tiny little fountain beside them. The waking-up part was hard. What's—? Oh. Oh, yes.

I lay there trying to think how I'd got home. I seriously didn't remember, but I noticed that I had hung up my dress, and my keys and bag were on the chair, so I must have been able to get in without disgracing myself. I looked down, I was in bed, which is always a sign that I was not totally pissed. I've never gone to sleep on top of my bed with my clothes on—that would have indicated that I was totally drunk. No, I had been fine.

What now?

Knowing how to deal with the loss of the one person who meant everything to me is something drama schools hadn't taught me. How can they? You can't have both. Young actresses think that they can have both. Perhaps for the first few years it works because you are still in the first flush of what could be a life-long relationship. It doesn't work. The sooner we find this out, the better. No, you can't have it all if you are an actress, possibly anything else—politician, writer, yes, why not? Or you have someone whom you find dull follow you around the world while the real fish gets away.

I wished Mum and Dad were still alive. I still miss phoning them. I wanted to pick up the phone and tell them, Mum on the kitchen phone and Dad on the extension in his study. But that's a fantasy. They had always lived up north in Manchester, never had any money, so they always disapproved if I talked for more than a few minutes.

"It's long distance, love, you'd better hang up—write us a letter instead." I wish they knew about the Oscar. Maybe they do. Mum was such a worrier. Now they were gone.

The phone rang. It was darling Steve.

"Hello, angel-face."

"Have you got my Oscar?"

"Of course, it is sitting right beside me."

"Good. Don't let it go to your head, baby. I want him back."

The morning became the afternoon. I walked around my apartment in a daze. I opened the door to get the newspaper—there it all was, photographs and all. It seemed like a dream. I had actually won an Oscar.

A huge basket of flowers arrived, then another from executives at the studio. All the people who worked with me seemed to send flowers that day. The clock on the wall was at the same time as it was yesterday as I was about to get dressed. It seemed amazing that I hadn't known the news this time yesterday. I knew that the last twenty-four hours would be the ones I would remember as the absolute climax of my work.

But then, I had lost Michael. How could anyone be so dumb?

But the one thing worrying me was that something might have happened to him, perhaps Peggy had been wrong. Maybe it wasn't just another woman, it could be something totally different. He had told me shortly after we had met that he had done an article on a Mafia-type executive in London and had exposed him in the press, and consequently the man was sent to jail. I remember how concerned I was because he seemed so nonchalant about the ramifications of such an article.

"Don't be such a worrier, Nicole," he laughed, patting my hand while we were driving down Piccadilly one night. I remember the conversation well.

"But you could really be in trouble with his friends who may try to do something to you. Then where would we be? Being a novelist is safer."

"But that's the stimulus of being an investigative journalist, you take the risks. If I ever disappear you can come and chase me." He laughed, turning to give me a kiss on the cheek.

"Be serious, it's no laughing matter," I said. "Why don't you just concentrate on writing novels? Give up the dangerous work."

"Everything involves some risk. If you didn't take risks you'd never do anything."

Thinking back to his words, I knew he was right. I was about to take a terrible risk, but I had to get away, no matter what it did to my career. Michael had disappeared and whether it was with a woman or a kidnapper there was nothing I could do about it.

I was going out of my mind with pain; I felt like I'd been in a car crash. It was panic time. I'd never thought of suicide before, it just wasn't my thing. But, I had lost him. What did I have to look forward to? I had achieved some kind of pinnacle in my professional life. Hollywood was not for me. I had made more money than I thought possible. I knew if I went back to London I'd chase after him, and the humiliation would be doubled. It was humiliating enough to be dumped, but to run after him would be far worse, and I couldn't get to him either if he had been kidnapped.

I had won the Oscar for playing the role of the wife of an investment banker who had embezzled millions in his company. The plot started where they had first met when in their twenties, at that stage of first love and tremendous ambition, without the temptations of business frauds, which came later. The whole story was about her terrible disappointment in him and her utter loneliness when she separated from him. I knew it was Oscar material as soon as I read it. But when an actress covets a role she rarely ever gets it, with the exception of Vivien Leigh *in Gone with the Wind*.

Some actresses *really did decide* that the life was too stressful and retired.

As I lay there in the sunshine, I couldn't help thinking about retiring as well, and doing something else.

The day progressed. I wanted to thank all the people I had not had time to mention in my acceptance speech. They did know, but, like me, they wanted recognition. I thought of Jeremy who had made a brilliant Shakespearean movie last year and wasn't even nominated.

I had enough money to retire, to do anything I liked. I want out—but where to go? Who needs to become a bimbo in La La land? I thought back to all the things I used to want to do if I ever had money. Deep down, I went back to my gut feelings. I'd always had dreams tucked away and I pulled out one of them. Suddenly it hit me like a thunderbolt. Italy! I want to go to Italy! Yes! To Tuscany. I want to go to Italy and paint. My movies will soon disappear but my paintings would keep me going and be on my wall, if not others' walls too, for as long as I liked. I wanted to paint Lake Como in the early morning sun. At the end of the day, I wanted to eat pasta and drink wine in a small bistro and listen to the Italians around me. Was I just being unrealistic? I suddenly remembered receiving a brochure ages ago about a summer camp for artists in the Italian lake district. I thought at the time that it would be a fun thing to do, every day going out as a group to paint a landscape, to have instruction and to have the companionship of other artists in the evening.

If I couldn't have Michael, I wanted to go somewhere that was beautiful—outstanding scenery, sensual pleasures, and be totally absorbed in my painting. Was I insane? I had lost control. How could I do this? Actually, I had been dreaming about Italy; funnily enough, in the dream everything was like an oil painting of Tuscany—sunshine on picturesque hills. I put on a CD of Maria Callas. I suddenly thought of Callas's pain over her lover and what comfort her singing must have been to her during that time.

Now that I had the Oscar, I realised I'd messed up my life. I should have married Michael, stayed in England, let him boss me around as much as he liked. Why didn't I see this in time? I would have been happy. All I wanted was him. The tears were coming, over-reaction from last night, I guessed, but I couldn't stop them.

I remember most of all his eyes. He was listening intently, he seemed so interested. I told him how I had started going to art school in between getting acting jobs. I felt his hand on my arm, looked down at the curly hair on his wrist around his blue leather watch-strap and wondered if I was sounding pathetic, especially as I said that being an artist was just as important as being an actress.

Sometimes I see people, especially famous people, and know that they are on such a high level of brilliance that I wonder they speak the same language. This is what I sensed about Michael. He was rich, I knew that by his clothes, he was successful and led a totally different life to mine. He introduced me to a new world, a new existence. He travelled, staying at the best hotels. I was spoilt forever as I can no longer stay in crummy hotels; just forget the B and Bs I was used to. He never bored me, he always had something new to say or to do. It was like being entertained by a king.

That first night in Cannes was memorable. Back in London we met for dinner. I wanted to see if I felt the same way about him as I had the night before, and I guess he did too. I took the plunge, it was the wine talking, and said, "I can't believe you're not married." I'd been wanting to ask him this anyway while we'd been talking.

We were both wary of what we said this time because we knew that we probably were going to sleep together even then, and we had to find out about each other beforehand. This time we were not twinkling at each other exactly, but analysing what we said to each other. Neither of us wanted to make a mistake, and I was as cautious as he was, especially since we had both been divorced. Thus began the most romantic period of my life. We became lovers. He had his flat, I had mine. He was divorced, no children, the timing was perfect. I couldn't believe my luck. We dined out, we cooked in, we made love, we drank wine, we watched television, went to plays but, above all, he made me laugh. He was very quick-witted and funny. It was instinctive, he couldn't help it.

He told me about his family, the country estate and how his older brother was in charge. They didn't get on, as his brother disapproved of his film and writing career, so he seldom went up north to the ancestral home. He kept in contact by phone but that was all. We talked about our former partners but he said his divorce had been five years ago, and there were no children. "How fortunate," I thought. His parents had died some time ago, so he and his brother had inherited everything.

A few weeks later, his agent phoned to say his latest book had been bought by an LA producer, who wanted to make it into a film. I was in the kitchen—I had moved in with him two weeks earlier and had sublet my flat.

"Who was that?" I asked.

"Good news," said Michael. "You won't believe it, but some guy in LA has bought the film rights to the book."

"Brilliant. How wonderful. Did they say who it was?"

"Yes, but I hadn't heard of him. All I know is that he just loved the book."

"Did they ask if you would write the screenplay?" I said.

"It hasn't been decided yet, it seems. They're working on it."

I put the dinner on the table even though I didn't feel like eating. "Michael," I said, "I knew that this book is your best, the characters are so realistic it's obvious it would make a great movie."

It was cause for a celebration so we opened a good bottle of champagne. As we were drinking it, it suddenly occurred to me that I would be perfect for the female lead in the film.

"Darling—"

"What is it?"

"I've just had a great idea. Could you possibly suggest to your agent that I could be considered for the part of Rosalind? I'd love to do it and who better than the author to suggest who could play that part? I know I'm not a household name, but if you get a celebrity for the male lead, then maybe it won't matter. It is such a great part. Michael, you have written the best role I'll ever play."

That night if bed, after we had made love, I lay there thinking it would be such a kick to do a movie as well as being in Michael's first film.

Nest day, he phoned Bill, his agent, and I was told to get my pix and résumé to him so he could suggest me to the producer. The next week went very slowly. Phone calls, deals, meetings for Michael. He hardly ever got annoyed or irritated but he didn't like to be messed about and have time wasted from daily writing schedule. He was so disciplined, which is another thing I adored about him. He wrote every day, no matter what he had to do. The study was his and there was no groaning or messing about, he just got on with it. No disturbances, please. I usually went out to the gym in the mornings to leave him in peace. The film business was taking time, not my request to be in it, exactly, but the complications involved, whether he was going to do the screenplay or not.

Finally, it was all sorted out. The screenplay would be done in LA and Michael could get on with his next book—he said he didn't want the hassle of fighting with them and living in LA. He'd been through it all before, five years ago.

We went walking on Hampstead Heath that afternoon. It was a lovely afternoon and the heath looked its very best—soft shadows with an almost deserted path.

"Now that the film business has all been settled, will you come to LA with me, if I do get the part?"

"I really don't have the time, love. This new book has to be finished in three months."

It was a blow as I really hoped he'd come.

"Why don't you give it up?" he smiled. "Become a writer."

"Me, a writer! Forget it, it's too hard." I once thought I could write but it was too difficult.

The next month I flew to LA. Two days of standing around a studio getting to know Steve, who would be my agent over there if I got the job. He was kind enough to take me for a short drive around Beverley Hills and we went shopping on Rodeo Drive. We stopped in the Polo Lounge for a drink and I discovered he was really a very nice guy. I had the film test, then flew back to London. Even though I'd been gone for less than a week, I missed Michael desperately. A real sense of apprehension hit my stomach when I realised that if I got the job I'd be in LA without him. I loved him with a passion. He was my Hemingway, Scott Fitzgerald and Graham Greene all rolled into one, as well as being the most sexual man I had ever known. I felt totally conquered and bewitched. How his wife could have left this entertaining, hysterically funny, loveable man I couldn't imagine. He was modest, quiet, even-tempered, generous, talented, good in bed and in the kitchen. His omelettes were heaven. Just like an Italian comedy or French farce, we were all food, wine, sex and sunshine. That summer was a perfect English summer. Lots of strawberries, ice cream and champagne.

On one of our picnics, when we were lying on our backs on a rug looking up at the blue sky, he told me that he had live in Capri and had a house there.

"Did you meet anybody famous there?"

"Quite a few, actually."

"Who, for example?"

"Well, Graham Greene, for one, although he was very old by then."

It turned out that Michael's father had been a writer, and as a young boy Michael had been taken to visit Somerset Maugham in his villa in the south of France (last Saturday we had gone to see Maugham's collection of pictures at the Theatre Museum) and had also met Noel Coward and Gertie Lawrence. His father used to stay with Coward at Goldenhurst. Maugham's house fascinated me and we spoke of the glamour, the sophistication of that generation. I sensed in Michael the same kind of elegance and cultivation. Perhaps it was from his Oxford days, a hang-over of the university life, but there was also that *je ne sais quoi*, a slight deviation towards depravity that didn't seem to fit into his nature. I once nearly asked him if he had ever visited a brothel or a massage parlour but I didn't want to hear the answer. Always in their biographies, these men, whether gay or straight, had some kind of sexual hang-up. I thought of Ken Tynan and of what Elaine Dundy, his wife, had to put up with. I remembered the day when I read about what Maugham, Coward and others got up to when on the Riviera, and it seemed as if their private lives were rather debauched and ugly compared to the American writers in Paris in the 'twenties. Perhaps I was being totally naive, but surely the expatriates were more enchanting to their readers.

There seemed to be something rather ugly lurking just under the surface. Perhaps I was imagining things but it was as if some of the extremely talented creative people had deep dark secrets, almost as if it was a kind of Faustian thing. Or was it that fame made you a different person, more immoral or desperate? Would it be my romanticism to think that Michael was perfect? Even though I was slightly shocked by his last book and the manipulations he had invented in the plot? The character I wanted to play was really rather dangerous, and I wondered why he had called it *A Snake in the Grass*. All very metaphorical, of course, but a bit too dark for me.

We walked back down the Heath. I wondered if he was as happy as I was. He said he was, but it was hard to believe he could be. I wondered if I would ever bore him, even though he thought I was creative. But he was far more creative, I knew that, but still his head wasn't turned. He had done the book tours, the celebrity interviews, the TV spots without being affected by it all. That evening we watched a film about madness and creativity. He didn't believe that you had to be slightly mad to create, like Van Gogh or Picasso or the other painters. So that was encouraging. The phone rang, it was Steve in LA to say I had got the part! I must have been slightly mad to accept it, but we were both really terribly excited. It was a great deal of money, more than I'd ever dreamed of. What a wonderful gift, via Michael! The days passed as I went about getting ready for the trip. Michael still insisted he was too busy to come with me.

On our last night in London before I left for LA we went to dinner at Rules. It was a toss-up between The Ivy and Rules, but Rules is quieter and more private. As we pushed open the door, we felt the usual rush of pleasure and anticipation, the aroma of good food and good wine. The menu hadn't changed. I ordered the salmon, Michael had steak and kidney pie. "How many times have you been here?" I asked.

"Dozens of times." He picked up the wine list.

"What did Graham Greene write in his novel? That they fell in love here over grilled onions." I paused, then said, "I hope you will come over to LA when you can."

"You know, I hate the place." he said, beckoning the wine waiter. "Is it stupid to ask you to be a good girl while you're out there?"

"Of course not. You know I'm mad about you."

Thinking back to that evening, it all seemed so simple. We trusted each other, we never even thought about anyone else. At least I didn't, and I believed he didn't either. We were both in love and I never had a moment's panic. Well, perhaps once or twice, but I was so trusting; we were like an old married couple. Afterwards we walked along the Strand

and down to Waterloo Bridge where we stood in the middle and looked out over the river. It was a lovely evening, with hardly any breeze. The city looked magnificent with the dome of St Paul's cathedral in the distance.

I'm going to miss all this."

"You sound as if you're going away for years," laughed Michael.

I looked at him and all of a sudden wished I was not going.

"Michael, you will wait for me, won't you?"

"What do you mean, wait? Where am I going? Of course, I'll wait for you, whatever that means."

My heart missed a beat. The possibility of losing him suddenly hit me.

"What's wrong?" Michael looked at me.

"Nothing, just a sudden anxiety attack. Give me a hug."

We hugged each other, then laughed.

"Just like a couple of teenagers, aren't we?"

The phone rang, bringing me back to the present. More congratulations about the Oscar. I knocked over the flower vase, the water went streaming across the coffee table, I grabbed the paperback, which was on the edge. The roses were top-heavy, so I went into the kitchen to find a larger vase. What a joy to have the whole ceremony over. No more screams at the sheer stupidity of it. No more sleepless nights. But I was finished. I am going to quit.

I put the roses in a bigger vase, wiped the table and picked up the paperback. It was a collection of stories by Somerset Maugham. I had been reading them in bed. What I most enjoyed were the exotic places and locales where he set his stories. Was I just being naive to think that one could be happier in those faraway places? Probably not. A faithless man is still a torture, whether it be in Singapore or Sydney. I could never understand the saying "A rolling stone gathers no moss"—was that a good thing or not?

The phone rang again. More congratulations. Now that it was all over I could talk as much as I needed, but they were new-found friends, not like back home. The idea of going through another film without any enjoyment was stupid. I had enough money to clear out. My head hurts, my head hurts.

Then Peggy phoned again, Peggy Roberts, a British actress, my closest friend for twenty years, we had known each other since drama school.

"Darling, I can't stop thinking about you. Are you really OK? Good! Tell me more about the parties. I want to hear everything."

"Peggy, it was overwhelming. The limo I went in was enormous. It's like a giant circus, gaudy and glitzy."

Her first call that day was more out of concern for me, as she knew how much I loved Michael.

"Where did you two go wrong? You must have known."

"I've thought so much about that—nothing went wrong, that's the weird thing. He just hated the separation. He was so lonely, he was a push-over for anyone who paid him some attention, let alone cooked dinner for him."

"You know it's more than that, Nicole."

We talked about the whole time leading up to the Oscars—I was doing another film, which finished a week before the Academy Awards, so I stayed on in California for the event. Peggy had been to hell and back after falling for Brian, a married actor, so she knew what suffering was all about.

"Listen Peggy, I'm not coming back to London just yet."

"What do you mean? You've finished the film, haven't you?"

"Yes, but I want to have a break. Just get away. I've booked to go to Italy."

I put my feet up on the bed. This will take some explaining. But Peggy understood.

But an hour later she rang again. "Are you sure you won't be too lonely?"

"There's no reason to dash back to London if he's gone away," I finally convinced her.

Steve came in to deliver my Oscar. He looked exhausted even though he was in bed much earlier than I was last night. He gave me a big hug and kissed me on both cheeks, then sat down on the sofa looking around at my living room. He was in his early thirties, thin and wiry, slightly balding with quick eyes and very agile; he could have been a dancer, I thought. His whole physique was healthy and I'm sure he worked out in a gym every day. The travel agent phoned back as he was sitting there. Steve heard my whole conversation, my plans for which flight I was taking, which airports, what times. He turned off his mobile phone and said, "We have to talk, Nicole, this is some kind of craziness you are going through, you have no idea what you're doing."

I felt guilty when I looked at him. I knew what he must feel.

"There is no way you can leave now!" The whole conversation was so tempestuous. "The offers will come pouring in now, you don't seem to appreciate the amount of work I've done for you. The old saying is true, it *is* a jungle out there, we have producers who will want to see you."

I had never met someone like Steve before, even though performers dream of getting an agent like him. He moved quickly, he was nobody's fool, he knew what he was doing and I was about to take away, or rather throw away, all that he had done for me. The whole American way of life combined with his street smarts was all wrapped up like a fresh bunch of exotic flowers and being handed to me within a big red bow. The things we had in common were all wrapped up in one big package of money, success and fame. He was the epitome of commercial know-how, contacts, press coverage, PR—all the trappings that go with winning an Oscar. He didn't care what the scripts were like, or who wrote them, just get the film contract. If I'd ever mentioned "artistic" or "intelligent" he would look at me as if I was some kind of prima donna. Besides, even if I were chosen to play Scarlett O'Hara that afternoon, it wouldn't have made any difference. The shock of being kept alive on my success of the Oscar by being given huge amounts of money just didn't touch me. I wanted out.

"Nicole, please consider me if you won't consider yourself. I can get contracts for you now that won't come again ever."

His eyes were looking directly into mine and I knew he was right.

"You will never get such an opportunity again in your career." He kept on and on as if he knew that he had already failed but wasn't going to give up so easily. There was no hostility, no meanness yet, but I wondered how long it would be before he would start to lose his temper. He was much too smart for that, perhaps if he gave me a long enough rope I'd come back. This, in the end, is what he must have decided because he suddenly stood up, pulled down his sweater, readjusted his jacket, and gave me another hug before looking deeply into my eyes and saying, "I'm just on the other end of the phone—let me know what you are going to do."

Suddenly he was gone, and there was a deathly silence. His words still hung in the air like weird premonitions. I knew he was right, I knew everything he said was true, he was talking sense and stark reality. I felt flushed with the common-sense and directness of his remarks, the reality of what he was saying. It was as if some doctor in a consulting room had said to me, "You are going to die in two months." Obviously, looking back, I was in shock, shock at winning the Oscar but also at the news from London. It was the same kind of shock as when the nurse had phoned me up and said, "Your mother died last night."—which of course still haunted me. It wasn't as if it was unexpected, I had half hoped that I would win the Oscar, but like mother's death, it was still a shock. Your body just seems to take over and your automatic pilot goes on, you go into top gear with all cylinders going, which propels you to do instinctively what has to be done.

Lifting out my suitcase from the closet was like lifting out the baggage of this whole experience to go into outer space, the residue of months of work and uncertainty. "Who will watch my movie in two years time?" I asked myself. But that isn't the point if you are a performer, is it?

I knew I couldn't stay in LA any longer, time was too precious; I wanted to assuage my anger, to follow my obsession no matter what I was messing up. Steve would have many clients knocking at his door now, perhaps another actress who would win an Oscar for him. I realised he was human; after all, he was not as horrible as most agents would have been to me, and I knew I would have to pay my dues somehow. I felt very irresponsible, embarrassed at letting him down, especially as he would have to deal with the media and all the problems in the next few days when I was gone. The only thing was, would he ever forgive me? When I had got Michael back, when things were normal again, would he ever speak to me again, let alone work with me?

That evening I started packing, still in a daze. I phoned the drug store for a delivery—hair colour, scissors and baseball cap; I then proceeded to cut my hair—it was cathartic in a way—coloured it dark brown, so when I went to the airport in dark glasses I wouldn't be recognised. I knew the newspaper reporters and photographers would be looking for me when they heard I had disappeared, so I made sure I would not be recognised. It would work if I was not too close up to someone. My career used to be the most important thing, but unless I can get him back it's all worthless. I'd think of a plan in Italy. I hated him. I despised him. I loved him with all my heart.

Chapter Two

THE PLANE TOOK AGES TO come to the gate at Milan airport. My clothes were all wrinkled, I looked like a gypsy. The stewardess gave me a washcloth to straighten up my face. I'd had lots of wine, which started me writing on the plane. The girl next to me had slept all the way with a blanket over her head. I decided not to, so I just started writing in my new journal that I had bought at a discount store months ago. Two movies were shown but I was not tempted to watch them. I walked up the aisle several times so I wouldn't get blood-clots in my legs, like they warn you.

Normally I hang about at the rear of the plane to chat to anyone who is as bored as I am, or I find the bar, usually at one of the stations in the mid-section, where most passengers who want an Irish Mist or Cointreau gather for an after-dinner drink, but this time I was not doing any of that. I just kept on writing, wilting at the edges. Have you ever noticed that the stewardesses often look fresher on landing than at take-off? How do they manage that? Maybe they sleep somewhere we don't know about. They take that little elevator down to wherever the food goes and sleep.

The driver was at the airport to pick me up to drive me to Lake Como, where I caught the ferry to Bellagio. It is a little town on the other side of the lake, and the view of it from the ferry takes your breath away, it is so beautiful. It is a gem. It rivals the best of the little hill towns of France.

The hotel seemed charming. All I heard was Italian and one British voice in the distance. However the receptionist did speak English and assured me that they were expecting me. A uniformed bell-hop took my luggage up to a first-floor room and opened the door. It was a pretty room, and when he opened the shutters I saw I had a tiny balcony with a magnificent view of the lake.

My soul is at peace. I am at peace. It must be one of the most beautiful places in the world. The ambience is so Italian but in the most artistic sense—not loud and noisy but gently pacifying. Almost operatic in a therapeutic way.

A surge of panic hits my stomach. Where did that come from? It went like lightning. A "someone-walking-over-my-grave" kind of moment. What am I doing here?

I'm just tired, that's all. Low blood sugar, probably. I need a drink. Fortunately, I didn't have much to unpack. I walked downstairs; there were bowls of fresh flowers on each table in the corridors, I walked out to the bar on another level. I ordered a Scotch. Sitting watching all the little boats come in and the ferry from across the lake, I wonder where these people are going. Some going home, some coming over for the evening and some returning from a day in Como. I pick up the menu, decide what I'll have for dinner, then open a guide book I'd bought at the airport before I left. Bellagio—not much about the place is written there. It seems Franz Liszt came here and stayed at a large villa not far from here. I decide I'll go visit it tomorrow morning. I feel better, more normal. The evening is still, there is no wind at all. The lake is suddenly becoming like glass. Unfortunately I am given a table in the dining room next to four American tourists who, I know, will either recognise me or want to talk anyway.

I got up and moved out to a table on the other side of the patio. My trouser suit felt tight, which is a sign that the weight is beginning to pile on again. I don't care, I'll walk it off.

The waiter is a true character. He kept staring at me. Dark hair, pale face, short, stocky. He was curious about me, I thought he recognised me but couldn't pin me down. He served me a delicious dinner, I chose the house red wine. Starting with a small helping of pasta with pesto sauce and a salad, the taste was glorious. I moved on to a crispy roast chicken morsel that had been sautéed in some sauce I couldn't identify, probably tarragon. My toes were tingling, my senses were tingling with pleasure at the sight of the lake, the aromas in the dining room, the touch of the pristine white tablecloth, of my dinner napkin, the crusty bread, the taste of the food and wine. Who would think that one could totally remove oneself from chaos, traffic jams, noise and smog in Los Angeles to a quiet exquisite Italian lake?

Michael had been like a dull pain in my gut all the way over in the plane. I wished I could have taken an aspirin, a valium, a potion to ease it. "Canst thou not minister to a mind diseased?" The pain was subsiding. Maybe it was the Scotch but I was suddenly reminded of a Noel Coward song—"When the storm clouds are gathering, or when the love light is fading in your true love's eyes, Sail Away." Coward said it all.

I knew Peggy or anyone else wouldn't be able to put up with me, I was pathetic. The past week had been one of the best and one of the worst in my life. Why is it that good and bad things almost always come together. An Oscar was something. I'd never really thought about winning one until Michael's book was made into a movie. "Don't fret about him," Peggy had advised when I called her from the airport. If anyone knew, she did. Nothing had come easy for her.

The aroma from the kitchen was drifting through the air. It was a mixture of grilled meat, garlic, some kind of baking, maybe a cake, but it was really delightful in the open air.

Tonight I would lie in a long hot bath and when I close my eyes I'll know I'm in a heavenly part of Italy—not London, not LA. Cities can be exciting but there is always the struggle to keep moving. Make your mark, make your name, circulate, be seen in the right places, the right clothes, the right boutiques. One of Peggy's favourite pastimes years ago was to walk down the King's Road on a Saturday afternoon to see what all the chic boutiques had in stock.

Suddenly I thought of Peggy in the "sixties! Swinging London, Mary Quant, mini-skirts—whoa! I read Quant's autobiography; at the height of her fame, she fled. She booked herself into hotels across Europe and took long hot baths, letting the water run constantly.

On the other side of the patio, I noticed a very elegant woman sitting on her own. I felt an immediate twinge of envy. She looked so well-dressed, poised. Age around forty, I guessed, with short, thick, brown naturally curly hair, a creamy peach skin and a pretty face. You could tell that her fabulous underwear would be very expensive, probably trimmed with French lace; her handbag would be neat, tidy with leather-bound gilt-edged address-book, glass case, an expensive compact with crocodile-skin wallet. I watched her as she ordered her meal. I couldn't hear if she was speaking in English or Italian.

Actresses, well, London theatre actresses don't usually care about clothes. It's really the last thing on our minds. The wardrobe department make us look glamorous if we have to be, so our day-to-day clothes are thrown on and we are out the door. Sweaters, pants, socks, shirts are the norm. This woman fascinated me. I had to meet her and find out about her although why would she want to do the same thing? Perhaps I was constantly making mistakes about other people. You can't judge a book by its cover, so why try? Would I, could I, look like her in real life, without the wardrobe department?

Perhaps Michael's new girlfriend is like her. Perhaps she has slinky underwear, is tidy, immaculate and uncluttered. He loves her for that? I had looked dowdy in London, I remembered, but then it was the weather, of course. It's so cold you have to wear a sweater, coat and sensible shoes. If you had a chauffeur who drove you from door to door, then you could look like this woman, I supposed. The total look. I tried to see what she was eating. She had the same carafe of wine as I had, so it was a guessing game. How she reminded me of Ellen. Same profile, same carriage, same hair. Ellen had been my room-mate at school and told me the facts of life late one night as we were lying in our beds in the dark. I remember I didn't believe her, I thought she was making it up to shock me. I pretended to believe her, though at the time I was determined to find out why she would make up such outrageous lies. It wasn't until the next morning that another girl verified what I'd been told. I stared at her and began to blush. Mother really didn't tell me much about the facts of life, I suppose that's normal. However, she did occasionally give me short lectures when she was in the middle of some baking or brushing my hair. She kept on telling me that getting married was the most important step in my life, that I should seriously weigh any offers because she believed that a man comes first, before a career. Even though I knew she was so old-fashioned I listened to her advice, which must have sunk in, as I began believing it. She also said things like: "The way to a man's heart is through his stomach." So if I met the love of my life I should know how to cook well, from roast beef to toad-in-the-hole, and she proceeded to teach me. Dad never wanted to eat out because he said he got far better meals at home. Since that time I have always loved eating out, and this place is one of the best.

The lake was unbelievably beautiful. I couldn't believe my luck. So often, you can find yourself in a dump. For once, I was pleased I had kept the brochure about this place; it really was as described, and I intended to chase up the address of the art school I had heard about. The scene was breathtaking and it soothed the pain. Who was it that wrote the poem about incredible scenery being sublime? Lord Byron, I think. The mountains on the other side of the lake were majestic, a certain kind of purple which, if you had painted them that colour, would seem almost totally unreal. I will go to Florence, Verona and Padua before I leave if I can.

My grandparents had spent their honeymoon on Lake Como, so in a few days I will try to find the huge hotel they stayed at in Stresa. My grandmother wore a cameo brooch that she gave to me shortly before she died, I wanted to see if I could find a cameo ring to match it. Being totally sentimental, I wanted to go back to those Edwardian times when the elegance of this lake area was filled with people like my great-grandparents; the atmosphere still lingered all around me in the old buildings with their wrought-iron balconies, the gas lamps and the uniformed staff waiting to give service to these elegant travellers. Large cabin trunks, silk dresses with umbrellas to match, gentle activities during the day and civilised conversation at night reminded me so much of what my grandmother used to tell me about her travels as a young girl.

The waiter poured some water for me out of the decanter and, yes, a basket of hot bread rolls appeared. I wouldn't have minded some civilised conversation just then. The hotel was set back from the lake, the patio where I was sitting was surrounded with huge palm trees, flowering vines which were lit up from underneath, as were the baskets hanging from the wrought-iron posts; the boats were only a short distance away, so you could see the masts bobbing up and down in the water.

The woman was eating a salad. I looked at the other diners. There were only two other people near me, an Italian couple who looked as if they'd been married for a hundred years and two other couples further away plus a surly over-weight man in a business suit who was drinking beer and reading a newspaper. No interest there. I ate the chicken, pulled apart the fresh crusty bread and drank the wine. After I had dyed my hair I knew people wouldn't recognise me so easily. An evening mist was beginning to form across the lake and a chill wind made me reach for my jacket. How much longer can I sit here looking at her?

She's reading a book now. When I ordered another carafe of wine I asked the waiter whether he knew if the lady was English.

"Yes, I think so, or an American." He shrugged and walked away. I guess they're all the same to him.

Half an hour later, after the wine had hit me, I got up, walked over to her and smiled. I just had to talk to somebody.

"Excuse me," I said dumbly, "I just wanted to say how much I admire your dress." Pause. "I'm an idiot" I said to myself, "What do you think you're doing? She couldn't care less what you think of her dress. Pathetic, stupid, oh, so boring. She really will think you are an idiot."

"Thank you. I'm glad you like it. It is one of my favourites. It travels well because it doesn't crease. Are you alone?"

She looked over to where I had come from, expecting to see a man, of course.

"Yes, I am."

"Sit down, will you have coffee?" Obviously she was a little high on the wine, as I was.

"No thanks, but I'll sit for a while. It's such a beautiful evening." The watch she was wearing was surrounded by diamonds, she had three rings on the third finger of her left hand, her nails were bright red, immaculately manicured.

"Don't I know you? You look so familiar somehow."

"Maybe we have met before." I cheated. I never like to say, "You probably saw me in such and such movie."

I felt as if I'd known her all my life. It was miraculous. It was probably the memory of Ellen, they could be twins. She suddenly took me back to my teen years again, back in London.

The waiter came and we both signed our checks and showed him our room keys.

"My name is Julia," she said as she reached across the table to shake hands.

"Mine's Nicole."

"Of course, you're the actress. I saw you on TV the other night. What on earth are you doing here?"

"Good question. I've retired, I guess."

"No you haven't. I love your work."

We looked at each other and smiled the smile of mutual admiration. We befriended each other. How many times do you strike up a conversation with a total stranger? Perhaps meeting Julia was supposed to happen.

The waiter came to clear the table and he produced a tiny brush to remove the breadcrumbs from the white, heavily starched tablecloth. His uniform was equally starched and immaculate.

"It must be one of the most beautiful evenings of the year—or is it always like this?" I asked him.

"Yes, this is one of our best days, because you can see the mountains, which are usually covered in cloud at this time of evening. It's very clear tonight." He brought a plate of chocolates, but we waved them away.

"I don't need to be tempted to put on five pounds," she laughed.

"Where are you from?" I knew she was American so that question wouldn't sound too pushy.

"Palm Beach in Florida, which is almost as beautiful, but not quite. We don't have the mountains for one thing, but it is always warm."

I wanted to talk to find out about her. It was a curiosity more developed, I believe, in actors. They are like magpies, taking any gems they can get. Character, personality, background, accent, opinions, work, jobs, anything they can use in their work.

Julia told her of her work as a fund-raiser for the Red Cross. She organises a ball every year and has at least $500,000 to raise. She works at it full-time.

"I love it. It is really a great deal of work, but I enjoy it."

"You must be good at it."

"I have been doing it for ten years and they do seem to appreciate my efforts."

"What a tremendous achievement. Things that really matter."

It seemed obvious, but if you are ambitious, surely the way you spend your days is most important. I was astonished to listen to Julia's account of what she did. She has "power" breakfasts at eight a.m.—my God, I'd be exhausted by ten a.m. Then on to another meeting, then home for a sandwich, standing up in the kitchen, or perhaps a lunch with other like-minded people. Afternoons were often spent typing up letters, sending faxes, telephoning and soliciting more funds, or asking people to accept invitations. It astounded me how busy she was, how much she got done. Acting in movies was so low-key compared to what she did. The work was not demanding, unless you regard the delay, the constant waiting about in your dressing room or trailer as work. Patience was the only real necessity. I couldn't imagine how she did it. It was so completely different from my life.

"My mother taught me. I just watched her, it was the only thing I knew how to do. Years of planning charity events, raising money became just part of our daily life."

The rich are different, I thought. Their problems are light years away from mine. When I was twenty I was auditioning, memorising, practising voice exercises when Julia would be getting dressed up in designer clothes, going to the hairdresser at least twice a week, attending charity balls, raising money at the same time.

It was the first time I had met anyone like her. It was difficult. I visualised her life in a mansion in Palm Beach. It was like night and day; I was not envious, but curious, perhaps. Meeting her seemed to put a new kind of perspective on my life. I found that she was just as curious about my life, only it did sound very superficial when I tried to explain what my daily life was like.

"Rehearsing a stage play, memorising lines, finding a character is far more satisfying than working on a film set," I said lamely. It was almost impossible to explain the tensions that build up on a film set.

She seemed so mature compared to my scatterbrain. I felt deeply worthless. What had I ever done for society? The emotion was admiration, awe at what she was doing with her life. Michael once took me with him when he visited a nunnery to interview a charity nurse who visited the poor and the sick year after year. Oh dear, our little problems sounded so terribly lightweight.

I looked down at my hands. They were shaking. Holding them in my lap, I hoped she didn't notice.

"Oh, look at the moon," I said. She turned. The moon was coming up over the lake. Same old moon. The one which sees us through so many emotions. I looked at it the night my mother died, I have looked at it in so many different countries. It is like a huge eye peering at us through our lives. Oh God, the moon. "Swear not by the moon, the inconstant moon." Why can't I be happy, I thought, this is such an incredible evening? I was beginning to miss Michael terribly, the pain just wouldn't go away. Where was my Romeo? It can't be over, I don't believe it. It's a nightmare, it's unreal.

"Don't look so sad." Julia reached out and touched my arm.

"Was I? Sorry about that, I must be tired."

I felt tempted to blurt it all out, but resisted the temptation, even though we were the only ones left in the dining room. She asked about my career, but I had to be careful not to sound like so many actors' biographies do: "Then I played this and then I played that." After a while, the waiter was about to put the lights out.

"It's getting late. I must go and pack," she said.

We got up and walked through to the lobby.

"Good night, I hope to see you in the morning. Please leave me your address," I asked her.

"Of course," she said.

Early next morning I woke just at sunrise. I pulled on my tracksuit and went for a run along the side of the lake. The view was wonderful. The lake was still calm, the fishing boats were all leaving the dock. The mountains were still shrouded in mist. The voices of the men came across the water, even from the boats a long way out. The path along the front was bordered by flower boxes and pine trees—the fresh pine scent mixed with the softness of the air was exhilarating. After a while I sat on one of the many benches facing the lake and rested. What Julia had told me last night was swimming around in my head. I felt so small in the run of the world. Damn this acting business. It is almost as if it was something you are born with, a part of your brain that is a congenital knot, like a withered ear, or a tissue that crosses over your brain, makes you want to dress up, make up and go on the stage. So child-like compared to Julia.

She didn't want to become someone else, or to act, or to spend her time thinking about imaginary characters, or their motivations: she didn't wonder why Shakespeare wrote the sonnets, or worry about next season, or whether a certain director liked her work well enough to hire her again. My whole existence seemed so superficial, what were my worries about employment and success compared to doing something really worthwhile with my life? Working for the Red Cross, working for any charity to help, not actors, but people who were starving, dying wounded or trapped in an earthquake. You do what you have to do. But do you? Just because you have spent your life working at honing your craft doesn't mean that it is the thing that you should be doing. People do decide to do different things if the struggle is too painful. I thought of Robert, who is a brilliant concert pianist, worthy of all the best concert halls of Europe, but he never got the breaks. So what does he do? Again, he realised that working for the good of mankind would be the ultimate role, handing out medical supplies, millions of dollars to the starving, eradicating poverty or sending McDonalds into African villages for a start. McDonalds are so rich they could afford to build one in every village and give away their hamburgers and shakes! A vanilla milk-shake to a starving child seemed so much more immediate than acting Viola in *Twelfth Night* to schoolchildren in

Manchester who couldn't care less. What bothered me was the time spent in the acting profession worrying about where your next job was coming from, and about contacts.

I kept running. My face was cold but my body felt warm. The exhilaration of just being alive suddenly took over. A great feeling of well-being came over me, I tried to stop thinking, to focus only on the view. The mist was rising from the mountains; it felt great to be alive. The whole place was so quiet, so peaceful that I wanted to stay here forever. Some people find mountains oppressive, especially huge ones like these, but I felt they were a kind of symbol of what we could achieve in life. "Oh pull—ease!" I could hear Peggy say.

The dull pain in my stomach was Michael of course, the act of running seemed to get rid of it, but, as soon as I stopped, it came back. How could he be so cruel? How could he not want to see me at all? Just cut off like a limb. Keep running. What did other people do in the same situation? Some run marathons, I suppose. I ran past an old man sitting on one of the benches, who was staring out at the lake. He seemed so lonely and sad. I would have liked to sit with him to talk to him about his life—did someone dump him, I wonder. Does he still remember? I felt I wanted to get involved with someone who actually lived in this paradise, but language was the problem.

Julia was having breakfast on the patio when I got back to the hotel. I stopped by her table and sat down. Just coffee and orange juice, I said, no, here comes a piece of melon.

"I'm so sorry you're leaving today," I said.

"So am I. But we must keep in touch. You must come to stay with me."

I knew that I wouldn't. Her mansion in Palm Beach would be too big, too tidy, too overwhelming for me. My brain couldn't take it in.

I watched her departure. Neat suitcases, neat luggage, but I couldn't put my finger on it. She was so well organised, so efficient, seemed not to be tied up in knots with anguish. Calm, put together, rich was probably the answer, but I was rich too, so that couldn't be the answer. She certainly wasn't dull. I could feel all these thought as if I knew I was the dumb one. Dumb. Just like why Michael had left me? I still didn't know. Well, yes, I did, he met someone else, stupid.

I didn't mention Michael to Julia. Talking about him is too painful. "The less said, soonest mended," my mother used to say. But it was nice to be distracted by her and find out about her life. Store it up in my "character" department. Good accent, elegant walk, there I go again. Stop it!

Did you know that when you are talking to an actor you are being automatically scrutinised? They do it unconsciously, your voice, your manner, your gestures are all going into a mind bank. Often to be used when creating a character sometime in the future. Your personality or character may figure in someone's next Lady Macbeth.

I walked into the village after seeing Julia off. She looked so dainty and composed. God, I could never look like that, or if I did, it wouldn't be like how I felt inside exactly. All screwed up. I kept walking along the lake beyond the town to the stunning villa I could see in the distance. Evidently this is where Franz Liszt the composer stayed with his mistress while waiting for the birth of their love-child. She had left her husband to follow in Liszt's footsteps—totally romantic, totally sublime. The villa was closed, so I sat on the grass at the top of a sweeping lawn crossing the area up to the hill beside the villa. The sun was shimmering crystals on the water between the pine trees lining the lake. What a story their lives would make. Now, there is a movie I'd like to make.

I took out my sunglasses from my satchel, also a camera and took some shots of the view. I came across the journal that I had started in the plane and began to read. It was, of course, my autobiography written in one big rush of energy, coupled with a constant flow of glasses of wine. It was the agony of finding out where I went wrong, like taking the wrong turn on an inter-state highway and not being able to do anything to get off.

Julia was the one who had stimulated me. Right now, she was sitting on the flight going back to the States. No anguish, no, that's not right, everyone has anguish. Everyone. A strange sleepiness came over me, the kind you get after a heavy lunch with wine, but I hadn't eaten anything. I lay down on the grass and closed my eyes. "To sleep, perchance to dream. Ay, there's the rub."

I woke up with a start, hot and thirsty with a crick in my neck. I could feel someone behind me. Shit! I panicked, then turned around quickly. No, it was only a tree.

Walking back into Bellagio, I wanted to photograph more. The sun was like a cannon ball in the sky through the clouds. How to stay here is going to be a problem. You meet dozens of people in the course of one year, but why is it just that one or two you connect with? If you are an actress, you meet dozens of actors, but only a few do you become close friends with—shared emotions. I felt this way about Julia; she had a profound effect on me. Why? Because I admired her.

As I approached the little shops, suddenly I heard two women speaking English. They were looking at some jewellery in a window. I stood beside them to see what they were looking at. A huge garnet necklace.

"Very expensive, but beautiful," one said to the other.

"Like how much?"

"At least a thousand pounds, I should say."

"At least a thousand pounds."

Right, they were English, I guessed. Pounds, not dollars.

They turned to move on and as they did so, they looked at me. They stopped and stared.

"Hello. My God, aren't you Nicole Bennett?"

I smiled; already I missed the recognition I was used to.

"Yes, that's me."

"I loved your last film. What are you doing here?"

"Having a holiday."

"Well, what a wonderful surprise. It's such a pleasure to meet you. Isn't this town fabulous?"

We started to walk up the pavement, which was very narrow with tiny streets criss-crossing the main street.

The women were friendly and admiring. It was almost as if they knew I wanted some company. New people who didn't know me. They introduced themselves as Fanny and Margo. They were both roughly my age.

Fanny was the prettier one, slightly plump, around five-foot-three with curly red hair done up in a ponytail, with a cheerful smile. Margo was tall and slim with glasses and long black hair. She looked far more serious than Fanny but also had a charming smile. They were each carrying a small canvas and there were spots of paint on their faces.

"Are you artists?" I asked.

"Clever you. Yes, we are, or at least we think we are," Margo replied. They laughed.

"Do you have any interest in painting?" said Fanny.

"Yes, in fact I do. Can I see what you've done?" I asked. They held up their canvases, still slightly damp, showing different scenes of the lake. They were really very good.

"You are both very talented!" I exclaimed. "I like what you've done. Did you paint all of this today?"

"Yes, we start early in the morning. We are here on an art course. A painting workshop. Come and join us tomorrow morning."

It seemed an incredible coincidence that the art course was still in existence. Fanny said with sudden recognition, "I knew you at drama school. Do you remember me?"

I didn't, but I pretended I did.

"You were in Mr Dance's class, weren't you? Guessing of course," Fanny queried and went on. "The best part was when he was the first teacher to let us choose our own monologues. Those days were so busy, everything was scheduled so close together."

"Do you remember, he kept going on about energy?" I said. "I can hear him now: 'Energy on stage is the real secret. Energy on stage is many things. Energy makes us move with precision, it is needed to get through a play.' Remember how he used to make us do all those exercises rolling about on the floor, and the deep breathing sessions. That was even before we started jogging exercises."

"But if we were meant to be actresses we were certainly not taught the disadvantages, like poverty for example, and men," laughed Fanny. "I never married, you know. My career was more important, and now I'm an old maid with nothing to show for it." Her smile was infectious, she obviously hadn't been to hell and back over a man, or maybe she was over it. I wished I was well over Michael.

"Come with us up to the studio tomorrow to meet everybody, perhaps you'd like to join the class," Margo said.

"I heard about these classes ages ago, but didn't think they were still going on. I kept the brochure for years, but forgot to bring it with me and didn't think I'd ever find anyone who could tell me where to go. I've painted as a hobby for the past ten years or so."

We all stopped to catch our breath after a steep climb up the slope to where the village ends. It was hot, so we started to take off layers of clothing. We looked back across the lake, now shimmering below.

"What happened to you after you left drama school? You sort of disappeared. We all wondered where you had gone. Where did you go?" Fanny asked.

"I went to Ipswich. Weekly Rep. Then I went home to look after my mother who was very ill. After she died I stayed on for a while and then went back to London."

Next day I went to the class. We walked all around Bellagio to paint landscapes. One woman would paint wild flowers or a tree, but most of us tried to paint the whole scene. At the end of the first session I walked back to the hotel with some kind of satisfaction. The paint was hardly dry, so I had to walk carefully. I put it up in my room on a shelf by the window.

"Not bad," I thought. I couldn't wait to start the next day.

In the morning, Fanny and I sat painting together and talking over old times.

"Perhaps you don't remember that winter. What did you do, Fanny?"

"I went into Rep in Glasgow. A horrible experience. I just got all the small parts. It's amazing how we all get sucked into the magic of theatre and end up doing awful parts in awful plays. The only consolation is the company's camaraderie and the contact or communication with the audience if you have a good part. Did you find this in making films?"

"No, there's no communication at all, really. I much prefer the theatre. But now, after my Oscar win, there are more film scripts than good plays. I really want to do more theatre. It's a terrible business, either everybody wants you or nobody wants you. You come down from the mountain very quickly!"

The painting expeditions always started early in the morning and lasted all day. I watched the others work; everyone had their own style. Some worked in watercolours, others with acrylic, which I favoured as well. "You have obviously been trained," our teacher and tour guide commented after seeing my first work. I was flattered by her compliment. We worked all day, then had a glass of wine in our usual cafe in the village, before going back to our various hotels.

I kept up a diary recording where we went each day. The beauty of the place, the satisfaction of painting, which was going well, helped slowly to take the edge off the trauma over Michael. Life was sweeter in my little Italian village doing such simple work. The painting classes were a huge distraction. I told the hotel desk not to put any calls through as I didn't want to hear from anyone except either my agent Steve or Peggy. It felt like I was in a new little world, just my new-found friends, this place and my work. Each day I would listen to the conversations, our teacher, the jokes, and try to create a new kind of vacuum as if my other life didn't exist any more, a sort of cocoon—a "let's pretend" world of paint boxes, canvases, friends and numbness. All of us were learning the technique of painting the perfect cloud; this seemed to be the most important task of the day. To think that painted cloud would be around, would exist longer than my interpretation of Cleopatra!

There were no men in our group for some reason. Just coincidental, they said, you can never tell, it's different each year. We didn't mind, as it allowed more freedom and girl talk at dinner. Each afternoon I dropped by the little shop full of pens, pencils and pads, where they spoke English, and they had a few paperback books in English. Some days we would catch the ferry to go across the lake to buy an English newspaper at the little tobacconist who also had a small library in the back of the shop where we found some books in English.

Margo and Fanny were full of questions about Hollywood, but I said I didn't want to talk about it at all, that I hoped they'd understand. They didn't, but let it ride.

"Why is it that sometimes you find that the most surprising things happen when you suddenly have to change your life?" asked Fanny "My life was so awful that I knew I had to do something. After my mum died I had to sell her house, pay off her debts, get rid of a lifetime of accumulated belongings, which was heart-breaking, then try to get myself back into the theatre. It was freezing cold, I caught the flu and when my dog was run over, I knew I had to get away. We all have to find something to do if we can't get work in the theatre. We desperately miss the magic, and this is a different kind of magic, don't you agree?"

It was like being back in drama school in a way, because we were not in the real world at all. We were creating and studying with the enthusiasm and energy of amateurs who haven't yet gone out into the professional world to find work.

I didn't confide in Fanny or Margo about Michael, but at night in bed I went over every detail, letter, phone call of the past few months. I tried to find the reason, the real reason Michael had betrayed me. I remembered how he had tried to talk me out of doing the last film, the film I got the Oscar for.

"Anyone can play that part, Nicole, it's not as if it is a monumental role. I'll write something better for you. Stay here."

"But I love that part—there is a real character there, and you got along very well before we met." We laughingly said that we would just have to commute to see each other. How little did we know? It was the wrong decision. I should have stayed. Do you ever know what is the best thing to do?

We sat facing each other over the coffee-table in his flat. I can still see him. He got up occasionally to walk around the room. He had on my favourite blue shirt. Would that I could rewind my life back to that evening and start all over again. Wipe out what happened. He really loved me then, which I just seemed to have lost sight of.

Each night I would dream about him, sometimes he was so close I would wake up expecting him to be in the room, vivid pictures of him talking to me, conversations I couldn't have made up. He said he was buying another house but would be living in it with someone else, and to keep away. It was a mansion, and I could see him through the window laughing with another woman. I'd be jolted awake with fright and realise it was all true. Maybe not the mansion, but that he was gone. Huge sadness racked my body as I lay there.

One of the women in the class, Marion, who had a cut-glass voice, had three daughters in boarding schools back in England. She seemed so together, so mature, totally in charge of her life and this was just a break for her. We looked at her with awe because she was managing a home, investments, children, a husband, all with such efficiency. If she wanted to sell her paintings after she returned home, then I could imagine that she would just pick up the phone and they would be in some art gallery by the end of the week. Done.

She reminded me a little of Julia and her charity fund-raising events. No anguish or stupidity about what you are doing with your life. One day, we sat next to each other at lunch and I tried to strike up a conversation. She was pleasant enough but distant. She knew my career but she wasn't impressed. I knew she would think along the lines of: "Anyone who is an actress is not to be taken very seriously as a person." Her paintings were good. It left me questioning my whole persona. I wondered if Michael had married someone like her. Mature, professional, stock market, bonds, stocks, but artistic as well.

Steve wanted to come over. He kept leaving messages at the hotel, so finally I called him.

"Baby, when are you coming back?"

"I don't know, I really don't know."

"You will be the death of me."

"No, I won't, just give me time."

"There is a script here that's been sent to you and there is a deadline."

"Send it to me, if you must, but I'm retiring, Steve, you know that."

"No I don't. You must get back here."

"I wonder why you don't just leave me alone!"

"Well, I'm coming over if you won't come back. I have to go to the Cannes Film Festival anyway. Why don't you meet me in Cannes? It will be fun. You can go back to your painting afterwards if you have to. You really should be there."

I put down the phone and looked out the window. The lake was like glass, nothing moving, no wind, absolute silence, with a heart-stopping view. Perhaps I'll paint this scene from this window.

Two days later Steve called again.

"Things have changed. You have to be in Cannes, Nicole, we need you there, they will probably sue you if you don't show up. You really are expected. Grow up! I've worked so hard for you. What do you think you're doing over in Italy at a time like this?"

His anger brought back all the bad feelings I had about LA and the terrific pressures involved. I was immediately hit in the stomach again by anger at Michael.

"Don't be angry, please, Steve. Please try to understand."

"Sure, I know, but you can't just disappear just because you have a domestic problem. You have to be in Cannes."

"But what if I was ill? What would you do?"

"You are not, and they know it. I promised I'd get you there."

"You shouldn't have done that. Call me tomorrow and I'll try to organise it." I told the desk I'd be leaving for a week, would then return, they were to save the same room for me. My tiny shell I could hide in. When I told the others they were all terribly excited, urging me to go. Unfortunately the art classes would be finished by the time I got back, they would all be gone. I had hardly any clothes to pack and they were mostly covered in paint. When Steve called again, we arranged to meet in Cannes. He said he would make all the reservations, I just had to get myself there. I asked him to go to my apartment, as he had a key, then gave him a list of clothes in my closet I wanted him to bring. "Get the green suitcase in the corner of the closet. If you can't find everything it doesn't matter. But bring all the T-shirts in the top drawer of the bureau and the long black dress in the closet. The yellow pant-suit next to it and there is a navy-blue blazer also." I just hoped he'd bring the right things, otherwise it would mean an expensive shopping expedition, which was the last thing I wanted.

That evening I said goodbye to my new-found friends at the art school and Fanny, and I promised to keep in touch, as well as to store my canvases till next year.

The hotel concierge helped me with the train timetables and in the morning I caught the ferry from Bellagio. Next stop Cannes.

Chapter Three

I TOOK THE TRAIN BUT had to change several times. The stations all had picturesque names. There were many back-packers in the corridor, as I sat there I remembered my last train journey as one of them. How simple life was then. If anyone had told me what a dilemma I would be in after winning an Oscar I would have laughed at them. If anyone had told me that I would have fame but not the man I loved I might not have become an actress. I might have been better off without the rat-race that life in the theatre is, the endless striving for recognition, for work, for fame. This line of thinking is so futile, you never can tell if things would have been better or worse, you do what you have to do, just hope for the best.

Suddenly a porter came along ringing a bell saying the lunch was now ready in the dining car. I noticed one young woman who was obviously travelling alone, sitting on her backpack in the corridor reading a paperback. I looked at the title: *English Romantic Poets*, a rather unusual travel companion.

I was ready for a good meal and for some company to distract me. I went past the girl and turned.

"Hello, are you travelling alone?"

"Yes."

"Where are you from?"

"Australia." She smiled, looking up. I remembered not being able to afford any kind of meal on a train in Italy as a student. She was obviously a student and I guessed about ten years younger than me.

"Would you like to have some lunch with me? Please come join me as my guest."

"Oh, that is so kind of you. Actually I'm starving. I ate my last orange an hour ago." She got up and shook hands with me. "My name is Patricia."

"Mine's Nicole. Come along this way, I think the dining car is at this end."

We threaded our way past all the backpackers along the corridor. It was good to see the obvious pleasure on the girl's face. I knew how she must feel. As a student I was always hungry on trains, terribly envious of people who could eat in the dining car, as I could never afford it. I remember in those days my idea of being wealthy was to be able to eat a sumptuous lunch watching the fabulous scenery whizz past. Now at last I could do it. We were shown a table on the mountain side where the train was shielded from the sun. The table was laid with a white linen tablecloth, fan-shaped napkins, a vase of fresh flowers in the centre. I reached for the wine list.

Patricia looked out the window, then said she would like to freshen up a bit as she saw her reflection in the glass when we suddenly went through a pitch-black tunnel.

She disappeared, then came back with hair combed and the slight smell of soap. She certainly looked a lot better. Over lunch, which started with a shrimp cocktail, then lamb chops followed by crème brulee, I found out that Patricia had come from Australia to study painting in London.

"So why aren't you in London painting, Patricia?"

"Well, I studied painting for a year there, but I promised my parents that I would go back home after that."

"But you came to Italy instead, or are you on your way home now?"

"I don't want to go home, I'm looking for an excuse to stay in Europe, I need a good reason to stay, a reason that my parents will accept, they're paying for me, after all."

"Why don't you want to go home?"

"I'm supposed to get married when I do."

"Nothing wrong with that, is there?"

"This boy I'm supposed to marry is obsessed with me, I left him because he was too possessive, he wouldn't leave me alone."

"A lot of girls would prefer their boyfriends to be possessive, to want the girl all to themselves, be jealous if she showed any interest in any other man."

"In moderation perhaps, but mine was impossible, we had rows about it."

I wondered whether my love for Michael was possessive. Was he an obsession? What is true love? To be in love was an obsession. The talent needed to be a good actress is almost like an obsession: you are always thinking about it, just as you are about the person you are in love with. The talent is to keep everything in motion.

I tried to change the conversation. "Where else have you been in Europe?"

"I spent some time following in the footsteps of Byron, Keats and Shelley, I went down to see the Chateau de Chillon on Lake Geneva, you know where Byron wrote such wonderful poetry. He always epitomised the spirit of the Romantics for me. It's stupid to say, I suppose, that I have great spiritual hunger," (as she looked down at her plate). We laughed.

I said, "And here am I on a kind of emotional diet, trying to stay slim and be reasonable."

She continued "I'm reading a book about the Romantics and the age of Romanticism with its escape from reason, its awareness of the sublime, which is all tied up with the love of nature. Look at those mountains, for example." Turning to the window she added, "They go with Beethoven, his Ninth perhaps, and Byron would have called them sublime."

"Sublime yes, but why did he write so much about despair?"

"Because sometimes nature is indifferent and cruel, even though we love it so much, and the same thing applies to men," she said.

"But the Romantics wanted freedom, as you said, an escape from reason. I really only liked Byron's poem about the prisoner in the Chateau and his indifference to being released."

We discussed our favourite poetry, then went on to our favourite composers. The time flew by. Patricia knew a great deal about her Romantic poets as I did about Shakespeare. We quoted verses back and forth. I finally finished with the actor's version of Keats:

"When I have fears that I may cease to be

I have another drink, or two, or three."

The train pulled into the station at Nice, which was Patricia's stop. She was going to see Picasso's museum in Antibes the next day. I gave her a big hug and said, "Keep in touch, if you get to London give me a call."

"I will, I will. Give me your telephone number, do you have a card?"

We exchanged telephone numbers, finally saying goodbye.

As the train pulled out, I watched her walking along the platform. She turned and we waved to each other. I envied her peace of mind; it compared well with her boyfriend's obsession and brought home how my obsession was still with me. I was tired of thinking constantly about Michael.

Sitting in the train looking out the window, I let my thoughts roam. It seemed ironic that after all the years at drama school, waiting for a break, getting the first job, struggling in London to break through to success, with lots of tears, poverty and hopelessness, that when I get to win an Oscar, the success just dissipates when the man you want just wipes all that effort away. Not to mention your ambition and hopes.

I couldn't believe it would happen. The force of sexual energy could be so horrendously, shockingly all-consuming. All I want is to be with Michael, wherever he is. No matter what he is doing. But then, he is always doing something interesting, taking everyone he meets along with him in his enthusiasm. Good actors are supposed to be totally dedicated, aren't they? No matter what—but as an actress I was distracted by him.

Drama school was not only frustrating because you were always rehearsing and never performing—for a real audience. Doubts about the two-year course were always there, sometimes almost every week. Suddenly there would be a fit of depression, irritation and despair. I remember walking down the street, trying to memorise lines for my next lesson or just cloud-gathering, a huge cloud would block out my enthusiasm. My only rationalisation was that my work in the theatre might inspire or create thought, or might give some enjoyment. The other students may have had similar thoughts but no one dared discuss them. We were all too insecure and wanted to be regarded as serious students.

Had I any idea how many hours would be needed to learn my craft? What a crazy world. We were told about actors acting through the Blitz, touring in freezing trains, working in unheated theatres. I wondered if it was just plain old ego that kept us going. Total exhibitionism! Why do you think that your interpretation of Ophelia could be any better than, say, the past thousand actresses who have played it. At school, one of our drama teachers was an old ham actor with the Donald Wolfit Company years ago. He was so experienced, we all loved him. He knew everything about technique. In the lesson he said, "Whenever you have a speech to deliver that is particularly awful, always give it out as though you considered it the finest piece of literature that was ever written and the public will accept it. An audience has an instinct very like an animal, let them see that you are afraid and they are likely to turn and snap at you; face them boldly and they will eat out of your hand."

I thought back to my first showcase. Everyone hoped that the agents they had invited would show up, we all knew that we would be out in the real world before long, walking on tight-ropes between auditions, agents and jobs without the safety net of our school friends' support. Stark reality. Poverty, huge barriers of rejections, blows to our self-esteem.

"What are you doing now?" was a question everyone asked when you went to an audition. You couldn't say, "Nothing," "Nothing, nothing," "Resting," or, "Walking the streets."

What am I doing now? "I'm writing a play," was what I came up with, because you didn't need to say you weren't working because you were working. No one questioned that because as an actress you could indeed be writing a play. They made their notes during auditions and every time they said their goodbyes you wondered why you put yourself through such humiliation—face-to-face rejection by people who probably don't know as much as you do. I used to take the tube home, looking at my fellow-passengers, analysing their faces automatically, the clothes they were wearing and wondering what ambitions each one of them held in their heart. Not bloody acting, I'm sure.

To have to work yourself up to do a monologue, out of context, from an epic play takes a hell of a lot of imagination, and a kind of spiritual energy that depletes you especially if the people auditioning you appear indifferent. If they said, "That was wonderful," but still didn't hire you, it would at least assuage the anguish and the stupidity of auditioning.

During these times, you have to have someone in mind who inspired you in the first place to take up acting. To reach your goals you have to keep remembering the artists who stimulated you in the beginning.

How totally wrong I had been to go off and go to LA. It wasn't the classical work that I had been trained for. In movies there was no feedback from an audience. Your timing and characterisation were very superficial. The lines you had to say were not immortal. Money was the only reward. I wondered how many actors had sold out.

Suddenly the train whistle interrupted my thoughts. We were arriving in Cannes.

The town was a madhouse. But then I expected it to be. Steve had managed to get us two rooms at the Carlton Hotel, where all the action happens during the Film Festival. It is on the Croisette, the street that runs along the front, by the beach, the row of hotels, boutiques, restaurants and bars, packed, jammed side by side, facing out across the Mediterranean sea. The Palais des Festivals is at the end of the Croisette where the main films are shown.

"Steve, this is absolute bedlam," I shouted at him as we threaded our way though the groups of people on the pavement near the Carlton.

"Just don't lose me," said Steve as he ploughed on.

Hundreds of people crowd into this town for the Festival, most of them seem to be between the Carlton and the Palais. Steve had arranged interviews for me with what seemed to be all the press invited. Radio, TV journalists were everywhere.

Outside on the terrace of the Carlton in the sun, cigar-smoking producers, aggressive distributors were noisily making deals, discussing contracts, drinking, laughing, swearing a lot, in general looking pretty unkempt. People wove their way through the cane-backed chairs and small tables, patting each other on the back, sometimes joining a table or just circulating—"working the room". I recognised several of our producers but kept on walking as I had no intention of being questioned.

A huge crowd was gathering round the front door of the Carlton. I looked over, it was Hugh Grant who was arriving. He looked tired, no doubt jet-lag. I saw Vanessa Redgrave stop to talk to a fan in the lobby, Julia Roberts was being interviewed in a room, next door to mine, which was crowded with reporters.

"Hi, Nicole," I heard a voice behind me. I turned round to see Howard, one of our producers. He seemed friendly, thank God. "Good to see you, time for a drink? I've got a great suite with a balcony."

"Yes, why not?" I needed to be cheered up and to mend a few fences. The terrace was too crowded, Steve was resting. I followed Howard down the hall. The suite was magnificent. We went out on to the balcony to look at the crazy crowd below, the azure sea straight ahead with the luxury yachts moored nearby bobbing up and down, their white decks glinting in the sun.

"Oh Michael, where are you?" my heart cried out.

Howard opened a bottle of champagne that was sitting in a silver bucket and poured two glasses. It was ice-cold.

"Here's to you, kid."

"Here's to you, Howard. You are incredible."

We clinked our glasses as I held my glass of golden amber up in the sunlight.

"This is a moment to savour, Howard."

"You have got to be the prettiest girl in Cannes, Nicole."

"Oh come off it."

Then followed the most seductive play I had yet to encounter. It was like the scene in *Some Like it Hot* when Tony Curtis convinces Marilyn Monroe he is impotent, then challenges her to seduce him. Only Howard was much less handsome than Curtis, heavily over-weight, and unshaven.

"But Nicole, you could at least try. There is nothing worse than sexual frustration, you know." His tone of voice indicated that he thought I owed him something.

"I think there are lots of things worse than that, Howard. Real grinding poverty for one, a painful incurable illness, grief over the loss of a loved one, all kinds of things."

"We're talking about the here and now, I'm frustrated and I bet you are too."

He kept going on and on about it until finally I had to tell him about my problem.

"What problem?"

When I explained how being dumped by Michael had frozen me over. Sex didn't appeal at all. So I would be absolutely no good at the job. He kept insisting and I suddenly knew I had to leave, before things turned nasty.

"Behave or I'll leave."

"No you can't."

He got up, he came towards me. I was out the door.

"Damn him, the stupid man," even before I'd closed the door.

I ran down the corridor cursing him. What did he expect? Did he think I would even think of going to bed with him? The idiot. The incident made me sick. No need to go back to my room, I wanted to be with people to forget it ever happened. Luckily I met Steve in the lobby, I said I needed a drink. He looked exhausted. We walked down the Croisette to the Majestic—there were fewer crowds down there.

We sat under a palm tree beside the pool watching the bikini-clad starlets splashing about in the water. There was a heavy perfume in the air, the pungent perfume that I recognised as the south of France. I calmed down and looked cross the bay, it really was a lovely view of the Mediterranean. Steve talked on and on about his day, the contacts he had made, the irritations, the horrendous delays everywhere. The town was filling up with people pushing films.

"What are you thinking about, baby?"

I was thinking about Michael, of course, but instead I said, "Oh, just about when I was here ten years ago as a radio journalist."

"Really?"

"Yes." I had to keep talking, I didn't want to discuss Michael with him just now. "I wasn't a journalist exactly but I wanted to be here, so I brought a tape-recorder with a letter of introduction from the BBC so in case I wanted to I could ask anyone for an interview."

"What made you come then?"

"Well, I'd met an old friend, a journalist from the States staying in London; she looked me up on her way to Cannes. She begged me to come down with her to 'do the Festival'. I was out of work at the time, so what else is new? After she'd gone, I suddenly thought what a great opportunity I had missed, as I had just finished a screenplay so perhaps I could sell it at the Festival."

"That is crazy, you know that is totally impossible."

"I know it now, but not then. So the next day I got the BBC letter from a friend, then came down here. Only trouble was, I didn't know where she was staying."

"In this crowd?"

"I walked into a hotel near the railway station and guess what, she was registered there."

"The first hotel?"

"I'm lucky at some things. We had a ball. It was nothing like this scene now. There were the old-time stars. It was so elegant then, in fact, far more sedate, that I vowed to myself that one day I would come back here."

"If you remember, I had to drag you here," laughed Steve.

"I meant to come back here, but *not* when the Festival was on."

We had planned to have dinner at La Petite Croisette because Steve wanted to be there. The noise was deafening, because the place was packed with all the film people, mostly journalists.

"Please, do we have to stay here, Steve? It's awful, you can't hear yourself speak! I've been to Cannes before, I know a place on the other side of Rue d'Antibes. It's much quieter."

"Well, if you say so." He could see I was about to walk out of there.

We found the little restaurant I'd eaten in ten years ago, although I didn't recognise the owner. Must have sold out, I guessed. The meal was divine, with lots of wine with a cognac to finish. Steve was being very kind, just let me talk as much as I wanted to. He was an experienced listener, gradually I told him what I had been doing in Italy. He knew about Michael but didn't mention him.

"What if I tell you I've got a great script for you. Are you prepared to read it?"

I read it that night. I hated it. I hated the character and the whole concept.

I was up before sunrise and paced about the room wondering how I could tell Steve. I threw on my running clothes and went for a run along the beach. The sea was dead calm, the only people about were the boys raking the sand. The air was cool and refreshing. Another film . . . all that work for what? Getting up at five a.m., going to the studio then home to bed to learn lines and repeat the procedure for weeks.

I met Steve coming up the hotel steps.

"I'm just going to have breakfast, come and join me." As we waited for the orange juice I wondered if it was the time to tell him. Full ahead.

"I read the script, I don't like it, Steve."

"It's big bucks, sweetheart. You know that."

"But where will I have to go?"

"They are shooting it in LA."

"But the script says Africa."

"It will be in LA."

"But I don't want to go back there again, Steve."

"We'll talk about it later."

We finished breakfast and Steve led me around all day to various meetings and interviews. I wanted to get away from the Carlton and the crowds to see something of the town.

That evening I managed to slip away, just as all the beach restaurants were taking in their umbrellas and chaise lounges. I walked along the water's edge. The palm trees were black against the setting sun behind them. I wished I had my paints and canvas with me. The film crowd was nowhere to be seen. Most of them were in the festival's screening room or at the Palais. Everyone was pushing a film. Stars were pushing films, but I just couldn't work at it.

Walking along the sand, the water was calm, just little ripples breaking along the shore, I wondered where I had gone wrong. Does anyone know when they make an irreparable mistake that sets off a tidal wave? You try to be careful, to be aware of what you do, like making the right decisions. I was so much on my guard, I couldn't believe things had gone so wrong.

All I had been thinking about then was the theatre, becoming a professional actress.

The love and romance that most young people dream about I regarded as a distraction from my real work. None of the decisions I had made about my career in the theatre had been so bad, but how dreadfully I had messed the rest of my life, the most important part of my life. I thought back to when I left home.

The day I left Manchester to go to drama school in London, the breakfast scene was classic, Mother fussing about my luggage, money, tickets, laundry etc. It amused me to think that my parents still regarded me as a child, incapable of taking care of myself, even though we had already been to London to rent a small apartment near the school. I was full of ambition, determined to become a successful actress. Drama school was only the first step on my agenda, I was already planning where I wanted to go after that. Nobody could have dissuaded me.

Mum and Dad had taken out a second mortgage on the house to pay for my drama school, so I was determined not to let them down.

Chapter Four

THE SHOCK OF ARRIVING IN London after living in Manchester was considerable. People moved faster, talked faster and nobody seemed to have any time to spare. The city was enormous, I felt I needed to focus totally or else I could be easily distracted by all the attractions of the city. London was going to be more expensive than I thought, judging by the taxi fare.

The first night in my new apartment was unnerving. The light switches were hard to find. The apartment was freezing with only one radiator to heat the whole place. When I switched it on, it burnt off all the dust on the element and smelt awful. Now, whenever I smell that turned-on radiator smell, the association is of freezing rooms, poverty and hopelessness.

London after innumerable visits was not new to me, so there was no sight-seeing planned, only theatres to visit when time was available. The apartment belonged to a friend of my mother's who said I could stay on till I found something more suitable.

Finally around four a.m. I fell into a deep sleep, then woken by a car siren going off in the street at seven o'clock. Instant coffee and a piece of cake for breakfast gobbled up before rushing to the tube to arrive in time for the first day.

Nothing was done the first morning at drama school except to register, find out where and when the classes were, and who would be teaching them. At lunchtime I went into the cafeteria for a sandwich, finding a seat opposite a girl about my age. She was small, quite short, with lovely curly brown hair and pretty face.

"Hello, my name is Nicole. How do you do? Do you mind if I join you?"

"Not at all. My name is Peggy."

The place was almost empty, I was hungry and quite exhausted.

"Are you a new student?" I asked her.

"Yes, I am," she replied. "Where are you from?"

"Manchester—and you?"

"Bristol."

"What do you think of this place, Peggy?"

"I don't quite know, it's all been a bit of a shock. I expected something a little more modern, it's so dingy somehow."

We ate our sandwiches, brushing the crumbs off the table-top as we did so. The cafeteria was nearly empty, we rattled the ice in our paper cups holding water and sipped the remainder. I showed her the classes and teachers that had been assigned to me. She showed me hers. Basically we were doing the same course with the same teachers.

"Looks like we'll be seeing a lot of each other," I said. Peggy nodded and we smiled at each other.

"How long have you wanted to be an actress?" I asked her.

"Ever since I can remember, or rather when Mum took me to my first pantomime. How about you?" asked Peggy.

"Same thing, I guess."

"Did you have a stage mum? One who started you off?"

"Of course. It's our mothers who are the ones to blame. If we both didn't have stage mothers we'd be totally well adjusted," I said.

"Because they really wanted it for themselves, more than likely. They want us to be brilliant and as famous as Vivien Leigh in *Gone with the Wind*."

My mother didn't want to be an actress, she wanted to be a ballet dancer."

"And was she?"

"No, she married my father instead," I said.

Peggy leant across the table for the sugar, taking three helpings to put in her tea. "If nobody gives me a job after twelve months I'm quitting."

"That's too soon. You have to get out there and push."

"I heard of a boy who sent out two hundred résumés and got four replies," sighed Peggy.

"That's because he didn't put in a stamped addressed envelope."

The ones that answered just said nothing. They said they would keep his résumé on file."

"God, it's hopeless. Two hundred of them!" I was amazed. "*Two hundred!*"

"And he's still doing it."

"Is he any good?"

"I don't know, I haven't seen his work. Can you imagine, the cost of the mailing alone, not to mention the photographs?"

"Is that what we should be doing?"

"No, not yet. Let's wait to see what happens at the end-of-term showcase."

I leaned over to her and said, "Do you believe in the casting couch routine?"

"Do you mean, would I sleep with someone to get a play?"

"Yes, I'm asking you."

"That's hypothetical. It would depend on who it was."

"A really ugly fat producer, gross."

"It may happen."

"Well, I'll wait to see if it does."

"Be prepared, as the boy scouts are."

We both took our trays to the counter and said our goodbyes.

Thus ended my first day. During the next few months, there were voice classes, mime, fencing, ballet, singing and exercise classes. The acting coaches took each student for private tuition, every week we would have to learn new monologues for our professors who demanded almost complete interpretations of the extracts. I found that I had no idea how I compared to the other actors in the class as they were all working on different monologues in private, no one critiqued them except their professors.

Plays were announced and each of us discovered what characters we would be playing. Finally we were all drawn together to rehearse, to put into practice what techniques we had learnt during the first few months.

My fellow-students were all so similar to me—young men and women with one dream. We were all ambitious, determined, full of hope. The school wouldn't allow any of us to accept outside work, whether amateur or professional, several students had opted out when they had been offered a good job, not knowing if they would ever get the same opportunity when their schooling had finished.

During the months at drama school, several of the actors wanted to date me—"to form a relationship" they called it—but I was not interested, having decided to channel all sexual energy into work, become like a nun, casting all thoughts and yearnings aside. Sexual dreams about some of my professors always made me blush the next day in their presence, but composure quickly returned; being nervous about my monologue would be the natural explanation.

The months went by, my classmates and I went to the theatre together, sitting in the upper dress circle or gallery, comparing notes after the performances in a nearby coffee-shop or next day at school.

I phoned my parents every week, making the effort to be cheerful and optimistic even when at times I was filled with doubts and despair. The fierce competition between actresses was becoming very evident. Even though they were my classmates and confidantes, it was overwhelming when working with them how obvious it was that they were all competing for the lead in the end-of-term play. Whoever got the lead obviously would attract the attention of the invited agents who attended these showcases.

Warning signals went up when I witnessed the politics of some students eager to become the "teacher's pet". Most drama schools have their annual play, but if they decide to do a showcase of monologues instead, hiring a West-End theatre at lunch time if they don't have a theatre at their school, then it is important to appear either at the beginning or the end of the show. Most agents nod off during the middle!!

I decided to do Emily from *Our Town*—the speech in the graveyard—I knew I would have to fight for the right spot in the programme. Whom to approach about that? Suddenly it became the most important issue in my life. "I must be at the end, the end of the programme. It has to be me to end the show." It was a graveyard after all.

Meanwhile my parents decided to come to visit. There was a sofa bed in the living room, they were to come on Friday.

"Of course, Mum, it would be great to see you."

"I'd like to see how you're really getting on. You probably don't eat enough, don't get enough sleep, aren't looking after yourself properly, you've always been a bit slapdash, rush, rush, rush, never hanging up your clothes unless I made you, I don't suppose it's any different now."

"Oh Mum, you treat me like a child, I'm grown up now, or haven't you realised that yet?"

"I'll see just how grown up you are, if you are, which I doubt."

Oh dear, what a terrible intrusion. On the one hand, I wanted them, but on the other, felt totally disturbed and distracted. A whole weekend lost. My mother's voice irritated me, her accent was awful. How could she talk like that?!

We went to the theatre. They paid for seats in the stalls. I was grateful, realising how much was missed in a performance by sitting in the gallery.

Next morning over coffee my mother asked, "Is everything all right?"

"Of course, all I need is a wonderful agent after I finish next month!"

"Doesn't the school find you one, or at least help you find one?"

"Well, they put on a show at the end of the school year, invite all the agents; that's why it's so terribly important to do well at it."

After my parents went home, I worked feverishly sending out invitations to the showcase. The day approached. All the students were concerned that everyone they had invited showed up. The school did not have its own theatre, so they had hired a West End theatre and had decided to feature each actor in a monologue.

I went to the school principal to ask if I could be the last performer. After a week of waiting, the place was mine. It took me days to knock on his door, I spent hours rehearsing what to say. The speech was so final that it would be an anticlimax to follow it with another monologue, so he agreed—a small victory but an important one. The showcase was a success. Agents and producers were given wine and sandwiches beforehand in the foyer, then went into the theatre for two hours of monologues.

I stood backstage listening to all of them. I was critical of most, so it only enhanced my hopes for my performance, confident that the wonderful emotion of Emily's speech would win over any agents in the audience.

Suddenly it was all over. All the actors were now in the foyer bar mingling with the audience. Relatives, friends, acquaintances came up to them to tell them how marvellous they were. I had not asked any relatives, so while I was talking with the other actors, whose eyes were darting around the room, I felt a tap on my shoulder. I turned around to meet Arnold Baker.

"Hello, I'm Arnold Baker from the Flitcross Agency. I enjoyed your work. Here's my card, I'd like to talk to you tomorrow."

I could have kissed him or got down to kiss his shoes, but smiled instead, managing to give him a great twinkle.

"Of course. I appreciate your taking the time to come."

Arnold did what I'd hoped he'd do. He sent me to auditions. He told me what to wear, what to say, telling me to call him immediately after the audition. I first was devastated at the interviews. They were monstrous. At the auditions, there were at least twenty actresses who could have played the part. They looked at my photograph, taken at great expense by a photographer of note, my résumé, then after five minutes I was out the door. All that bother of dressing up, getting there, then meeting such rejection. I felt like a race horse being viewed for the next race. Although they didn't actually ask to look in your mouth to count your teeth, they certainly took notice of teeth, hair, body and bust.

Some actress, I remembered, had told me it was all to do with your boobs. Big boobs, big parts, she'd said. So I started putting socks in my bra, wearing tight sweaters to auditions. It seemed to work, but I sensed slight overtones that bothered me. Christ! Is the old story of the casting couch true? Not talent, but sex? No one had warned me of this—I had thought it had gone out with food coupons, and the innuendoes infuriated me. I took particular notice of the advancement of other actresses who were well endowed. One actress posed for a magazine wearing only high-heeled shoes and a string of pearls. She became a success overnight.

"It just might be true," I thought. One agent who met me at the showcase invited me to visit him at six p.m. the following Monday.

I dressed down, then was slightly disturbed to see no secretary there when I arrived. He led me through the office to the next room and I quickly observed that it was his living quarters. It was already dark outside, and there were candles alight on the coffee table. I immediately spotted some porno videotapes on the table, took in the red velvet curtains and the red velvet couch, and knew I had to get out of there.

"Would you care for a glass of wine, my dear?" he said.

"No, thank you, I'm not a drinker really."

"Let me pour you one anyway . . ."

Rapidly I assessed the situation, or rather seduction scene and decided that no matter what he had to offer me, I was not interested.

How naive of me, how stupid! This silly old man! But how to escape without giving offence? Who knows, he may be able to put me on in the West End.

When he told me to sit on the red velvet couch, I declined, saying that I was most anxious about my mother who was arriving that very evening to stay with me, and how I had forgotten to leave her the keys.

A quick getaway, but how embarrassing! In the taxi, I found herself shaking with anger. "*My God*! The dirty old man, how dare he! He's so gross. Would anyone I know fall for *that*?"

The next day I phoned him and apologised that I had had to dash off (as if he didn't know), hoping he would still be my agent and send me out for auditions.

Meanwhile "Arnold the Agent" as I called him, seemed genuine enough. He was young and serious and didn't seem to be interested in big boobs. He sent me to many auditions, telephoned me afterwards to report, when he would often say to me, "Don't take it personally; often they're looking for a 'Type'. You must understand if you can, that producers don't have much imagination. Even though you can change your personality and looks, it's what they see up front that they go by. Don't worry, we will find you a job."

Tirelessly I waited. Auditioning for crummy people who weren't worthy of even conversing with my professors at drama school; creepy, horrible types who looked like they were on drugs, often auditioned me. Sometimes I felt so degraded by performing for them. They looked at me in a rude kind of way, as if I was a bundle of meat, and treated me in the same manner; it was so difficult not to break down in tears from the sheer humiliation of it all. The build-up of the audition, the performance of the monologue, the instant emotion needed, effected from the technique you had learnt for hours, sometimes days, with your professor, often to be discarded within a minute.

If only they could be more polite, I thought. Manners would be very welcome. We are human beings after all, we have gone to drama school. We have learnt our techniques, history, often our parents have sacrificed their savings to pay our fees. It was hard not to feel self-pitying. We are broke, we are cold, we are desperate for a job, only to be dismissed by these rude people. Maybe some of us are more talented than others, but we still should have some kind of respect.

I got out of the taxi when the meter reached five pounds, trudged back home in the rain, my anger rising as I thought of how many times I had felt humiliated and abused by these agents. The other actresses seemed to be more resilient; Peggy, who had become a close friend, said she put her veneer on before she went out to audition. She mentally covered herself with it and let everything bounce off it.

"You must, otherwise you will be finished. Toughen up, give them the same back."

"I wish I was as tough as you seem to be."

Peggy had had an audition with the National, she knew people who knew Trevor Nunn. She was very confident, as she had auditioned there already. When she went in for her next audition, not with Trevor, but with an assistant, she was astonished when, as she approached him smiling with résumé in hand, he said, "Oh, I see you've had your teeth fixed."

She was so appalled that her teeth would have even been noticed.

"Yes," was all she could say. She was about to do a brilliant monologue, so what did her teeth matter? Christ, why bother? But she walked to the stage, and tried to erase the conversation as she withdrew into Joan La Pucelle from *Henry IV Part I*.

After drama school and the showcase was over, everyone dispersed. I was surprised that my new-found friends didn't keep in touch, except Peggy. They would meet at the same auditions, often having coffee together afterwards. No one was offering them work.

Six months later, I was desperate. The agent who had been so enthusiastic just disappeared. His phone number was disconnected. That was that. I never did find out what happened to him. Maybe he died or something and went to agents' heaven, if there is one. It reminded me of the joke about the young man who needed a heart transplant. When the doctor told him that two heart donors had been found, a young man who had died in a traffic accident and a theatrical agent, so which one did he want? The boy chose the latter, saying, "Because the heart would never have been used."

I began answering ads in *The Stage* newspaper. Nothing. More auditions with questionable characters. "Why didn't anyone tell me that it would be so difficult?" I kept asking myself.

Then one day, the phone rang—totally unexpected of course—it was about an ad I'd answered three weeks ago: "Juvenile lead wanted in weekly repertory company." The voice on the phone said he was Harold Murray, the Artistic Director of the Ipswich Theatre Company, they liked my résumé, could I come to Ipswich by Friday? Friday of that week. I was offered the job over the phone, they were that desperate. Evidently they had fired my predecessor, needing someone to start rehearsals the following Monday.

I phoned my parents who had given up hope.

"Guess what! I've got a job!!"

"Got a job? Where?"

"Ipswich. It's a very good repertory company."

"What will you be doing?" asked Mother suspiciously.

"Juvenile lead."

"Darling, that's marvellous! What did you have to do to get the job?"

"Answer an ad in *The Stage*, that's all. Probably the Artistic Director of the Ipswich Rep saw me at the school end-of-year show or something."

As I put down the phone, I realised how much my parents wanted me to be a success, after all the money they had spent on me. I knew that they hoped for something in return. At last some action, I thought. Go forward. Ipswich is not the West End, but at least it was a job.

It was around four-thirty p.m. when the train pulled into Ipswich Station. It was already dark. Mary Murray, the wife of the director, met me on the platform. Only six other people got off, so she had no trouble in recognising me, with my two bulging suitcases.

"Hello, you must be Nicole."

"Yes, how do you do."

"I'm Mary Murray, Harold's wife. Can I help you with those?"

She looked at the two cases.

"No, I'm fine."

However, Mary took one of the cases. We walked about three long blocks, then turned down a narrow street to their digs. Mary did most of the talking. She explained that the company of seven all lived in the same boarding house, which was run by a middle-aged woman named Milly. Milly cooked them breakfast leaving a cold buffet of meat and salad each evening for them, with a hot meal on weekends. She filled me in on the rules of the house, so by the time we arrived, I had a clear picture of how they all survived living together.

Mary had her own key, we entered without ringing; by then it was almost time to go to the theatre.

I met the company in the hallway and tried to remember all their names. Milly came down the hall from the kitchen. She seemed nice enough, and gave me a cup of tea after showing me my room on the second floor—one single bed, a wardrobe, a night table, a desk, an armchair, with a window facing south.

The other actors were friendly as they left for the theatre, which was only five hundred yards down the street. Drinking my tea quickly, I followed them down to the theatre. That evening I sat out front to watch the play. It was a new play called *Love for Six* which was little more than a bedroom farce with slamming doors and lots of action. I liked all their performances, making allowances for the poor script. I studied the audience, the people coming in and their reactions, as well as trying to listen to some of their comments in the interval.

I went around afterwards, feeling shy at meeting them again, having to compliment them after only having just met them.

"Darling, you were marvellous," obviously was not appropriate, coming from a yet untried juvenile lead.

The company then all crossed the road to the local pub, I was invited to join them by Mary who, sensing I might be broke, bought me a drink. Then Harold handed me the script for next week's play. We all sat around discussing the evening's performance; the bonhomie of the actors was a pleasant surprise, especially when they recalled their memory lapses or fluffs on stage. They obviously included me in their enjoyment although I had nothing to say, being rather in awe of them all as well as worrying about the next day's rehearsal and their opinion of my work.

All I can recall about my first day was the familiar feeling of excitement, then the sense of great pleasure, and that warm feeling of belonging as I walked back and forth to the theatre. I was now a true member of a respected repertory company.

That night, in bed, I read through the script. It wasn't very big as I was playing a character part. The part of the old nanny who makes three entrances is not very demanding. I would need all my training in make-up to become an eighty-year-old, no doubt would be powdering my hair as well. I was relieved it wasn't a big role for my first play.

Next morning as we began the first read-through of the play I was nervous. The actors were curious to hear me read. However, it all went well. Then after the morning break (coffee in chipped mugs made by the ASM, the young assistant stage manager) we went up on stage to start blocking the moves. By the end of the week we would have to be word-perfect, know where to move simultaneously, as well as master our own interpretations of the characters we were playing, communicating it to the rest of the cast.

During rehearsals, we were very sensitive to criticism. Lucy, who was of a certain age, well over fifty I should think, played the main character parts.

"Darling, don't walk like that," she whispered to me. "Take smaller steps across the stage."

She was right. The director gave me the same note at the end of rehearsals that day.

"You walk like a lumber-jack. Do take smaller steps, more from the waist."

Oh dear, it was embarrassing, as I'd had no idea. I knew I took long strides but I didn't think it was so bad.

Next came the make-up. Not enough! The lights can make you look like a ghost!

Lucy had a huge wardrobe, her room must have been full of clothes. She took great care of them, often lending me things. I liked her even though she kept to herself, didn't come to the pub after the show or hang out with us. It was probably the age difference—she had heard all our chatter about missing props, corpsing and forgetting lines many times before.

"Don't forget to find some new cushions for next week's set—we can't have the same ones over and over again, the audience will recognise them," demanded Harold as I left the theatre that day. I had offered to help the ASM find the props.

The main street stores gave us many of our props as they got a credit in the programme each week. They didn't like lending things such as cushions as they couldn't sell them afterwards if they looked shop-worn, or rather theatre-worn. Heaven forbid if we spilt anything on them.

The heaviest work was done on Sunday—changing the stage from one set to another, learning lines, packing, sorting props and furniture, all of which had to be returned to whoever had lent them to us. Life was so hectic, every hour was filled. Little did I know how I would look back on those days with envy later, when unemployed, waiting for the phone to ring. Actors often say that they got more experience working in their first repertory company than at any other time.

My parents took the train to Ipswich every so often to see the show, staying overnight at a local hotel. We would have a meal together, and sometimes they'd come to the pub to meet the other members of the company afterwards, otherwise no one save the locals saw our work. Reviewers from London didn't come very often except if we were doing a new play, so we all just got on with it.

All of us tried to avoid intimate friendships as the atmosphere was so tense; we lived in each other's pockets, so to speak, the thread of friendship could easily be broken with the tension of working together. Mary had her hands full, being married to the director, and their off-stage scenes were an indication of the fragility of that relationship. Sometimes we would come into the theatre to hear them screaming at each other in Mary's dressing room. Often we would hear her throw things. We never really found out what their rows were about as they would stop shouting when they heard us come in, one of them slamming the door, rocking half the back-stage area, stamping out. They used to go at it hammer and tongs, then all of us would go creeping around keeping very quiet, trying to find out which one of them was seething so we could avoid the unhappy spouse.

We would go quietly to our dressing rooms and start to make up. I shared a dressing room with Lucy.

"Lucy, please try to watch me tonight, see if my walk is any better."

"Well, it certainly is since Monday. I've been watching you—as long as you keep to small steps you'll be OK."

Trevor Lockwood was the juvenile lead. He was tall, blond and handsome with cobalt-blue eyes. I immediately felt a chemistry, but it didn't register with him, I thought. He seemed preoccupied often going straight back to the house after the show, probably to learn lines, but it seemed more that that.

I wasn't sure if he even noticed me at rehearsals, for he never spoke to me after the show.

I developed a crush on him. Perhaps because I had been living a convent life at drama school, the feelings which had been repressed suddenly came alive in the less rigid daily routine of a repertory actress. It was such a joy to be working at a theatre that the desire for more enjoyment bubbled up.

Trevor knew he was a good actor. He had been with the company for just over a year, so he was familiar with the instant characterisation that was necessary for each new script. Like all the others in the company he was writing off to larger companies around England, also requesting auditions in London. All of them knew they needed to move on but knew never to give your notice until a new contract was signed. I was devastated when, three weeks after I started with the company, Trevor announced that he had landed a job in London and gave his two weeks' notice. I went up to him after rehearsal and congratulated him. I wished him good luck, wanting to say much more but was too shy to do so.

"You will be so successful, you are such a good actor," I managed to blurt out. I cringed as I said it because it sounded so gauche.

"Thank you. I hope so."

It was then he said the thing I'd hoped he'd say.

"You're a good little actress, keep at it. It's not talent, you know, it's persistence."

"I hope you will let us know how your new job goes."

"Of course I will."

But I knew he wouldn't. The minute one leaves, it is a whole new world. Too hectic by far.

However he came back after three weeks, to see the play, mostly because Mary, who was playing an important part, had asked him to come to see her performance. It was good to see him again, even though he stayed for only two nights at our digs I managed to have a long chat.

"It's not that I am getting such wonderful parts, but in London there is more chance of being seen," he said, "Don't be so glum, you are learning here all the time."

After the second show we went to the pub, when Brian, who was our character actor and a struggling playwright, suddenly opened up after a few drinks.

"I want to be able to live like Noel Coward, to travel in style, to go abroad—imagine having an opening night in the West End and not even being there. Writing plays, partying, going to the theatre, meeting terribly important people must have kept him very busy. How did he do it?"

"He worked every day writing, you silly twit," Trevor remarked.

"He knew the kind of plays he wanted to write and he wrote them," said Brian.

"But what motivated him?" I wondered.

"Money of course," laughed Trevor. "That was what he needed because he was supporting his mother most of the time."

"But she took in boarders," insisted Brian.

"No, he moved her to the country."

"He knew everybody. Most of the time he was socialising. Read his diaries."

"I know, I already have."

"Lunch with the Queen of Spain, tea with the Queen Mother."

"His diaries read like a super-star, royalty, trips on luxury yachts, homes in Bermuda and Jamaica."

"But he worked for it. Look how much he wrote. He worked hour after hour. Up at six-thirty in the morning. He knew what he wanted. You get up at six-thirty every morning and write, maybe you'll get on private yachts, then have opening nights on Broadway."

I think it was the six-thirty a.m. bit that really did Brian in. That really got to Brian.

"Well, the creative juices have to be running pretty strongly in you veins to get started so early."

Brian was upset. He had confided in us his deepest feelings, his personal ambition, we were knocking him down.

"Never mind, Brian, we love you," said Trevor. He got up to get his coat.

But it must have stimulated Brian, either through anger or embarrassment, because his face was flushed.

"You know it's all about the relationships you form at school," said Brian. "It's all right for you. You just want to act. I want to write plays as well as act. To be able to live like Coward would be marvellous, in that it would be international travel with the right kind of people. Besides, his plays will always be remembered."

Then, as if struck by a stroke of lightning, I realised that the plays we were performing were totally forgettable. I knew immediately that, above all, I wanted to be with a company which did Shakespeare, Coward and the great playwrights. Did I have a choice?

Eventually it dawned on me that eight performances a week in a forgettable play was a waste of energy and ambition. We discussed this as we walked back to the digs in the freezing night air.

"I'd rather be doing a Christmas pantomime for children who would remember their first visit to the theatre. Children who were enchanted and very moved by what they saw on stage," I blurted out.

"'I loved your performance,' "all the locals say; these are people who had never been to the West End. "Shit! What am I doing here and why did my parents pay so much money to have me stuck in Ipswich?"

"Only you could change that," said Trevor.

"Now, I have to get out of here, do something that is more important than weekly rep. More important than amusing a geriatric crowd for two hours."

We all staggered back to the house, feeling slightly better from the drink and the camaraderie. It was a wrench to see Trevor go the next day.

The director's wife, Mary, liked me from the beginning. She was about ten years older than me—tall, thin, lovely, long black hair which she wore in a French roll at the nape of her neck most of the time. She played the female leads. Sometimes we walked back to the digs together rather than go to the pub with others after the show. I admired her, envied her secure position as the director's wife and lead in the company. I watched her in rehearsals, learnt a lot about her technique, how she worked on her roles. When I was given a juvenile lead role she helped me, not only running lines but with costume and characterisation.

During the past months I had been going down to London to audition on my rare days off. Then one day it happened. I went to the theatre before the others, as our ASM was on holidays and I was covering for her. I unlocked the stage door, turned on the lights, put the kettle on for tea, turned on the heat, checked that no one had broken in backstage to steal all the costumes—a recurring nightmare of our director.

I stooped to pick up the mail, then was surprised to see, among all the bills and notices, a buff-coloured envelope addressed to me. It was totally unexpected. The letter was from the National Theatre director, offering me a six-month contract. I stared at the letter, reading it through several times. It was one of those monumental moments in your life that you never forget. I was in the women's dressing-room which consisted of a long wooden plank along the wall with a cracked dingy mirror behind it, with not too many working light bulbs above. I sat down. The letter said, "We would like you to join us . . ." Join us! This, after months of no, no, no, we don't want you! It was a combination of joy, complete shock, emotion and a kind of terrific relief. I had forgotten to hope after so many auditions, almost as if I had given up unconsciously, then suddenly it all happened. I knew my life would be changed irretrievably in four weeks' time.

I heard voices, I pulled myself together as the other members of the cast were showing up for rehearsal. Harold came in first, I took him aside and showed him the letter. I made the excuse that I had to go to the post office for stamps, dashing out before I greeted the others. I didn't want to be there when they heard the news, as I reckoned there would be a lot of forced smiles and congratulations mixed with envy as we all dream of receiving such a letter. I wanted to spare them and me that initial confrontation. I knew that no one else had been to London for an audition with the National recently. They had almost forgotten my weekly trips to London.

The rehearsal had already begun when I got back, so I could sit in the stalls till coffee break, letting the news sink in, at the same time trying to concentrate on the rehearsal.

The worst part was over as I knew after the announcement that I would be leaving, that all of them did wish me well and then thoughts about their own careers would be examined that night. But I had another play to do after the present one, so it was back to work as usual. It was coffee-break time. They all got their cups and gathered around me. "Great news, Nicole!" they all said, and I felt as if they really meant it. That evening after the show, I wrote accepting the offer asking for more details of when to report for rehearsals.

The last two weeks seemed endless. It was difficult to concentrate, I spent every spare minute going through my possessions and clothes, trying to decide what to throw out and what to take with me. I had two huge suitcases of clothes, always needed when you work in Rep, but I left them all in the wardrobe department of the theatre. I wouldn't be needing them.

Just before I left, Mary came up to my room as I was packing, to have a farewell chat. She sat on my bed and we talked. We finished a box of chocolates I had discovered in a drawer. She was on a talking jag.

"As your career develops, your needs as a creative artist begin to satisfy the effort, so does your need to widen your life unfold; once you reach one level, then the next one comes into view. Bigger parts give you less time for other things. As time goes by, as you grow older, the need for emotional support, for companionship becomes much greater. It's obvious friends help but you must deal with any intimate relationship with great caution. The need is great, but so are the consequences if you fall in love, which I did. How can all that work and effort be disregarded so lightly for a relationship often doomed from the start. Actresses are so gullible, more so than any other profession. Maybe because we are children and need recognition no matter who gives it to us. I'm not talking about the boy next door—the stage manager, the director or the leading man are more likely."

We talked for an hour along the same lines until we were both too sleepy and decided to say goodnight.

The last play was a comedy. Our regulars were in the audience. Wednesday matinees were full of couples from the near-by nursing home. They often talked to each other during the play. There had been a small paragraph in the local paper about my new job, so many people came that week to see my performance out of curiosity I expect it helped the box office a little. The last week was fun, a few cast members threw parties to say goodbye and I was let off helping to dismantle the set after the show on Saturday night. However, I did buy the fish and chips and beer for all of them that night and stayed to help put away the props. My replacement had arrived the previous Monday, so I was showing her the ropes all that week. After the fish and chips I hugged everyone and said goodbye as I was catching the train to London early the following morning. Actors always remember the friends they have made in those first jobs in rep, and we all said we'd keep in touch but rarely did. You see their names later perhaps in *The Stage* or in the TV guide, but I never met any of them again, unfortunately.

I was surprised how well Peggy took the news, as obviously she wanted a job with the National as much as I did. She met me on arrival back in London.

"We have to celebrate, let's go to the Ritz and have some exotic drink."

"I'd rather have a party here."

"No way. All that cooking, food, etc. Let's go out."

We went to the Ritz, sat in the Palm Court, drank Manhattans, ate all the nuts, then took a cab to the Savoy, went upstairs into the American Bar and ordered two bullshots, as we knew Noel Coward always drank them whenever he was there. We got giddy and a little tight. We decided we were in a movie, all we needed was for Hugh Grant to walk in. We listened to the singer at the piano, then later went up to her to ask for some requests. Her name was Ruth, she joined us at the table when she had her break.

The room had emptied so the three of us chatted on, once again eating all the nuts and olives. Three bullshots later we stumbled into a cab, Peggy dropped me off at my flat.

Several weeks later, I was asked if I'd like to go on tour to America with the company. I said, "Yes," of course, delighted to have the opportunity of visiting New York. The first few weeks had been nerve-racking, to say the least. Little did I know that except for three or four of the more senior actors who had been at the National for years, all the company were nervous and worried about their own work at rehearsals. However, the pleasure of rehearsing at the National after the rep company was immense. The hours each day raced by.

A week before the tour was to begin, my mother suddenly became ill. I took the first train north on Sunday morning. When I was in the hospital, the doctors said they would have to operate or my mother would lose a kidney—nothing desperately serious, but worrying. My father was distraught and sat by her bedside every day. Fortunately they had a small staff who could carry on the business but I still felt very guilty when I had to leave on Monday afternoon, several hours after the operation. I wanted to stay on with my father but he said there was nothing much I could do. Returning on the train, eating the sandwiches I'd brought from home, the realisation of how binding a theatrical life was suddenly struck me. If an understudy took my place, it would only be a matter of time until I would lose my place in the company.

Chapter Five

A WEEK LATER THE COMPANY left for New York so at least I knew that the crisis was over, and that my mother would recover. The company were doing three plays in New York—*The Merchant of Venice, All's Well that Ends Well,* and *Romeo and Juliet,* which we had been doing in London for the past three months, I was playing Jessica in *The Merchant of Venice* and the nurse in *Romeo and Juliet,* Peggy was playing Juliet and understudying Portia in *The Merchant.* We had been working constantly on the plays, inventing new moves and stage business to keep the productions fresh. Because of the difference in size of the stage in New York we had to make adjustments to each play with regard to effects and movement. I was still worried about Mum, she wouldn't talk on the phone for long, so I tried to write to her every day, even though she wasn't that interested in the day-to-day details of our theatre news.

Dear Mum and Dad,

Greetings from New York! This is my first news bulletin from the great USA.

Fortunately the critics liked the play, so we are sold out for the six-week run. We can't get over the hospitality of the producers and their friends, it is like a huge theatrical feast, we are so stimulated by all the action.

The first night Peggy and I dumped our luggage at the hotel, then took a taxi to the famed Algonquin Hotel. We'd read so much about it, the famous Round Table in the

Rose Room where Dorothy Parker with the writers of the 1920s ate lunch, trading quips and gossip. It was just as we imagined it to be. We had martinis in the lounge, soaking up the atmosphere. The spirits of all the theatre people who stayed there seemed to surround us, from Noel Coward and Gertie Lawrence to Cole Porter and Scott Fitzgerald. We then walked over to catch our first look at Broadway, then to find the theatre where we would be playing. The Great White Way was teeming with people, the neon signs were bigger than anything we'd ever seen, the noise, traffic and sirens made it like a movie. The atmosphere was exhilarating. We went to Sardi's for dinner. Again, the whole place was bubbling with energy and excitement. We were fascinated by the clientele, listening to the many accents around us. All the waiters seemed friendly, much more so than in London. Afterwards we walked around the theatre district taking in all the billboards, names up in electric lights, the stretch limos, the fashions and the crowds.

What is it about New York? It is almost too much. The jet-lag overcame us both, so we got a taxi back to the hotel. Too much for one day.

Must go. Take care of yourselves

Love
Nicole

During our stay in New York the usual things happened, nothing that couldn't be fixed. We went sight-seeing, shopping, were given parties or dinners after the show. Members of the company got to know each other much better than we would have done back home. We were in a kind of residential hotel, a short-term place with kitchens where we could make cups of tea to have something hot if we didn't want to go out after the show. We saw as much of the city as we could, taking our cameras with us. I sent masses of photos back to Manchester.

Peggy and I started writing a film script when we had time in our dressing rooms. It was all about our time in New York, we put members of the cast in it, changing their names of course. We had the idea that anyone could come from around the corner and we would be on to Hollywood, things were happening so fast! Producers, agents, critics, newspaper people, interviews, articles were all mixed up in a big pot of introductions, cocktails and parties. Spinning into fame, we thought.

The nightlife was incredible. We usually went on somewhere to wind down after the show. There was nothing like these places in London, even if there were, we all had long distances to cover to get home. Here in New York, your hotel was only a few blocks away. On Sundays, after the matinees, we'd either be invited out to someone's home in Westchester or Connecticut or we'd spend it in Central Park. We took the Circle Line boat, which goes all the way around the island of Manhattan; there are spectacular views of the Statue of Liberty.

The city enthralled us—we had never seen such luxury, even in London. Often we were invited to supper by some wealthy patron of the arts, I was astonished at the affluence. There were marvellous penthouses with patios overlooking Central Park and huge reception rooms full of chandeliers and antique furniture.

At one of these parties, I met Tom. It would be a cliché to say it was love at first sight. We both went up to the buffet table at the same time and reached for a plate.

"Sorry, after you," he smiled.

"Everything looks delicious, doesn't it?"

"It does indeed. I enjoyed your performance this evening very much."

"Thank you."

"Would you have a few minutes to spare? I mean, I have an empty chair over there, if you'd like to sit down. I hate eating standing up."

While he was helping himself to the food, I sized him up. Quite short really, about five ten, say, but not fat. Wiry brown hair, blue eyes, well dressed in sports jacket and tie.

"Come, I'm over here." He gestured towards the windows. We discussed the play, then in the American way of asking direct questions I asked him about himself.

"I'm a lawyer. I started late, as it took me years to decide what to do, even though my father was a lawyer. I took a year off to travel so I'm just starting out, really."

"What do you intend to do?"

"Follow in my father's footsteps, I suppose."

It turned out he lived in Chicago but was here as a guest of our hostess, a friend of his, on a short trip to New York. He was funny and warm. There definitely was chemistry. He told me about his journeys and we laughed about all his mishaps. I asked about Chicago, his work, then he asked me about *All's Well that Ends Well*. During the conversation, he casually dropped in the information that he had been engaged to a Chicago girl several years ago, but they had broken it off.

"How do you know so much about Shakespeare?" I asked.

"I've read all the plays; I took drama in college, I would have liked to become an actor but there was too much family pressure."

"In what way?"

"My father and his father were both lawyers, so it was understood I would go into the firm. I am going back to join them in Chicago."

He kept on with questions about the production, the other company members all gathered round listening to his praise.

"He's gorgeous," Peggy kept saying. "If you don't want him, I'll have him," but Tom only had eyes for me.

I tried to find out more about him, enjoying many suppers with him after the show. He had been in London once and wanted to return that year but I was careful not to encourage him because it would only complicate my life.

The company were all wondering and worrying if they would be kept on when the run was over, when we went back to England. No one knew if they would have jobs or not as their contracts were only for the American tour. We realised that casting was already under way back home for the next season.

On our first few dates I left Tom at the front door of my hotel, yet after several passionate embraces, I realised that we both wanted more. I knew he was a kind, decent person with a great crush on me, which I found immensely flattering. No one had really courted me before or taken such an interest in me. Peggy was no help in advising me what to do about the situation. Peggy was madly in love with one of the actors in the company, they were already sleeping together every night. He had left a wife behind in London, so I wondered what would happen when they returned home.

"I'll worry about that when we get back, Nicole, but right now we are just not thinking about it."

"But you will suffer dreadfully if you think it will be the same."

"Don't nag me. Things will turn out all right."

The last night approached, I had spent the day packing for the next day's departure. After a magnificent party in one of those Park Avenue duplexes, Tom and I were on top of the world after many glasses of champagne, we didn't even stop at the door, as it seemed so natural for Tom to be with me that night. We were both slightly drunk, staggered onto the bed laughing and pulling each other's clothes off. We made love, which seemed so natural, even though I had never made love before, it just was the normal thing to do. The champagne had lifted any inhibitions I had, so it was just a tremendously exotic and exciting time for me. I had no idea if Tom felt the same way.

We had told each other about their previous encounters, although I had not divulged that I was a virgin and Tom had said he'd dated a few girls, but that's all he would say. The night was incredibly exciting. I'd no idea what to expect but it all seemed right, somehow. I instinctively felt as if he was meant for me, that we were meant for each other. The whole experience was sort of religious, primeval—losing my virginity, I felt like quoting from Romeo and Juliet, especially as every word I knew by heart. The whole world was beautiful.

Next morning, he wanted to come to the airport to see me off, but I knew he would be waiting around the airport for ages, so dissuaded him, and said I would write. We made love again, then I insisted he leave, go to work, to let me go with the others to the airport. I felt slightly embarrassed about the whole episode even though I had known it would be inevitable. Peggy was full of questions on the way to the airport, so I told her what had happened.

"And about time too, he's gorgeous."

"Perhaps we were too drunk to know if it was a good thing to do."

On the flight back, everyone was quiet, reflecting on the great time they all had had in New York. Many slept, even though everyone was apprehensive about the company breaking up.

It was raining, of course, as we arrived at Heathrow early the next morning. We went through the procedure of collecting our luggage at the carousel, and as each of us got our luggage we would wave goodbye, hug the actor closest to us, then push off, all of us with a pang in our hearts. It seemed unreal that we were all going our separate ways. The family was breaking up. Peggy and I shared a cab, dodging the rain pelting down. It was unbelievable that it was all over. No one had been at the airport to meet us, which was a bit of an anti-climax, so Peggy said she'd like to stay over before she went home to her parents. Her lover had gone back to his wife; she was confused and bewildered. I kept silent about it all.

That evening we had a post-mortem after a serious shopping trip to Tesco's to replenish the refrigerator, drinking two bottles of wine, going over the past six weeks in detail.

"I wish I'd never gone to New York, actually, then this would never have happened," said Peggy. She was already on the rebound and feeling desperately hurt. She became hysterical and vengeful. One night she talked about wild schemes of revenge. Brian parked his car on the street, not in a garage, so she said she was going to buy some tins of white paint and pour them over his car after dark, letting down the tires as well. I managed to talk her out of it, thank God.

What was worse, neither of us had been asked back to the company. Our agents had informed us just before we left the States. We were devastated, as it meant we were back waiting at the phone, back to zero. Most of the men were back, but the women were not. For some reason, there were no parts for them to play.

We looked at each other wondering what would happen next. The visit to see the family, of course, but then what? Peggy suddenly knew she wouldn't see her lover again, as he had said on their last night that his children needed him, that he couldn't leave his wife at that time. She felt used and humiliated, but it was, as I feared, an American romance.

Peggy couldn't stop crying. I took her a cup of coffee in the morning, tried to console her. Nothing I said seemed to help. Peggy's eyes were red and puffy. She looked terrible. Her face was swollen as well, the mascara had smudged over her forehead and pillow.

"I must phone him!"

"You were told not to do that. If you do, it will only drive him further away. He knows where you are."

I was delighted when Tom called a few minutes later. He missed me already. As I was talking to him, I looked out the window watching the rain. The raindrops were pouring down the kitchen window, I could feel a chill breeze coming in through the door. The wind was bending the trees outside in the street, I watched two passers-by trying to hold on to their umbrellas against the wind.

Listening to his voice, the words he was using, love, love, love—it meant so much to me after consoling Peggy for the last hour or so.

"What are you doing?" he asked.

"Unpacking, talking. Peggy is here."

"Well say hello to her, give her my love."

"I'm going to see the new Neil Simon play tonight. Wish you could come with me."

I found that I really missed him, his energy and positive, confident manner. Here we were, two miserable actresses, holed up looking at the rain, with no jobs. We talked for about half an hour, then he said he'd call the next day. The whole city seemed lifeless after the frenetic buzz of New York.

I put the kettle on for the third time that morning, neither of us wanted to do anything but sit and talk. The weather was depressing, we both said we missed the sunshine. Peggy decided to stay over rather than go back to her place. She needed me desperately, wanting to go over the love affair step by step, which after a while bored me enormously. It's funny how love's so blind, I thought. Peggy couldn't see it. However, in the next few days, I realised that I too had fallen in love.

Going out to buy groceries, as someone had to, I bought a huge bundle of flowers to give to Peggy, which only set her off again. She begged me to phone Brian at home so she could talk to him. Actually I thought he was terribly cruel not to have phoned her by now. He knew she was staying with me. I felt very tempted to phone him to tell him so, but I knew it wouldn't do any good. She was almost hysterical with grief. "How can he cut me off just like that, as if I didn't mean anything to him? He just used me, that's all. I can't believe it. He's a real shit."

She began crying again. Every time the phone rang she thought it was going to be him, but it wasn't. It was difficult to fathom the depth of her anguish. I knew I would have to get her out somewhere to distract her. That evening we went to the Green Room Club, staying until the actors who were in West End plays came in for a drink after the show. It was nice to be with them, working actors.

Peggy went back to her parents the following week, which was rather a relief because she was beginning to depress me with her agony over Brian. I did phone him once so Peggy could talk to him, the only thing he said was he would get back to her shortly.

It seemed ironic that both of us had the use of Shakespeare's description of anguish in words. We both could both recite poetry about what Peggy was experiencing. The whole repertoire of unrequited love, the pain, the indescribable cruelty was what we knew from our work, but it failed in our own lives to enable us to express our own feelings. Shakespeare of course had experienced all these emotions so there was nothing new for Peggy to feel. After playing Juliet, she could recreate Juliet's suffering very easily, but it didn't seem to help her with her own, even though she kept saying some of her lines over and over again.

During the next few weeks I realised I was deeply in love with Tom and missed him terribly. We talked on the phone every day but it wasn't enough. I wanted to be with him. The constant rejection at auditions, the waiting, the unemployment was dire. Then it all happened. I suddenly felt different, not at all well, and my period was late. The next day I went to Boot's to buy one of those pregnancy kits. I'd seen them on the shelves, never thinking I would buy one. Walking back to the flat, I realised that the contents of the little bag that I was carrying could change my life. It was what I had suspected. I found out that I was pregnant. Of course, it had to be Tom. That one night we had slept together. Neither of us had taken any precautions, we were too much in a hurry, with all the champagne we had simply not thought about it.

That day was unforgettable. I sat at the kitchen table, watching the rain, wondering what to do. Of course, I told Peggy.

"Oh Nicole, what *are* you going to do?"

"Marry Tom, I expect."

"But does he want to?"

"Yes of course, although he doesn't know it yet."

"What are you going to tell your parents?"

"Nothing, they would be so upset."

"Maybe they would be pleased."

"If I'm married they would be, but I'll wait till I am before I tell them."

"*If* you get married."

"Tom will marry me, I'm sure of that."

It didn't take much soul-searching on my part. I was very despondent about my career, nothing was happening. No calls, no job, I felt I needed a complete change anyway.

Seize the day, get up and go. Most actors said if they hadn't made it by the time they were thirty they'd give it up. I didn't want to give up acting, I could always work in Chicago once I was married, Tom was there waiting for me. New horizons, a new life, it must be better than waiting by the phone every day. But only time would tell. It was like setting out on a new adventure. No matter how ambitious you were, it is depressing when nothing happens. Nothing was happening for me in the theatre, not even the promise of a part for the moment; how many parts are there for a pregnant actress? Not many, I couldn't think of even one. It'll be nearly a year before I can work again. Still, it'll be a rest of sorts.

I decided not to tell my parents why I was going to the States again. They would be so upset, so shocked. They would be totally disappointed in me, would blame themselves for allowing me to go to London at all when they could have prevented me from going. In which case my present situation would never have happened. I was so worried myself I didn't want them worried as well. If they knew how much we were in love it would make such a difference, but of course they didn't and they would still be hurt anyway. So the idea was to get over there as soon as possible.

Chapter Six

THE NEXT MONTH WAS FILLED with hectic long-distance phone calls, trying to arrange everything from our wedding to where we would live. Saying goodbye to friends, sorting everything, finding tenants, sub-letting the flat, putting lots of stuff in storage. Starting a new life. My career was put on hold. However, I felt as if I was acting in my own movie, my own life for once. It all seemed like a dream. Suddenly everything was changing, I really never thought I would marry quite so quickly. To save money we decided to get married in the States. No big wedding. Just us. Tom's parents had died ten years earlier, and he was an only child.

Theatre friends raised eyebrows. "Mid-western America?" Let us know how you like it out there."

"Will do."

He must be a great catch."

I was growing up, getting married, sharing a life with another person, having a baby. It was all happening so fast I didn't have the time to reflect on my actions, it was too hectic getting things organised. I reserved two nights in a posh Chicago hotel, then we married in a little chapel, the day after I arrived.

I insisted I stay at a hotel overnight alone on the first night before the wedding, to have some kind of suspense on my wedding day, as we had always believed you shouldn't see the groom until the ceremony. Don't ask! That morning I woke up and lay there thinking, "This is my wedding day," and suddenly missed Mum and Dad, wishing they were here. The only person I could tell was the hairdresser in the hotel salon that morning. It seemed kind of unreal, as if it was a dream, but my morning sickness quickly brought me back to reality. Tom had invited several of his friends to the wedding and they came back for a champagne supper afterwards. They seemed to stay for ages, we couldn't wait to get rid of them. Surely they knew we wanted to go to bed!

Tom was busy working on a case, so we promised ourselves a honeymoon later. During my first week there I started out to explore our neighbourhood. First I'd drive Tom to work, as we had only one car, then I drove all around the district. The supermarket, the post office were the first places I looked for. Then, leaving the car, I walked down to the park, a rather small park near the post office. There was a children's wading pool and swings, so the place was full of children. I chatted to a couple of mums but I felt very out of place. They were light years away from me.

"Are you going to stay in America?" one of them asked me, as if I looked like a freak. I became slightly paranoid talking to them, as they seemed to be patronising me, my clothes, my accent, my hair. Most of them were friendly but terribly curious which bothered me.

"I have something to tell you, Nicole," he said about a week later, just as we were going to bed. "I should have told you before but it wasn't the time."

As we lay there in the dark, side by side, he spoke quite quietly. I felt a wave of anxiety go through my body about what he was going to say.

"I have to tell you that I don't have that nest-egg I hoped we'd have. My accountant called me last week and it seems I owe far more in taxes than I had ever imagined. He has arranged that I can pay it off in instalments, but for the first year or so we won't have very much money. I know you will want to carry on with your acting of course, but with the baby coming you won't want to work for a while."

I just lay there in shock. How could he be saying this now? I sat up on my elbow and looked at him. "You mean we're broke?"

"Not really, but it will be tough going for a while. I'm really sorry to have to tell you, but I thought you'd never come here if I told you before you left."

"But what about things for the baby? Clothes, furniture etc. and all that stuff."

"We'll manage. If you find you're bored while I'm at the office, maybe you could get a part-time job while you're waiting for the baby."

I got out of bed, went to the bathroom and sat on the toilet. We were up the creek—or rather I was. I couldn't believe what I'd got myself into. No use panicking, time to think about it in the morning. I went back to bed.

"Are you all right?"

"Yes, just tired. Let's just go to sleep and don't worry. We'll think of something."

A month went by, it was mid-June when I found a job in a cardboard-box factory, folding boxes all day, the place had only an overhead fan in the storage room. They couldn't afford air-conditioning, it seemed. It was another world. The other women must have thought me quite odd, with a British accent and no idea about baseball or hockey. It was a total immersion programme into the local women's lives. The heat was terrible. I would try to avoid going to the local cafe to have lunch with them so I wouldn't have to answer their endless questions. I took the gum they offered me and learnt to chew the way they did, to keep from appearing totally uncool, laughed at their dirty jokes, taking a swig from a Coca-Cola bottle every so often.

In the evenings, Tom and I would go out for a walk in a nearby park just to get out of the stifling apartment. It was only slightly cooler. We sat down on a bench facing a small fountain which had no water in it. Tom seemed preoccupied most nights, but I knew I had to talk to him about our future together. He was very involved in building up his law practice, so he was concentrating on his present clients as well as he could, in an effort to gain more business from word of mouth, and get new clients. But, increasingly, I found him dull. He never seemed to have anything to talk about anything except his work. Lawyers don't have much of a sense of humour, or at least he didn't. He didn't talk at all about theatre, mainly because we were living in a suburb and he was too busy to drive into town to see a show.

"I suppose you don't want to take time off to go away this summer, Tom?"

"We can't afford to, really. It's not just the money but losing the contacts I've made."

"Would you ever consider moving to the East Coast?"

"You mean New York?"

"Somewhere like that, or Washington, somewhere I could get work in the theatre."

"Not really, Nicole, it has been hard enough to get started here, at least I know everyone here."

Later that night I lay in bed wondering how long I could stand the heat and the loneliness. I missed Peggy and the theatre, it was as simple as that. Phone calls were frequent, but not the same thing.

Tom sensed I was still awake, turned over, and put a hand on my stomach.

"You'll feel better once that baby is born. It's the waiting that's getting you down."

It was far more than that. The whole scenario was impossible, I could see the outcome of it all. I'd really burnt my boats, as my grandmother used to say. I still had a lot of living to do. I lay there in the dark, willing myself not to speak my thoughts out loud, as it would only upset Tom and get us nowhere. I was beginning to feel we were wrong for each other. I suddenly didn't want to be a lawyer's wife, with no life of my own, no career of my own. This is not what I want. Maybe I'll end up hating Tom. I had made a huge mistake.

I waited till I heard him breathing regularly and had gone to sleep, then I got up, closed the door and went into the kitchen. The night was humid, I opened the window but there was no breeze at all, I wished a thunderstorm would come to clear the air. It felt like a scene from a Tennessee Williams play; woman pregnant, desperate, sitting in kitchen drinking beer in the middle of the night, like the beginning of a murder scene. "She picks up the carving knife and kills him." I tried to keep my sense of humour, trying to dramatise it, but it didn't work. What am I going to do? It was too late to call Peggy, she was tired of me complaining to her anyway, and she didn't want to give me any advice.

Tom, like all young husbands I guess, was working every day to give me a better life, to give us all the things we wanted, like a better house, a bigger car, all the things to go into a house, a savings account to put something aside for vacations. But I was in the wrong town. I tried to analyse what I did want. I couldn't go back to London as I had sublet my flat for a year. If I feel like this now, what's it going to be like after the baby is born, I'll be more trapped than ever?

The clock ticked loudly on the kitchen wall, it was the only sound in the house. The refrigerator stopped humming and I wished we could afford air conditioning. I knew I should just resign myself to the situation, as there was nothing else I could do. Tomorrow I would buy some paints and a canvas or two, then try to start painting again. At least I'd be doing something even if I never finished them.

Reading helped. Every book was like a journey, entering into someone else's life. It helped with the boredom. Perhaps I could paint enough canvases to have an exhibition. I could try writing a play, or joining a writers' group. The trouble was that most of the women I knew were so totally different in their ways from me. They spent whole days in the beauty parlour having pedicures and manicures whereas I couldn't afford that. Their homes were spotless with matching china, cutlery, curtains and carpets. I felt like an outsider. Tom's business friends invited us for barbecues and cocktail parties, but most of the wives, local girls who had lived here all their lives, didn't want to be anywhere else at all. Happy, contented, well, most of them housewives who were raising children. Well, what's wrong with that, I asked myself? Except I didn't want to be there any more. I'd met Tom on his one and only jaunt to New York, I had obviously misread him and his enthusiasm for the theatre. He really wasn't that interested in it at all. Our time in New York was like it never happened. I found out that the only Shakespeare he knew was what he remembered from school. I realised this ages ago. He was kind enough, trying to please me in a dozen different ways, but perhaps it was the complete change, not only in my daily life but also being in a new country with no support system, which disillusioned me. A family circle would have helped. Perhaps if his parents had still been alive, their age, wealth and experience would have helped me settle down. We could have talked about Tom's childhood, his youth, I could have entered into their world where I could talk to people who were well-travelled.

There seemed to be a whole world out there that I was missing. The wealthy patrons who entertained the company in New York seemed to be out of reach. Although the class system in New York differed from the traditional one in Britain, where even poverty-stricken aristocrats still mattered, the sense of old money, and lots of it, permeated the lives of our hosts and hostesses. We saw glimpses of this world when we were invited to the prestigious clubs of New York, the equivalents of the Athenaeum and the Reform Club in London. Here in Chicago, we were living in the suburbs, so there would be no chance of meeting sophisticated people with the cosmopolitan charm and conversation to be found in the upper reaches of society, whether in London, Chicago, Hong Kong or Lisbon. Tom's father had been a member of the Travellers Club, which I had once visited in London. I knew we were too young and too poor to expect to be invited to such places.

The huge gap between the two levels was almost unbreachable. Some women, in their determination to breach the gap, sleep their way to the top, to gain access to the rarefied air of cosmopolitan society, whereas the men have to reach the upper level either through family connections or by outstanding financial success. Actors don't belong to this world, but the wealthy patrons provide stepping-stones to oil the business of show business, with grants, by backing shows, supporting theatres, entertaining actors, buying blocks of tickets and in these ways making it possible for actors to live.

Most of all, they are appreciative of artistic endeavour, even though none of them want to be actors themselves, they seem to admire our productions. I had mistakenly coupled my associations with these people, including Tom, with an expectation that my stay in New York would be replicated in Chicago. Now it was clear how mistaken I had been. There were no cosmopolitan dinner parties where we lived. Tom didn't belong to any cultural associations, nor did he have the time to socialise except with other lawyers; the very rich lived in another part of town. Not that I missed them exactly, but now and again I thought back to those great hostesses in New York and wondered if they were still throwing parties for visiting actors and artists. After Tom had told me we would not have the money to travel, I panicked. The other wives wanted me to go bowling with them or bring a dish to a pot-luck supper, which was a novelty in the beginning but desperately boring after the first one or two. I was a square peg in a round hole.

The pregnancy began to show soon enough, so I quit that job because of having to stand all day, and searched the newspapers for more work. I must have spent the equivalent of three hours each week looking. Things got worse. The rent was put up, the car broke down and had to be traded in. Then one day Tom broke the news that the firm wanted him to move to a small town five hundred miles away. It seemed to be the last straw.

"Five hundred miles away?" I said. "I would have to find another doctor, another hospital . . ."

"People do it all the time," Tom said, getting himself a beer from the fridge.

"But do you realise we would have no friends there? You may have your office and colleagues but you'll hardly have time to socialise or help with the domestic chores. Darling, I really don't want to go, I'd rather stay here."

"But we can't afford to keep two places, pay two lots of rent."

Every day I'd pore over the newspaper, reading the want ads, hoping I would find a solution. "Leading lady required to take over in road tour of *My Fair Lady*" is what I would like to have seen. But that Sunday I saw an ad for a "live-in" child-minder. No housework, no cooking, just to look after a one-year-old, with a private air-conditioned apartment included plus salary. I put the paper down to think about it. I smiled and thought of *The Lady* magazine in London, where the most proper people advertised for companions and nannies. It's not considered unusual at all. Unemployed actresses read them with foreboding as a matter of course, even though we joke about it. That evening I confronted Tom after dinner. I told him that I didn't want to move with him, but I didn't want him to give up a good opportunity.

"I've thought about it all," I said lightly, "so I came up with an idea which might work."

"What is that?"

"Well, I could get a job as a nanny and live in with a family, just till the baby is born."

"What are you saying? You'd rather do that than move with me?"

I didn't want him to guess the truth, that I was bored with him, bored with sitting home alone all day with nothing to do but housework, that I had decided I didn't want to move at all, doctors or no doctors.

"I want to be near the hospital, not five hundred miles away in a new town. If I stay with a family, we will save money." Shit, this is more difficult than I thought it would be. He was looking at me in a strange kind of way, curious but hurt, I think.

It was a lame excuse, I know, but I could tell he was thinking about it. It certainly would be a relief, a load off his mind if he had to work long hours to know I was happier. Then I showed him the ad in the newspaper.

"All right, we can drive around to have a look at the area."

Next day we got into the car, then after a look at the map found the address in the newspaper. It was in a very nice part of Chicago. The house stood back from the street surrounded by trees. The area was quite beautiful, I noticed air conditioners on all the windows! That's it, I decided! I called the number to make an appointment for the next morning.

The interview went well, I told the couple that my husband had been transferred, I wanted to stay in the city to attend the clinic where my baby was to be born, so they took me.

The life of London had gone. It was as if it happened in another century. I was totally changed by America. Everything was bigger, the cars, the houses, streets, cities and shops. Huge aisles in the supermarket—not like in Tesco's; everything was cleaner—the interiors of people's homes, buildings, restaurants and transportation. People seemed cheerier, healthier and happier. It was so different from London life. I grew accustomed to it. Moving in with the American family was one step further removed from Tom, it was even more strange and foreign inasmuch as I had to adapt to the family's way of life.

Each day I would bathe, dress and feed the little boy. Then take him for a walk to the park, come back, play with him, read to him and each day I spoke to Tom. After six months the winter came. The routine was almost the same. I stopped writing to Peggy as I didn't have anything to write about and her letters always upset me when I read of her weekly activities. The winter in Chicago was as cold as the summer was hot. Tom was moving back to the city, I was house-hunting so we would move into a new place on his return. The family were all going to Florida for three months, so they knew I wouldn't be travelling with them. Absence makes the heart grow fonder, Tom and I were quite excited about having our own place again.

I left the family after the first snowfall of the season. They closed up the house for the winter. We had only been in our new house for a week when I slipped on the ice coming up the front steps. Then everything started to happen. An ambulance came, the men picked me up as I lay on the steps. I knew instinctively that something fatal had happened and I felt rage when the man put me in a wheelchair and said, "Don't cry, you're going to have a baby" which started me off again. What an idiot!

It was all over in a matter of twenty-four hours. I lost the baby, after an overnight stay in hospital I was released. Boom. Just like that. *Boom, boom.* It all happened so fast I don't remember too much about it, except I seemed to be weeping a lot. I'd got used to the radio, which was playing rock music in the ward. I imagined a huge orchestra with the conductor trying to end the symphony which had a long finale. *Boom.* Another great final note. *Boom. Boom.* There were great chords striking, but I don't know who was playing them.

Tom picked me up at the hospital and dropped me back home. He had an important meeting he couldn't cancel at the last minute. "So is that all right, Nicole?"

"Oh of course, just let me off at the front door."

I sat on the bottom step of the stairs for quite some time; I felt nothing, like a zombie. The house was silent. The clock was still ticking. I felt kind of numb. I wandered round the house just touching things. Miles away in a cloud somewhere. Unreal. I stared out at the snow. "Somewhere over the Rainbow blue birds fly", why did that song come to me then? Maybe if there was a God, then He had taken a hand in the events that had just happened, and for a good reason.

That evening after Tom had come home slightly earlier than usual, as we sat over dinner he suggested that maybe I should take a break.

"Go away for a while."

"But where?" I got up to get the ice cream from the refrigerator. I still hadn't got over the fact that you could buy thirty-four varieties in the States. I was working my way through them.

"Well, phone a travel agent for suggestions."

"The idea of going back to London in mid-winter doesn't appeal at all."

Tom had the distraction of his work. The whole episode, or rather that whole year was easy for him because he could work. I was pleased that he was taking it all in his stride. It was easier to cope without having him fussing about. Well, he wasn't the fussing type. It would have been easier if I'd been working too. My loneliness was about not being on stage again. You're never lonely when you are on stage. It is appearing before an audience in a theatre that makes you feel you belong. But I wasn't ready to go back to the battlefield.

Next day I studied the travel ads in the paper, the Bahamas looked good with all that azure blue water and palm trees. I decided on Nassau in the Bahamas. I felt like Shirley Valentine and smiled at the memory of her talking to her kitchen wall as I packed my bags.

"Hello, wall, I'm at least doing something at last," I said to the bathroom wall.

Little did I know that it was the beginning of a totally new life. If you can remember the joy that Shirley Valentine felt by taking that holiday to Greece you will understand how I felt. My theatre life drifted further away as I removed myself still further from the dreariness and cold of London, then from the icy wind and indifference of Chicago to the heavenly azure green waters of the Bahamas.

Chapter Seven

THE BRITISH COLONIAL HOTEL, SET back in a huge garden of trees, a botanical park of dense tropical trees and flowers, was my destination. The lobby smelt of jasmine and hibiscus. The decor reminded me of a Mayfair townhouse. Pale grey carpets, white furniture, pale pink roses and tropical flowers on the front desk, an exclusive air of heady perfume, deep luxurious carpeting with slow-moving ornamental fans hung from the ceiling. It was almost French in the mixture of superb elegance, fresh flowers, soft air with the tinge of humidity to make your skin glow immediately.

After checking in, I was shown my room. The louvred shutters opened out on the densely planted garden and thick foliage below. The bed had four posters with carved wooden pineapples on top of each poster. Later I was told that pineapples were supposed to bring good luck. The room had light yellow walls, white furniture, yellow drapes, the bed had a white bedspread, the bathroom too was white with fluffy yellow towels. Crystal goblets and a split of champagne in an ice-bucket suggested welcome. I felt rejuvenated, and delighted with the whole place. I opened the champagne and drank it sitting on the balcony listening to the wind in the palm trees and admiring the tropical flowers growing around the window. Dinner was served on a large stone patio that was surrounded by flame torches illuminating the palm trees and casting giant shadows across the area. I started with turtle soup, then tried the grilled grouper Bahamian style followed by coffee spiced with the local rum topped with whipped cream.

That night I had very strange dreams. It seemed as though I was back in Chicago and Tom was coming towards me saying, "Why did you leave me?" In his arms he had a small baby which was crying, I began walking towards them with tears streaming down my face. Suddenly there was a small abrupt cry, then we were separated by a huge bus driven by a Bahamian who was in a native costume. You couldn't see whether they had been run over or not. I jumped back quickly, which woke me up. I did not know why it seemed so tragic to wake up crying.

Every day I sat by the pool for so long that I often watched the sky turn pink with a brilliant sunset each night. At five o'clock a calypso band played around the pool and I was introduced to the now well-known calypso songs. The music was charming. Each evening I walked down to Bay Street to window-shop before choosing a restaurant for dinner, as I didn't want to eat every night at the hotel.

Most mornings I went to the beach to swim in the pale green-blue water. I knew the salt water would help heal me. For me the whole world seemed changed. The months of feeling ill, bored and depressed slowly slipped off me like an old skin, I felt renewed in spirit at one with my inner self. The euphoria of being alone, not having any resentful or hostile feeling towards another human being was like having a huge weight lifted from my shoulders. I hadn't realised how much resentment I had been harbouring that suddenly felt washed away. I felt youthful again, as the pain diminished the memory of the miscarriage it subsided in the sun, and my spirit soared.

One morning I went down past the hotel pool, which was in the centre of the old trees in the garden, to the pool-side bar. People simply sat around in the bar, mostly chatting at random to whoever was sitting beside them, often young men trying to pick up girls or girls trying to pick up young men. There was a lazy, happy atmosphere, if anyone had any problems they simply didn't talk about them. I fell into conversation with a girl about my own age, discovering that she was an actress.

We exchanged the usual show-biz talk . . . . where did you study, who have you worked with, what have you done, etc?

Her name was Rita. She was almost the American equivalent of me, three years of drama school, summer stock, bit parts in TV and still searching for a brilliant agent who would get her launched.

"Are you married?" I asked after our second Margarita.

"No, not yet," replied Rita "I haven't met Mr. Right yet." I kept asking her questions so she wouldn't ask me any. "What are you doing in the Bahamas, apart from having a good time?"

"We, the company I mean, are putting on a few plays down here, we've been doing them in New York so we don't have to rehearse. They're mostly one-act plays because of the heat, as we don't have air conditioning." She laughed. "Why don't you come along to see one or two? Tonight we're doing *Albee's Zoo Story*." She got up to have a final dip in the pool, dropping the towel she had around her. I was amazed to see what great shape her body was in, not much fat anywhere. I was still working on losing ten pounds, which I'd put on over the last few months.

"I'd love to, I will. It's ages since I've been to the theatre, it's even longer since I've been on stage."

"It's a pity all the plays are fully cast at the moment, otherwise I'm sure there are quite a few parts you could have played. Still, I could ask the director for you."

"Would you? It would be wonderful if you could."

After she had had her swim, she came over to say she had to go to get ready for the show. "See you later, Nicole. Don't be late."

As I watched her walk back to the hotel I felt quite elated at the possibility of working again. I would be back in harness again doing what I loved most. The stimulation of studying a part flooded back, the energy and enthusiasm raced through my veins. It was quite an intoxicating moment and I felt quite dizzy. It had been so long since anything had stirred my spirit. I ordered another drink. I looked forward to seeing their plays and went at eight o'clock to see the show and talk to the director afterwards to see if there was anything for me.

I was invited to join them after the show. We all sat around outside on the terrace discussing the night's performance. The second act had been drowned out by a sudden downpour when the rain hit the tin roof above and I just couldn't hear the actors. However, the plot was simple enough to follow.

Rita introduced me to their director, Jim Jordan, who seemed very laid back about the downpour because he had been through worse things than a rain storm. He looked like a tennis pro with his trim figure, tanned skin, quick movements, dressed in white shorts and T-shirt, his black hair curling around his ears in an endearing fashion. I noticed his hands, in fact I always look at men's hands. His were long and graceful. He looked about forty but could have been older. It was hard to tell.

"At least we don't have gunfire around us as we had in Vietnam," he said. Turned out he had been head of entertainment in one camp over there, putting on reviews and plays for the troops. I was surprised and rather shocked that there seemed to be an immediate chemistry between us. Rita watched us talking and she obviously noticed it. Who knows if I was treading on her toes, or rather territory? I was determined to cut it short, so stood up and said goodnight, feeling as though it was the best thing to do, having asked Jim about any parts available.

"It would be great to be able to work with you all." But as I expected, there was nothing available, all the roles had been cast. Still, the mere fact of looking for a part somehow stimulated me. I knew that my spirit had been jolted into action, the passion was still there and I had to get back to acting. Why had it taken me so long to realise this? But where and how? New York was probably out of the question, but London was a distinct possibility. I should really write a play with a good fat part in it for me. Why not start it now? Certainly, I had all the time in the world. I hunted for my exercise book, which I found at the bottom of my suitcase. I read through the notes I had written ages ago making a few new ones as well.

Next morning I met Rita at the pool again, it was good to see her. I knew that I couldn't put off for much longer answering questions about why I was in the Bahamas, especially as the whole company had shown such hospitality towards me the previous evening. I told her everything and asked her to keep it in confidence. She offered to help, but I knew that any advice is almost impossible to follow without a conviction of one's own.

"But as you trained in London, Nicole, wouldn't you be better off there?"

"But could I face the miserable climate of London again, the lecherous agents, casting directors, the perpetual struggle, the cut-throat competition?"

"Well, maybe you could try it for a month or two," said Rita.

"I guess. I still may have useful contacts there, but if I was working none of these circumstances would really matter. I don't think Tom would object as long as I was happy and busy, I know he is feeling guilty about not being there when things went so terribly wrong, so a little solitude would probably ease his conscience."

"Why not phone him to sound him out?"

I knew that Tom worked long hours at his office, so I waited until I was sure of catching him at home. First, I told him about meeting Rita and the acting company staying at the hotel, then I made my proposed trip to London sound merely an extension of my holiday, though in some corner of my mind I realised that it was more than that, something in its way as decisive and fateful as my marriage had been and with unpredictable consequences. Tom, oddly enough, seemed relieved, perhaps he hadn't been looking forward to my return just yet, maybe he too needed a break. Whatever the case, it was decided amicably that I would go to London to see how things went, then we would take it from there.

Thank goodness money wasn't a problem any longer, a busy practice had finally rescued us from the poverty we had endured when we were first married. He was able to let me have enough to support a couple of months of unemployment if necessary. I had learnt to live on practically nothing, I knew I could stretch it out for at least a month longer.

Being in the Bahamas made me realise the importance of the sun to one's psyche; it really does give one life force, energy, the passion to continue to pursue one's goals. To my surprise the atmosphere of the island, the flowers, the warmth, the sunshine all combined to do something else to me, it aroused sensual feelings that had been long dormant, reminded me how I had felt when the first stirrings of teenage desire had impinged on my consciousness. I felt like a young girl again. Perhaps it wasn't just the atmosphere, maybe meeting Jim and realising the chemistry between us was responsible, not that anything would come of it. I was determined not to complicate my life at this stage, but just to enjoy the warm hospitality of the Bahamians, their music, their *joie de vivre*. Each day it would amuse me to watch the Bahamian waiter carry above his head trays full of colourful tropical drinks with hibiscus flowers and toy umbrellas stuck in them, smiling as he weaved his way around the pool tables to deliver the Bahaman mamas, the Pina Coladas, the rum punches to the thirsty patrons. When the calypso band started playing, and you'd had a few drinks, it was almost like heaven. I decided to try to write a play, so every day I would make notes by the pool, at least I felt I was working at something.

Next morning when I was working on my notes I saw Jim coming towards me and when he said, "Another dull day in paradise," I was at a loss for words. I smiled and said lamely, "It beats working."

He pulled up a chair and sat down. "What are you writing?"

"I'm trying to write a play."

"Well, that's working," he said laughingly.

"But it's not going very well."

"Can I ask what it's about? Or is it too soon to say?"

"It's a one-woman show but I'm having problems with it."

He smiled at me and beckoned the waiter over. "Would you like something cool to drink? I'm having a rum punch."

The waiter approached with his tray and smiled. "Sir?" he said.

"Two rum punches, please." He looked at me and said, "If you don't want it I'll drink it."

We sat there chatting, drinking the rum, for about half an hour, discussing a plot for the play.

"Would you like me to rub some writer's block—I mean sun block—on your back, because it's looking very red?"

"All right," I said, handing him the bottle. I turned over and closed my eyes. He made me laugh. His hands caressed my shoulders, it felt wonderful. It had been so long since somebody had touched me, had stroked my body. He kept stroking far longer than necessary, and because I didn't ask him to stop, he knew the effect it was having. I remember reading a newspaper article about how many people who live alone go to a legitimate masseur just to have someone touch them, let alone the people who go to the other kind of massage parlour. It seems we all need to be touched and have bodily contact to remain sane.

"That's enough," I said to Jim, as I turned over and put the straps of my swimming suit back on my shoulders. Right then I was tempted to rush him back to my hotel room and seduce him, he had excited me so much, without knowing it. What difference would it have made if we had had a passionate hour or so in bed? I badly needed it and the combination of the rum, the massage, for that's what it was, and the hot sun was almost too tempting to resist. I'm sure most other people would have jumped at the chance. Life is short, go for it. But instead I steeled myself, afraid what emotions would erupt if I let myself go. Besides, I thought he might talk, especially to Rita. Smiling once more, I turned to him lazily and said, "You're dangerous."

The moment passed and I shaded my eyes with my hand to look up to him and said, "That was lovely, thank you. I feel great."

He smiled and said, "Any time." We saw Rita walking towards us, and I wondered if she had seen him rubbing me with sun cream, not that it mattered.

"Good afternoon," she said, and sat down beside us "Isn't this just an incredible day? I can't imagine living anywhere else after this place. It is so hedonistic. Why do we all keep struggling, I mean why bother to achieve anything when we will all be forgotten in a hundred years' time if not fifty?"

Jim ordered her a rum punch and another one for me. She had saved the day, or rather a possible seduction with perhaps dire consequences, like me ending up in a hysterical crying fit.

She went on, "Here we are, worried about our careers, when we are nothing more than drops in the ocean. We will be swept out to sea and all our little worries mean nothing in the divine order of things."

"I didn't know you were religious," remarked Jim.

"Well, think about it," said Rita. "If we were all religious, we would know that we are here as God's creatures and he would tell us what our place is in the universe, what we should be doing, and when things last so short a time nothing matters very much, even acting."

"You still have to pay the rent," laughed Jim.

"But don't you understand that this place makes you question your whole existence?" she said.

I agreed with her.

Meeting them both certainly made me focus on what I wanted out of life. They had rekindled my passion for the theatre in the most unexpected way, rekindled my passion for living and I knew that time was of the essence. It was serendipity to find out these facts in such a lovely place.

Once again I was packing my bags and wondering what would happen next. At least I was on the move and some choices had been made. It was sad to be leaving Nassau, the land of the sea and sun. Who knows, maybe I would return one day.

Chapter Eight

NOTHING HAD CHANGED. IT WAS as if I had never left. It was raining, naturally. Peggy met me at the airport. She had insisted that I stay with her until I decided on my next move, as my apartment was still rented.

"Nicole, you look fabulous. What a tan you have. Is it out of a bottle or what?"

"Don't be silly. You know where I've been," I answered laughingly. We kissed and hugged each other. She had put on weight, but looked quite cheerful. Her hair was still full and glossy. That evening we sat up late into the night catching up on each other's news with all the heartbreak about my miscarriage and her unrequited love affairs. She had finally got over Bruce, thank goodness, and was seeing someone else.

"Not another actor, I hope?" I laughed.

"Yes, but he's single, younger than me, but adorable." She handed me his photograph.

"Not bad, not bad at all. I'm not going to ask what the age difference is." He looked like a young Laurence Olivier. I put the framed photograph on the table as I looked around the room. Her apartment was full of books, plants and photos of the plays she had been in. It was very bright, as it faced out onto a small garden. Peggy told me of her disastrous tour around the provinces which lasted nearly a year, but her agent was so annoyed with her for finally quitting the company he hadn't sent her more work. She was waiting to hear about a film audition she'd had three days ago.

"That's one thing about England I missed, the English garden," I said, cutting off some cheese, piling it on a cracker. "Look at all your lovely flowers."

"It's all the rain we get. I've got to get out there to do some weeding soon."

"I'll help you. I love weeding."

"That's one more thing I don't like about touring, the garden goes to ruin while I'm away."

"Can't you get someone to come in?"

"I tried, but they never show up, or so my neighbours say."

I got up to pour Peggy another glass of wine.

"I don't have to tell you that the London theatre scene is in bad shape, and for the next generation it will be more so."

"Why do you say that?"

"Well, for instance, school visits to theatres and concerts have been drastically reduced. The government is withdrawing huge sums and subsidies for the Arts, so there will be less and less work for us. Look at Covent Garden. We finished the building the best opera house in the world but there is insufficient money to run it. We desperately need a subsidy again to support all the good work that can be done in the theatre. It really infuriates me, so much so I envied your break away and even your time in Chicago."

"Oh please, I wouldn't wish it on you."

"At least it was pastures new."

Peggy was working in a library to make ends meet, so she was gone all day. I insisted on paying my rent and for all my phone calls.

I asked Peggy, "Whatever happened to Trevor? I'd like to see him again."

She made a face and put up her hand. "Oh Nicole, that's not a good idea." She put down her glass on the coffee table, turning towards me.

"Why not? I know him—you know we worked in rep together."

"I know you did. But I guess you haven't heard—he's been ill."

"Ill? But he just had a smash hit in London last year."

"Yes, I know. But there were really big problems after that. He got in with a bad crowd who were on drugs and all kinds of things, evidently."

"I can't believe it. He was always so ambitious. What's he doing now?"

"He got married, of course, I guess you heard about that."

"Yes, I knew about that."

"It was really his wife that got him out of trouble."

"Well, where is he?"

"He's in a psychiatric detox centre. Not only was he on drugs, but alcohol was a big problem too. I mean, alcohol is bad enough, we all drink too much, but it was worse for him."

I couldn't believe it, even though Peggy kept confirming it. Poor old Trevor. I had to see him. After about a dozen phone calls to various departments in the hospital, doctors and so on, I managed to get to see him the next day.

"What a dump," I thought, walking through the corridors. The walls were green and there was linoleum on the stairs. It felt cold and damp. I was very apprehensive, almost nervous at the prospect of seeing him again, it had been so long. I thought of the line "But that was another time in another country" but, of course, it wasn't another country. When I walked in the room he was lying on the bed, reading, but swung his legs off when he saw me.

"Don't get up, Trevor, I can sit by the bed."

All that morning on the way to the hospital I was remembering the crush I had on him at Ipswich and how I chased him, therefore I was quite embarrassed about meeting him again in case I gave myself away by blushing or saying something ridiculous or inappropriate. I needn't have worried.

"Hello, Nicole. It's kind of you to come."

I gave him flowers and he gave me a quick kiss on the cheek.

"Thank you, that's really sweet of you, Nicole."

He looked terrible, about twenty years older, with touches of grey in his hair and sunken eyes. I was shocked to see how much weight he'd lost, how different he looked since I'd seen him last. He got up and walked to the window. I looked around the sparsely furnished room, just the bed, a chair and a table, I was pleased I'd brought him some flowers which would cheer the place up a bit. I couldn't believe that this was the same man, my lovely handsome leading man.

"I only just heard you were here. I've been away."

"Yes, I heard you got married. In Chicago, wasn't it?"

"That's right, but it didn't work out. You got married too, didn't you?"

"Yes, last year. Her name is Gillian, she's a teacher. I don't know where I'd be if it hadn't been for her. Dead, probably. She's been wonderful." He turned to look at me, and said, "I'm sorry to hear that your marriage didn't work out. Is he an actor?"

"No, a lawyer."

"Serves you right. What made you marry him?"

"I thought I was in love. Also I was pregnant."

"Oh dear, what happened?"

"In a nutshell we married, but I lost the baby, then I found that his work was more important than me. I tried to make a go of it but it was no use. It's only a matter of time before we get a divorce. He won't want me staying here in London, I know that, so I think we will part amicably enough. He's not really interested in the theatre anyway, or my career, he doesn't have the time, he's so ambitious. Love dies when it's met with indifference."

"Then I guess you will divorce."

"I was terribly lonely out there, I missed my friends and the work of course."

"Couldn't you have got work out there?"

"It was all too difficult, and besides, I was homesick for London."

"That's pretty sentimental, isn't it? You mean you missed the misery?"

I smiled at him. "There's misery and there's misery."

"Tell me about it!"

"I'm sorry. Tell me about what happened to you."

Trevor explained things that I had already heard many times before from actors, people who devote their lives to a profession in which rejection, humiliation and long periods of unemployment are an essential part of life.

"When I got the job in the last play we got married during the first week, I thought everything would be fine but after six weeks into the run I got so bored with the part, and wanted to be with Gillian so much, I thought I would go out of my mind. I needed a fix to be able to go on stage every night."

"That's terrible, Trevor," I said gently.

He went on to explain: "Gillian would be gone early in the morning each day and I'd leave just as she was getting home in the afternoon, so we never saw each other, so I used to drink during the day. Oh God, let's change the subject, please, I don't want to talk about it."

We asked each other about news of other actors, it was almost as if we wanted to hear about their failures as well as about their successes. Trevor said that Brian had come to see him and told him he was giving up the business.

"I asked him why," said Trevor, "and he went on and on, as if I didn't know."

"It's the stress of waiting mostly, constantly waiting either for money, a part, or a phone call, or a director, or rehearsals, the run itself, the boredom, the time wasted in spinning wheels. Then after the waiting comes the high of the performance, the constant stress of relationships, and the whole bloody business."

"He was trying to do too much, doing telly in the day and theatre at night."

"We never know when to give up, do we? But tell me, are they treating you well?"

"I guess, but we don't have any 'happy hours'. I suppose they're over for me anyway. I feel much better. It is going to be a long haul. Brian went over all the actors he knew who had become alcoholics. Cheerful, eh? Just what I needed! He just kept saying it's all part of the business."

We spoke until a nurse came to get him for a group session—to talk more, I guess. I gave him two big kisses and hugged him before I left. The struggle not to cry was tricky. He now had Gillian so at least he would be taken care of when he got out.

Going back to the apartment, I stared out the window on the bus ride, feeling depressed at the outcome of his biggest success so far, and thinking just how difficult it would be for him to get going again. He really will, though, I'm sure of it. We all go through rough times when we're out of work. It's all about security and having nothing to look forward to in the future. At least I knew that Tom would support me even if he did divorce me, until I started earning again. I wondered when he would actually start proceedings. Suddenly we passed Teddington. Why did I remember that name? Ah yes, it was where Noel Coward had lived. What did he do to escape becoming an alcoholic? He just kept on creating wonderful characters, I suppose. I looked at all the little semi-detached houses we were passing, wondering what all the people who lived in them were doing, and whether Coward or his plays had any place in their lives. Or Shakespeare, for that matter. What did the theatre mean to them?

I sat by the phone for a week, making calls, called my old agent, Tony, trying to find out casting information, to get leads as to who was doing what, and reading all the trade magazines and newspapers. Finally, I thought I was almost forgotten. It's bad enough being available all the time in London and going from one show to another, but if you go away for six months, unless you're huge, you're forgotten. That reminded me to call the casting director of the National. I knew her from three years back. I was given a time for an interview. "No need for you to audition." Well, the day came for the interview, and although they were all very friendly and seemed keen, there was no further follow-up. When the phone rang, it was nearly always for Peggy—not anything important, but at least I heard the sound of the phone. The weather was foul. No one seemed to care that I was back. Finally my old agent called and started sending me auditions. They were miserable. "What have you been doing?" I felt like saying "Living! I've been living." but instead I gave them the old line that I had been writing, writing a play. A writer is better than an actress, because the profession is so over-crowded it is frightening.

The following week I got a part in a fringe production. No pay, but at least it was a job. The theatre was well regarded. Every day we rehearsed in a freezing hall in Tottenham Court Road, it was just like starting out as a drama student all over again.

The play got good reviews, so for a while I was happy enough. We were all hopeful that the play might transfer to the West End, but the money men decided that it was too big a risk as the producers were not well known enough. Peggy got another tour, leaving me after two weeks while I stayed on alone in the apartment. The turmoil of trying to adjust to a much smaller world, that of the treacheries of survival in the theatre world, was constant. I knew that family, what I called my "outside life" was after all terribly important to maintain some kind of equilibrium. It almost seemed to be masochistic with the constant struggle and rejection, travel and regular hours notwithstanding. Maybe it would only be a matter of time before there would be rejection in my other life.

Tom was being very understanding, but he was no angel so he couldn't keep on living a saintly life without meeting someone else, so I knew I might lose a husband and a best friend. If I couldn't get a job in the next month I would return to Chicago, I decided, to a normal if humdrum life; at least I would be a helpmate and wife. I would have those roles after all, just not nothing. The fringe job was over, then I suddenly had an offer to do a play in Eastbourne with a possible transfer to London—Eastbourne, not even Richmond or Leatherhead. It was an Agatha Christie murder mystery, *The Unexpected Guest*, an old chestnut—but then when I thought that *The Mousetrap* was still running in the West End, there may be a chance. Surely London could stand two Christie plays running simultaneously.

Then another offer came just before I accepted: a new play at the Adelphi. Brilliant, just what I wanted.

I was surprised because I realised that you can never tell what you will enjoy doing in the theatre and what will disappoint you. Sometimes what you look forward to with great anticipation proves not to be a happy experience. Expect nothing and you will not be disappointed, anything good that comes along will be a pleasant surprise. I don't know if this is a wise way to live, or whether it leads to pessimism and a gloomy disposition. It probably does, so I decided to be optimistic, make good things happen, or at least behave as if they are going to. The new play at the Adelphi seemed promising, it was West End rather than fringe, the playwright's previous successes boded well for this one, there were no real duds in the cast and the director knew his business, so all in all there were grounds for optimism.

How wrong I was. The play only ran six weeks . . .

———◆———

The seduction scene at the Carlton this afternoon with Howard had really shaken me, I couldn't wait to get back to London to find Michael. However, the sunset over Cannes had been glorious. I was sitting on a rock overlooking the blue-grey silvery Mediterranean Sea, thinking about my time in LA. It was the hardest thing to realise that other people were happy here in the South of France. Looking at the starlets posing topless on the beach every morning with a group of photographers around them, they looked elated, happy, so too did the people drinking and eating at the cafes all along the Croisette. Two girls walked towards me, they were laughing and joking together, eating ice-cream cones. I felt so out of place somehow. I stared at them; they looked so carefree and gay, whereas I felt as though I were in a nightmare, that it wasn't really happening. Tomorrow I'd wake up and it would all be a dream. I'd roll over in bed and there would be Michael. He would say that it had all been a mistake, and he had never meant to treat me as he had, for he loved me and he couldn't live without me. I'd feel his kisses on my mouth and weep with joy, asking him why he'd been so cruel and I'd say to him, "I just had an awful dream." He would hold me and say, "Don't worry about it." I'd feel his soft warm skin which was so sexy and run my hand over the curly black hair on his chest. He'd smile his wonderful smile at me and we'd make love.

"Watch out!" someone yelled.

"Damn." I stopped dead in the middle of a pedestrian crossing.

"Merde!" The driver screeched on his brakes and gestured to me, leaning out the car window. We stared angrily at each other. I was too angry to reply, and once I knew he had definitely stopped, I continued across the road.

The girls had seen me and the car approaching and had shouted out to me. I waved to them from the other side and shouted, "Thank you." They waved back and I walked back to the hotel.

"I could have been killed," I said to myself. The shock of the incident gave me a huge jolt of adrenaline. Anger and revenge brought me back to reality and action. I suddenly made up my mind to go back to London, find Michael with or without his wife, and to confront him no matter what the cost. The whole thing was so dreadfully mortifying.

Chapter Nine

BEGINNING WITH THE LAST THREE weeks, from the dash to Italy, then on to Cannes with Steve, the time seemed to be far longer. I was determined to find out what had happened. The last two days in Cannes had dragged on, I couldn't wait to get back to London to hear all the details, Michael's explanation, a blow-by-blow account, even though it might be like hammering on the head, down, down, down. In the depth of my soul I knew no matter how much it hurt I had to see him. Like a sailor in distress, I was straining to sight some far-off white sail in the mists of the horizon. No matter how much it hurt, surely it would help to know the reasons. Peggy had just left on another tour so wouldn't be there to hold my hand.

I felt as if the plane would never land. Fortunately, my tenant had moved out so I went back to my flat. After dumping my stuff, I took a taxi to Michael's flat when there was no answer to my phone call. The locks had been changed. After Peggy had found the note left for me, he must have gone back to collect more things and had the locks changed. I felt somehow violated, this had been my home after all, where I had been so happy. The tears came in the taxi going back to my flat. I knew it was going to be humiliating but not as bad as this. I couldn't find him.

I phoned his cottage in Scotland, he wasn't there. The two of them had just vanished. His agent said he had phoned to say they were going away, but that was over a month ago. Could it be that they had gone to Capri? He had never taken me there so I wouldn't know where to find them if I did go. I had no address or contacts for him.

Every day I looked for his car; if a red Volvo went by I'd look first at the number plate which I knew by heart. There were dozens of red Volvos in central London, but I never saw his. It was just an instinctive habit. I thought I saw him from behind a couple of times, but it never was him. The constant searching was tiresome. Someone once said if you stand in Piccadilly Circus long enough you'll meet everyone you've ever known. I wondered how long it would take.

Presumably, he would have a phone in Capri, so I might get an address, yet it sounded rather doubtful to risk a journey for that. I felt too humiliated to phone any of our friends—to admit I was looking for him. They'd quickly think he had left town because I was back. I phoned Yvonne, a former girlfriend. "Did you hear about Michael?" She had, but she knew nothing. It seemed stupid to go to the police when he was probably just on an extended holiday and I'd make a complete fool of myself. Anyway what did I want to say? Congratulations on your marriage? How does she measure up to me? Total blank. The insult was not that he hadn't let me know and that they had just gone. The bastard! Who was she?

The light was blinking on my answering machine—next to my Oscar—when I got home. I reached over to the machine and knocked the statue over. I stared at it on the floor. To think that this little statue was what I had always wanted, it represented years of striving, now it just represented loss—loss of everything that made life meaningful to me. As I rewound the message, I thought that maybe, just maybe it was him. I pushed "play". No chance.

It was a message from the travel agent that Michael used for his overseas travel. We had talked to him last year when we thought of going to the South of France. The voice said that Michael had not been in touch with him at all, and his assistant hadn't heard from him either. Very strange. Perhaps it was his new wife who had made the travel plans, she could have easily arranged it all. A huge spear of jealousy pierced through me. I couldn't bear to think about it. Forget him, I muttered, don't torture yourself. That was another life. It's over. He's gone. It will never be the same.

The pain in my heart was unendurable. Sitting on the floor, I rocked to and fro in agony. Love is pain and anguish, shame, ecstasy, heaven and hell, the sense of living more intensely, and unutterable boredom. It means freedom and slavery, peace and unrest. Now the lyrics of every love song haunted me. But I needed him. I missed him dreadfully. Would I ever see him again?

The phone rang again. The call was from a jeweller's shop in Bond Street where Michael and I had bought several little brooches on our way home from lunches at the Ritz. Again, it was the same answer. No, sorry, we haven't seen Mr Rodham for the past two months and he hasn't made any purchases here. Good. At least he hadn't taken her into our favourite little shop.

Where could they be? They could have gone to Australia, South Africa, anywhere in fact. He had probably finished his new book and was taking a break somewhere. The Bahamas? Mexico? I just wanted to know. Would it have made me feel any better? The image of them travelling together, enjoying each other, laughing, drinking, making love, sickened me and I knew that I'd have to snap out of it or I would go insane and do something crazy.

Hell hath no fury like a woman scorned. I wondered who wrote that. Is there a quotation for an actress who puts her work first only to find out she has sacrificed her private life, or does that sound too simple? A quotation about ambition of course would be the more appropriate one. Fame is the spur. Do you ever feel that the timing is the most important thing? If only I hadn't wanted to be in the film, if only I hadn't wanted to be an actress, I could have been happy—a career girl at home, for example, with a computer, perhaps, or with six kids, or with both. Pretty little blond-headed boys with a lovely husband and a white picket fence and no worries.

The next morning I couldn't get out of bed. The despair of another day without Michael. There was no stimulation, no reason to get up. How could anyone leave such a gap in one's life? How could some other human being take over your whole existence? I couldn't talk to anyone about it, I knew that they would give advice. But I didn't want any.

That evening the phone rang just as I was locking the door to go out for groceries, I dashed back in and caught it before the answerphone kicked in.

"This is Patricia calling, is that you, Nicole?" I heard the Australian accent and remembered the girl I had taken for lunch on the train, two weeks ago, on the way to Cannes.

"Oh I'm so pleased you're there. I thought you might be still in Cannes. I'm at Victoria Station. It looks as if London is completely sold out. I can't get a room anywhere. I do hope you don't mind me asking but do you know anyone I could possibly stay with? Remember you said I could call you if I was stuck."

"Yes, yes, of course. Listen, get a taxi and come right here. You can stay here with me."

"Oh, thank you so much, Nicole." I could hear her begin to cry on the phone.

"You've no idea what the crowd is like down here. I've waited for over two hours." She was now sobbing into the phone.

"Come on over and we'll cheer ourselves up."

"Oh, thank you so much. You're an angel."

Well, the groceries will have to wait, that's for sure. I remembered what it was like when I first came to London. You needed all the friends you could find. I quickly tidied up the place and dusted, pushing things in drawers, whipping round with the vacuum cleaner (Dirk Bogarde again) and pulled out some clean sheets from the closet.

Fifteen minutes later the bell rang and a very bedraggled Australian was on the doorstep. She had her backpack by her feet; she looked exhausted. I welcomed her arrival as it proved to be a timely distraction of sorts; it made me feel better trying to help someone else, taking me out of my loneliness and thoughts of Michael. I decided to concentrate entirely on her problems.

You were the only person I could reach," she explained, shaking her umbrella at the door.

"Never mind that, come on in and I'll make a cup of tea." She seemed so grateful, her eyes told everything, and it did make me feel better.

"I was crazy not to have made plans earlier but I was desperate." She took off her wet raincoat and shoes, leaving her backpack inside the door.

I took her coat, hung it up and asked her, "Where have you been since I last saw you?"

"I went to Nice, then up to Paris. I stayed with some friends there, then they left, so I had to move on." I made the tea, then afterwards we continued talking over a glass of wine in the kitchen while I cooked dinner. We had to make do with pasta because I had no meat in the freezer, but at least I had the makings of a salad and leftovers of an apple crumble.

It turned out that she had met a Frenchman in Paris and fallen for him like a ton of bricks. They spent a whole week together before she found out that he was married. He said he was separated, at least, but she got fed up with him making phone calls wherever they went, and finally decided they weren't business calls—he was calling his kids. She felt humiliated and resolved to leave Paris to get away from him.

"I couldn't believe I could be so taken in by him. It's true you know, that French charm is irresistible."

"I hope you took precautions," I laughed.

"Yes, of course. I insisted. Can you imagine me arriving back home unmarried with a baby? It would be my parents' worst nightmare! How could they explain it to all their neighbours shopping in the supermarket—they all have 1950s' morals!"

Next morning, we sat having coffee in the kitchen and she said she had to go back home because her money was running out.

"I'm just afraid, if I go back I'll never get to England again. It's just too expensive to come over here and I'll be stuck. I'll probably get married, have kids and that will be that. So many of us go home and suddenly ten years have gone and we are all suburban housewives, with all the mundane work of bringing up a family."

I knew she probably had no other choice.

"Couldn't you get a job and stay on?"

"I've tried, but it's almost impossible. I'm not qualified for anything."

It was Peggy, still on tour, who came up with an idea when I told her about Patricia.

"Why don't you let her stay on in the flat, she can take all your messages, just in case Michael does call while you're out, at least she'd be company for you, which you badly need, and she probably does too. Job-hunting is depressing at the best of times."

Patricia came to the shops with me. We bought bagfuls of groceries, a couple of bottles of wine, fresh bread from the bakery, and lugged it all home. She insisted on buying me some Australian wine.

"I really like being in London but it can be very lonely, and I don't even like travelling alone any more. That's why I was so vulnerable when I met that rotten Frenchman," she said. "It's no fun, perhaps it is time to go home."

"Maybe we can find you a job so you to stay on. A nanny perhaps. They are always in demand." I told her about my job as a nanny in Chicago, how much I had enjoyed it and how hospitable my employers had been. I sent her out to buy a copy of *The Lady* magazine, and when she got back we sat down and turned to the Help Wanted ads in the back pages.

"Companion wanted", "Nanny wanted", there were lots of them.

"Here's one—'an American family needs mother's help. Liberal time off, two young girls'—why not try that one?"

We wrote to three different box numbers. I helped her compose the letters, she went out to mail them. Nothing ventured, nothing gained. Patricia was very much like me, she needed people. Perhaps writers spend their time creating their own characters with no real need to talk to them, but both of us needed to communicate with others. As an actress, it was essential to sink oneself into a character. By burying myself in work, I felt that the agony over Michael would be diluted. It was, as it were, that in putting on my make-up, or somewhere in my pot of grease-paint there was another personality that couldn't be touched by human grief.

Two days later the phone rang, the call was for Patricia. I detected an American accent and immediately thought of the ad.

"It's for you, Patricia."

She was in the kitchen ironing. She'd washed everything she had in her backpack, and she was ironing everything including T-shirts. I went into the kitchen while she was on the phone, ironed a few things, listening with half an ear. The conversation went on for quite some time, she came back into the room smiling.

"You'll never guess," as she ran her hand through her short blonde hair.

"What?"

"That was the American family we wrote to."

"And?"

"He is a movie producer from California, just here for three months working on a film and they said if things worked out I could go back to the States with them. I have an interview tomorrow morning. She sounded really nice."

We went out that night to celebrate; even though she hadn't got the job yet, she felt that she had, besides we were very cheered that she had got a response. We walked down to Joe Allen's, the big show-biz restaurant in Covent Garden. It was there, over some food and a glass of wine, that I told her all about Michael. We had eaten there so many times, Michael and I, it was still painful.

Patricia had seen the movie of course, but hadn't realised that Michael had written the book.

"Is that why you went to Italy immediately after the Academy Awards then?"

I nodded.

"How awful. How could he do such a thing and not tell you?"

I poured another glass of wine. It felt good to be able to talk about it to someone new, someone who could be as sympathetic as Patricia was. Peggy was sick of the subject, I knew.

"So when you got back to London you couldn't find him? That's unbelievable. Did you try the internet? You can find anyone that way."

"No I didn't. As you know, I haven't got a computer. He does all his work through an agent so he wouldn't easily be found."

"Do you really want to find him? I mean, he's been so terribly cruel, why could you want ever to speak to him again?"

I spread some butter on my bread—what the hell, I didn't care if I put on weight at this stage. It was delicious.

"Because I'm still in love with him, and I'll do anything to see him again. I suppose you think I'm crazy?"

Patricia smiled and said, "Not at all. It's just that it might be even more painful for you if you did see him, or talk to him."

"I'd risk it."

The waiter brought some cheese and we ordered more wine. Patricia looked lovely. She was obviously enjoying herself.

"It's amazing you can't find him. I guess you've tried all your friends, phone numbers etc. etc."

"Everything. I think they've gone away somewhere."

"Don't worry, we'll find him somehow." She picked up her wineglass, smiling at me.

"Here's to finding Michael, and to my new job!"

Early next morning Patricia left the flat for the interview. Before she left I sat her down at the kitchen table, insisting she eat one of my pancakes with syrup, then some toast and coffee. I sat opposite her, admired her make-up, only a touch of eye-liner and very pale lipstick.

"You look great today. I do hope it goes well."

"If I like the kids, then it should be OK."

I cleared the table as she left, wondering what I'd do that morning. More detective work, more groaning, more hyperventilating.

"Wish me luck." She was out the door.

I washed up the dishes, made the beds, and went to buy a paper. When I got back, Peggy had called, saying they were staying on in Bristol for another week. I made some more tea and sat down to read the paper.

There was nothing in it about Michael or the film except the ad in the entertainment pages. I certainly wasn't tempted to see it again. It was still only eleven o'clock—the day was crawling. I checked the clock to see if it hadn't stopped.

I wondered how I could get through the day, so I decided to check through my wardrobe, always a terrible job. There were so many things that I never wore, either because they were too tight or too difficult to put on, or the wrong colour. I lifted out a dress I liked and decided to shorten the sleeves, they were too long and too tight. I searched for a pair of scissors; they weren't in their usual place in the kitchen drawer, but after I found them the sleeves came off. Sewing the hem around the new sleeve-length was calming. Sewing and ironing are so calming on the nerves. "I wonder who's sewing on his buttons now," I muttered.

Sitting there talking to myself, it suddenly reminded me of the play I was in, called *The Wardrobe Mistress,* when I had to sew on stage for an hour talking to the audience. Even though I had a thimble—does anyone use a thimble any more?—I used to prick my finger every time I looked up to speak. The poor lady had spent her whole life backstage making and sewing the costumes of great characters she dreamt of playing herself, from Juliet to Liza Doolittle. It was a sad little play, but demonstrated the loyalty of backstage staff including her and all the dressers. I enjoyed playing her. She had guts, especially as someone tells her, "Your future is behind you."

Bugger Michael, where is he? He must know I'm back from Cannes. I ached for the sound of his voice, but he didn't even have an answering machine I could listen to. Just before two o'clock Patricia was back.

"Well?" I said, opening the door.

"I got the job," laughed Patricia.

I hugged her and asked her what happened. We went into the kitchen and sat down.

"They were really nice people. She is very chic, the children seemed very well behaved but asked a lot of questions. Nice house in Hampstead, nice housekeeper too. Then the husband came in. Guess what? Have I got news for you! He knows Michael!"

"What?"

"Yep! He knows him."

"How did his name come up?"

"Well, it's a long story really."

"Tell me!"

"They wanted to know where I was staying, I guess they wanted to find out if I was working with another family. I said I was staying with you, and they said, 'Not THE Nicole Bennett?' I said, 'Yes, that one.' He knew all about the film and how Michael had written the book, etc."

"What's his name?"

"Schwartz, Bill Schwartz."

"No, I don't know him."

"Anyway, they know Michael, and he said he knew he was out of town. He thought he had gone to Capri. Does Michael have a place there?"

"Yes. He did once, anyway."

"Well, that's where he must be!"

Just then the phone rang. It was Peggy, wanting to know about Patricia's interview. I told her that Patricia had found Michael for me. "Would you believe it? She got the job and the family, who are American, know Michael and say he's in Capri with his wife."

"Go for it, Nicole. Go to Capri and harass them. Give it a try, he must be there. You won't do anything till you see him again."

She was right. I desperately needed to see him and find out the truth.

Patricia agreed with her and thought I should go.

"But will you be all right here if I leave you on your own?" I said.

The family want me to start right away, so I'll just come back here on my days off, if that's all right with you."

"Of course. Let's have a look in my wardrobe to see if I can lend you some clothes." As we sorted through skirts, sweaters, slacks and cocktail dresses, some of which were out of date but still in good condition, we swapped life stories. I told her about my parents in Manchester, and without any money my determination to become an actress.

"That looks great on you," I said, as she tried on a blue wool two-piece suit with white collar.

"You're sure you don't want it?" she said, turning to look at herself in the mirror.

"No, please take it. The skirt is too tight on me, and the colour suits you beautifully."

We both enjoyed laughing over some of my worst fashion disasters, including a yellow and black striped tent dress which made her look like a zebra or a giant wasp. It was tiring so we stopped for tea. She told me about her coming to England.

"I didn't know what kind of clothes to bring with me to London. Some people said to just bring jeans and sweaters, others said you need to dress to go to the theatre and concerts."

"Yes, I love getting dressed up."

"I imagine actors like to see people dress up for the theatre. Nowadays people don't seem to dress up at all, which seems a shame. You know it was my grandmother who paid my fare over here, and she loved to dress for the theatre. I spent my first week here retracing her footsteps."

"Your grandmother?"

"Yes, she came over several times buying antique furniture to take back to Australia for her shop."

"She had an antique shop?"

"Yes, in fact two at one stage. She used to go to all the auction houses. I think she would be shocked to see Leicester Square now with all the crowds. It looks more like the Third World, with all the litter, all the hamburger bars on Shaftesbury Avenue; it must have been so different when she was here."

"Where did she stay?"

"The old Regent Palace."

"But that's such a dump."

"It wasn't then, it was a very elegant hotel. She told me it used to have a large Palm Court filled with white wicker furniture, lots of palm trees of course, an orchestra which played for tea, all under a large glass dome which is supposed to be still there. The art deco dining room is supposed to be still there too, but it's all boarded up. She used to go to see the Changing of the Guards the first day she arrived. She was a true royalist who loved anything to do with the monarchy. We were brought up to regard England as home."

"Well then, you must feel right at home already."

"The funny thing is that I don't. London seems to be totally different to what she described. The place seems to be full of people like me in blue jeans with backpacks, even going into those fashionable restaurants. Granny used to talk about the Regent Palace, and how staying there was a real treat. Those days have gone, together with the British Empire. Granny used to have a little weep every time she heard 'Rule Britannia' played in the band-shell at Regent's Park, or saw the Queen Mother. She belonged to a whole generation who felt close emotional links with England. They considered themselves Englishmen living in Australia, and called England home. Remember, we fought for England in the two world wars, and the European conflicts which started those wars meant little to them, but any threat to England did."

"Did your grandfather fight in the war?" I asked.

"No, he volunteered, but was turned down on medical grounds; he was too deaf, it seems, but her brother was in the army and was killed in France."

"Yes, so was my grandfather."

Patricia continued, "You see, her generation were very loyal to Britain and they completely adopted their political and cultural traditions, from royalty to band concerts in the park. Now that's all gone, now we have to face up to the fact that we are an Asian nation."

"Do you really think so?"

"Well, it's only a matter of time."

"It's funny, come to think of it, you don't see many Australians in London these days."

Patricia laughed and said, "That's because we can't afford it, the exchange rate is horrendous and a lot of the older Brits, even though they are fond of us, still call us colonials and their welcome is always tinged with patronising amusement."

"Not any more, surely?"

"Well, my professors at art school were all very much like that. Almost as if we couldn't produce any serious art if we were from down under. I think it made them feel superior. They're worse with us than they are with Americans."

"Yes, I know what you're saying, at least I think I do."

"How will you feel about working for Americans?"

"Fine. They are more like Australians than the British in their way of life. They don't have the class system as you do here. I still can't get over the fact that it all depends on what school or rather what university you went to when you're trying to get a job." She got up and rinsed our cups in the sink. It was so nice to have her around to talk to, and I knew I'd miss her.

"Is it the same when you're trying to get a job in the theatre?" she asked.

"It depends. Obviously if I had been in one of the dramatic companies at Oxford or Cambridge I would have had a head start because of the tremendous contacts you make up there. Lots of students go on to be directors and playwrights, so if you know them it helps a lot. It's even better than the Royal Academy of Dramatic Art or some of the London drama schools because you keep your university pals for the rest of your life, whereas the agents who come to your showcase see you just once, and if they don't sign you, that's it."

"But you didn't go to university, yet you did pretty well, didn't you?"

"Yes, however, I would have liked to have gone. If I had any advice to give a drama student, I'd say, get an Oxbridge accent if you can't get to university."

"They say it's just a matter of who you know in the art world if you want to get on," Patricia said bitterly.

"Don't worry," I said. "It's exactly the same in the theatre. I found that out by looking at Ellen Terry's family tree and following John Gielgud's career. And so it goes. You find out soon enough if you're on the grapevine. The branches of success always help."

"Is it true what they say about the casting couch?" smiled Patricia.

"In a way. There were great stories in Gielgud's day about Binkie Beaumont chasing actors around his office and unless you were a homosexual you didn't get very far. I suppose nothing's changed very much but I've never had to sleep around for a job, at least."

The next morning Patricia left for her new job and I decided to go to Capri.

Chapter Ten

IT'S ALWAYS A SPECTACULAR SIGHT approaching the island of Capri by sea. There really isn't any other way to get there, of course. You can take a boat from Naples or Sorrento or Positano. I didn't want to go through Sorrento again because of a tragedy that happened when I was vacationing there with a writer friend years ago. He committed suicide during the time we were there. I had to arrange everything afterwards, contacting his family, dealing with the police. He was a writer who had been so deeply depressed by his writer's block that he just gave up. We had decided to take a week's break between my rehearsals and went on a share basis at the hotel, taking a charter flight, sharing a room and our expenses. The old hotel was right on top of the cliffs. When we were given our room I opened the French windows and shuddered to see a sheer drop way down to the rocks below, but a beautiful view of the sea. I closed the window quickly. It rained every day and bad weather is always worse to endure in a hotel room than back home when you can always find something to do. The charter flight didn't leave till the weekend. I got tired of shopping, the television was in Italian, I'd sent off all my postcards and there was nothing to do. It was too cold to swim, and who would want to in the rain? The hours between lunch and dinner seemed an eternity. There were no English newspapers and I'd finished my book.

He started to drink heavily, sometimes at the hotel bar or in one of the bars in the main square. The drinking made it worse, he had nothing to do, he couldn't write, I usually walk a lot but it wasn't pleasant in the rain. One evening I had been out getting some fresh air after dinner, and when I came back to the hotel I saw him in the bar so I went straight up to bed.

I heard him come in much later when I was half asleep, but I was grateful that he didn't put on any lights and I fell back to sleep again.

About three o'clock I was awakened by a cold breeze across my face. I reached for the bedside lamp and quickly discovered that he wasn't in the other bed, and the window which was directly above the cliffs was wide open. He had jumped. I couldn't look down as I closed the window and started weeping and groaning with shock. There was a note, and in it he just said he didn't want to live any more, that all he wanted to do was to write, but that all he wanted to write had all been written before.

Passing those cliffs reminded me of the whole episode, which had been a nightmare. I often thought if we hadn't had that room he wouldn't have done it. The invitation of that huge window made it too easy.

After the boat arrived at noon, but the time I had found the hotel and unpacked it was nearly two p.m. I walked down the tiny alleyway into the square. It was so hot, I kept mostly in the shade. The cicadas were singing away. The place was full of spiritual energy. The whole island was so exotic, colourful and stimulating. I bought a bottle of wine, some pastries, then went down a pathway till I came out to a small clearing overlooking the sea far below. The rock was warm from the sun, so I sat there drinking the wine from the bottle, watching the boats coming in from Italy, the people like tiny dots below coming off the launches. The wine went to my head and the truth seemed clearer. What's the matter with me? I must be mad to come here alone. Some women don't, they go in twos everywhere, to keep themselves secure. But in the end, you are responsible for your own actions. You pay for everything. Every decision is important, who you work with, who you sleep with, what jobs you take—what your agent tells you is sometimes wrong. What you do is sometimes very wrong. I hadn't wanted to chase Michael in London because it was so humiliating in front of my friends and his—however here in Capri I couldn't care less what the fishermen and locals thought of me. Nobody knew who I was.

The little alleyways and paths were fascinating. I searched for the bar that Graham Greene used to frequent. I had remembered to bring a book about him, so I knew where to look. It was a very tiny place but I sat there having an aperitif, hoping someone who spoke English would come in. The air was still very hot, but cooler inside surrounded by the white-washed walls with the large fan overhead. Shortly afterwards, two men, slightly older than me, entered and sat in the corner. They were speaking English all right, but not as clearly as I hoped, as there was a radio on behind the bar.

After I'd had two drinks I introduced myself. One was named Don, he owned a boat here, but seldom used it. Bruce, an Australian, was visiting from Sydney. They were mostly talking about the house repairs and supplies they needed to fix up Don's roof. Not the intellectual conversation I was expecting, and worse, they'd never even heard of Michael. For the next two days I spent most of my time wandering about trying to find anyone at all who might have been able to give me any kind of information about Michael, where he was, who he was with, how he looked, anything at all. But nothing. Finally, after going each evening for a drink at the same bar, on the third night I met a man named Peter Marsh, who had known Michael when he was living here two years ago. He was about the same height as Michael, just under six feet, thin and loose-limbed. He was pleasant-looking, neither handsome nor plain, with a deep tan and sun-bleached blond hair with a slight wave in it. He was wearing white shorts and a blue polo sports shirt. After buying a drink at the bar he came over and asked if anyone was sitting at my table. I smiled at him and asked him to join me. He sat down and I noticed his hands. They were long but not large for his size, beautifully shaped and at the same time strong. I thought that a painter would be pleased to paint them. He had rather high cheekbones, and his grey eyes were deep set and his lashes were thick and long.

I told him I was doing an article about British writers who lived on Capri, but I don't think he was fooled for a minute. I took a chance and asked him if he knew Michael.

"Why Michael?" he said.

"Because he's quite famous now and I'd like to interview him." A lame excuse.

"You should interview him then back in London."

"The only trouble is he doesn't seem to live there any more. Would you know if he is on the island?"

"Well, he was here for a couple of days last week. We had a drink together, but he told me he was going to Rome to do some research for his book."

"Did he say if he was coming back?"

"Yes, he did. He said he intended to come back here from Rome."

"Good, then I'll stay on and wait for him."

"You could interview me if you like, I'm a writer." He laughed.

"Are you serious? It's too much of a coincidence. What do you write?"

"If you let me buy you a drink I'll tell you." He got up and went over to the bar. "It's a gin and tonic, isn't it?"

I watched him as he spoke fluent Italian so easily to the barman. My antennae went up to signal that I might get carried away. I made up my mind there and then that I was not going to have any kind of affair, no matter what, with anyone on the island. I just hoped that this man wouldn't come on to me. I needn't have worried, as during our conversation he told me he had come to Capri after the death of his wife whom he adored. Evidently she had died in a car accident together with their son some time ago. They had a house here but hadn't been back for quite a while. He also said he'd rather not discuss it, so I switched back to talking about Michael.

"Michael and I are completely different kinds of writers, he is far more literary than I am, and he always argues that my books are too commercial. I suppose he thinks they sell better than his," he said, lighting a cigarette.

"By the way, did Michael have anyone with him when you last saw him?" I asked, trying to sound casual.

"Yes, I think so, although when I met him for a drink he was alone."

He walked me back to my hotel. I felt relieved to have met a friend and one who wouldn't expect any physical involvement. We were both hurting, but in different ways, so maybe we could help each other just by being there for each other. I lay in bed listening to the cicadas, feeling pleased to be on the island away from London, with the thought that I would be able to stay on till Michael got back.

Every day I went to the little beach on the other side of the island to sunbathe. The water was glorious. Each evening I would find a little bistro, order pesto, pasta and red wine. I fell in love with the island, even thought about living there as Michael had. The lowers, the sea, the visual beauty were a balm and comforting, somehow different from Nassau—more historical, mystical, inspiring poetry and operatic themes. I was making lots of friends who lived there most of the year except in the winter. Beach people, I called them, because we really had little in common.

Peter had become a support system, a real friend, and finally I had told him my whole story. He was totally sympathetic.

"Nobody is worth that much suffering."

"But I'm still in love with him."

"Obviously, but it's over, Nicole, you know that."

"There is always the possibility that things are not working out and he might be missing me."

"You would have heard from him, if that were the case."

"But I'm here."

"You pick up your messages, don't you?"

There weren't even any "hang-ups" on my phone, so it was clear there were no calls.

Every day we would meet after he had done his quota of words for the day. He was completely different in character to Michael. Although I could see some of the same characteristics in his nature, he was kind, considerate and intuitive, but he wasn't Michael. I was fixated on Michael, still.

The island was a joy to discover. There were many archaeological sites, Peter, knowing most of them, took me to see them. He was more of a scholar than Michael. They had both gone to Oxford, though Peter had been three years ahead of Michael.

"Enough of past history, Nicole, let's go meet some living legends."

"What do you have in mind, Peter?"

"I've been invited to dinner at the Palazzo Ricci, it's well named, the family is as rich as Croesus, has been since the Renaissance, it isn't polite to enquire how the first Riccis made their money but they've been hyper-respectable for generations, they even have a title. They asked me to bring a guest. Would you like to come?"

"That sounds lovely. Thank you for asking me, but what on earth shall I wear?"

"It'll be in black tie, so you'd better wear something dressy."

The house was enormous, with breath-taking views from the front steps. We went into a most elegant house full of antiques, chandeliers, Persian carpets and gold and silver ornaments. The guests were equally elegant, to me they seemed the height of sophistication and glamour; most of them were Italian. I had to struggle to follow their conversation, but there were a few people speaking English, which helped. Peter stuck close to me, sitting next to me at dinner, so I wasn't completely at sea. It was one of the most romantic dinners I'd ever attended, seated there under a great chandelier, with huge bowls of flowers on the long table facing me. The three crystal wine glasses, the silverware in front of me, gleamed brightly; my napkin was hand-embroidered as was the tablecloth, all the staff were in uniform. Needless to say, the food and wine were perfection itself.

At coffee afterwards on the balcony overlooking the sea, one of the Italian men who had been sitting at the other end of the table at dinner came over to me. He spoke in English. He was about my age, very handsome and distinguished looking. I'd had several glasses of wine, so felt like flirting, my defences were down. My good intentions were swept aside by the exhilaration of the evening. It was a hysterical fifteen minutes. The chemistry was immediate. He flirted back. We asked each other, if we were married, would we speak in English or Italian? I said it would have to be English since I don't speak Italian, and he suggested that we run away together. We were flirting so much I never did find out if he was married. It was as if a dark cloud had lifted suddenly. The sheer enjoyment of it all, unexpected, gave me a jolt of exhilaration. It really was quite intoxicating, a once-in-a-lifetime evening—like your first glimpse of Venice or one of the chateaux on the Loire.

"What do you do?" I asked.

"I'm in business."

"What kind of business?"

"I export wine from my estates."

"And where are your estates?"

"Mostly in Tuscany."

"How wonderful. Perhaps I *will* run away with you."

It was a terribly frivolous conversation resulting from the wine, the conviviality, the sumptuous dinner and the exquisite surroundings. Of course, why wouldn't I meet a romantic handsome Italian? The evening cried out for it and this time my stars must have been in the right constellation. I looked into his deep brown eyes, which matched his light brown hair, and gave him one of my most dazzling smiles. His smile in return was even more dazzling than mine. I noticed he had lovely teeth. We exchanged cards, I wrote the name of my hotel on the back of mine. I glanced at his card. It had a gold crest on it. A Count, no less, imagine that!

After dinner, Peter walked me back to my hotel.

"That was some experience, Peter, worlds away from the theatre."

"No, it's just theatre of a different kind; they put on a show, it's entertainment, it's the way Italians live."

"It's a world totally removed from our daily lives, isn't it? It's another culture, another tradition that one would have had to be born in. It's not just the language, all the ground rules for everyday life are different, don't you yourself feel a little bit at sea?"

"It's different, I grant you, but it doesn't bother me in the slightest. I can follow the language by now."

"It's not just the language. I felt the same way when I lived in Paris, even though I spoke French. I just love Italy though; wouldn't it be wonderful to star in an Italian movie, wouldn't it be a dream come true?"

"The dream would have to be dubbed, I don't know if drama can be," laughed Peter.

"You don't have to make fun of me. But thanks for taking me, it was a marvellous evening, and thanks for not letting me just sink or swim."

Alone in bed that night, I thought of what it would be like to be born into a rich Italian family who had a huge palace in Rome and a huge villa for the summers, either here on Capri or possibly on Lake Como. I wondered if I would have gone into the theatre if I had been born Italian. So many actresses dream of being in other people's shoes that dreaming of being Italian, French or German is just par for the course.

A corner of the curtain had lifted for a moment and I caught a glimpse of a world rich with colour and significance I had not dreamt of. I hadn't achieved anything compared to these people, who were rich, had great homes, connections, tradition and practised the great art of living, or the art of great living (it's called inheritance, I suppose). But maybe I could meet a rich Italian aristocrat, give up the theatre and marry him. Forget it, I don't even speak the language. I finally fell asleep.

Next morning Peter announced that he thought he would have to go back to London.

"But why, Peter? What do you have to go back for?"

"I have to see my publisher, there are some problems to sort out."

"But I don't want you to go, anyway you hate London, you avoid going there if you possibly can."

"I know, I know, but I haven't been there for ages. You've had a bit of a break now, so who don't you come back to London too? Get back to work. Obviously Michael is not coming back here. He had a deadline for his book, I know."

"You never told me that."

"Well, I really didn't want you to leave the island."

There was really no reason not to now, and without Peter it would be so lonely, even though we hadn't become lovers. Still, he had been terribly helpful.

That evening, over the usual glass of wine in our local bistro, he suggested again that I go back to London. I looked at the flowers entwined all around the elaborate wrought-iron balcony, at the sea below, and savoured the aroma of the garden beneath us, the colours, the warmth, the visual delights.

"But this is heaven, how can we leave it?"

I then realised he was right. Work was the answer, not sitting in the sun. I had to admit I was getting slightly bored. Bored with paradise? Everybody seemed so happy that night, the bar was filling up and we watched the sun go down in a blaze of fire. It had been a healing experience but it was time to move on, make something of my life. As if he was reading my thought, Peter reached over and touched my hand.

"But you mustn't try to find Michael."

"You can read my mind. I only want to find out the truth, why this happened."

"The truth?"

"You know what I'm talking about."

"The truth doesn't matter, Nicole. It's only a matter of time, just as in my case."

"Yes, I'm sorry. I keep forgetting what you're going through."

"It just takes time, Nicole, you'll see."

"Why is it that if a love affair fails you always blame yourself?"

"I don't," announced Peter. "It takes two to make it happen."

"Well, maybe women are different, they blame themselves, I blame myself. If I hadn't gone away, if I hadn't been so preoccupied with my wretched career and paid more attention to Michael, he wouldn't have gone off and married. He should have married me, I should have given up the theatre, he was more important."

"Crying over spilt milk is the most futile, most useless thing in the world. Let it go."

"Maybe the dinner you took me to opened my eyes, Peter. Maybe I should marry some nice, rich man and try to be happy. I'm not happy struggling away trying to become famous."

"You *are* famous, Nicole."

"Only for as long as I keep getting great parts, and no one can guarantee that. However, if I'm rich, with any luck I'll stay rich. I don't want to struggle any more and the theatre is a constant struggle, I'm tired of the fighting, I'm tired of the theatre, I'm tired, period. I need to be looked after, some good man to take care of me from now on, and in return I'll be good to him."

"You want to sell yourself?"

"I'm selling myself every day in the theatre, I have to make the anonymous audience love me. Wouldn't it be far better to make some man love me, I wouldn't be selling myself, I'd be a wife, not a mistress."

"But your motive would not be love, it would be comfort, security."

"Life's not that simple, not for women anyway."

Each day I had been doing some painting. Some days it went very well, other days, disaster. I did mostly small canvasses as they were easier to handle and carry around. They were all very similar, pictures of cliffs, the water far below, fishing boats near and far away. Flower pots on balconies, white-washed walls behind them. The sunlight was magnificent, and I knew that even though they were all alike I had captured my time there.

"You should take all these back to London with you, then have an exhibition," Peter suggested. He was my biggest fan. I stored my canvasses at his house as there was no space in my hotel room.

"This one, for example, is beautiful." He held up a scene of the marina with the boats all tied up together in the shade.

"Do you realise that marina is the one that Noel Coward wrote about? *In a bar on the Piccola Marina.*"

"Life came to Mrs. Webster-Brewster," I continued. "Yes, I realise that, but I didn't want to paint the bar. Too obvious."

"These would fetch some money."

"But Peter, I'm not known, who would buy them? You have to be a name, you know that."

"Well, maybe my friend Marg can help, she has a wiz PR firm."

"I think I'd rather keep them for myself. Just to remind me of these pleasant times."

"Whatever you say. But it is part of the creative impulse to want to be admired, and recognition is very important."

We put the paintings back in the corner of his living room, where I noticed a huge canvas bag.

"What have you got in this bag?" I asked.

"Oh, that's my book bag," he laughed. "Come on, let's go and have our usual." We walked down the rocky path. The perfume of the flowers was heavy in the air. The hot dusty smell of the red geraniums greeted us as we sat out on the terrace. Someone was cooking a steak. It smelt of onions and garlic with lots of butter. I would never have come to Capri if I hadn't been looking for Michael. So I have had some kind of consolation.

"I am intrigued about your book bag. What's in it?" I said as I sipped my drink.

"Oh, my book bag, well it's full of my favourite books which I take with me wherever I go. Then, on rainy days or boring days, I can delve into it. I've got plays, novels, biographies. I'll lend you some if you like."

"We do need a library here in Capri. Yes, I'd like to see what you have. Are you ever bored here, Peter?"

"When it rains and my work is not going well, but then that applies wherever you are."

"Were your first attempts rejected?"

"Of course. I think I had at least thirty rejection slips for my first novel."

"God, how did you keep going?"

"With great difficulty. But every writer goes through it."

"Who would want to be a writer?"

"You get used to it. If you didn't, you'd stop writing. Acting must be just as difficult."

"It is difficult in a different way. You have to wait until someone chooses you. Chooses you for a part, but there is a lot of rejection, some people just give up, like writers. If only they knew that success might be just around the corner."

"Graham Greene got rejected at first," he laughed. "I've just been re-reading a biography of him and trying to relate the themes in his novels to what he was going through in his own life. It's been done before, of course, the influence of his religious conversion to Roman Catholicism in particular, but I'm more interested in the women in his life and how they appear, thinly disguised, in his novels."

"Why did he live here?"

"Lived is hardly the word. He used the island to escape from England."

"Like we both have," I said.

It was obvious that both of us would soon have to return, Peter had to see his publisher and I thought the activity and action in London would be more of a distraction and help him recover from his grief, so I encouraged him to leave. It didn't look as if Michael was coming back here, so I had to decide what I was going to do next; however, I wasn't sure I wanted to leave just yet.

The next day I walked to the ferry with him to see him off. I hated to see him go but I wanted to wait just a little longer in case Michael did show up. I waved to him as the goat pulled out and realised suddenly that he meant a tremendous amount to me. Was I falling in love again? He had been so kind to me with such understanding I knew he was exceptional, so much better than Michael.

Chapter Eleven

WHEN I GOT BACK TO the hotel, there was a letter from Carlo. He was the Italian I had met at the Riccis' dinner party. It was an invitation for dinner the following night. If anyone had told me that I would be swept off my feet by an Italian Count, who was an outrageous flirt, kissing your hand and all that sort of thing, I know I would have told them to stop being ridiculous. But, nevertheless, that's what happened.

I wondered where he was going to take me for dinner. I chose my lightest blue shirt and my new white pants, gold sandals and a silk scarf of blue and yellow stripes, hoping it was not going to be too casual. Thinking back to that enormous house with all the servants and luxury, I knew he must have expensive tastes. I smiled, and thought that I do too if I'm not paying for it. Nevertheless, I was a little apprehensive, hoping that my conversation wouldn't bore him or that he would find me a let-down after that evening which had been so magical. I needn't have worried.

That first evening he took me to a most elegant restaurant on the island, we couldn't stop smiling at each other almost as if we both knew what was going to happen. The meal was chosen by him, and of course the wine. What is it about expensive wine that makes you feel so euphoric? I had rarely drunk very expensive wine, so I could feel the reaction immediately. It's almost as if you have suddenly got a new brain, a more intelligent one, your thought and conversations are on a much higher level. Your subconscious is guiding your emotions, everything is far more civilised and comprehensible than before.

The wine, the first bottle with the salad, was a Malvasia, slightly sweet, very slightly fizzy, but delicious. The salad was basically aragula, with chopped olives, bits of shrimp and endives and rather too much olive oil, which meant I had to wash down every bite with a good slurp of Malvasia, so that by the time the next course arrived I had begun to feel even more civilised and brilliant. The second course was a small bit of fish. I asked Carlo what it was; he said it was probably swordfish, which I had never eaten before, but it tasted all right. The wine with it was a very dry white wine, a burgundy, Chateau Ausone, unspeakably fine and delicate, probably wickedly expensive (I found out later just how expensive it was!). By now I was undoubtedly a genius. The third course was lamb, thin slices but plenty of them, grilled to perfection, with hearts of palm and the tiniest new potatoes, the wine was naturally Bordeaux, Chateau Kirwan, not the most famous name perhaps but the best wine I had ever drunk in my life up to that point. Albert Einstein, I thought, was probably not as bright as people believed, he couldn't even keep his cheque book straight.

We found out all about each other over dessert; by the time we got back to my hotel we felt as if we had known another all our lives. I got my key at the desk, took Carlo by the hand—he didn't say a word as I led him to the elevator, nor did I. When we arrived at the door of my room I put the key in the lock, turned it, pushed the door open. Carlo followed me in, I closed the door, then he took me in his arms.

We couldn't wait to get our clothes off. He kissed me all over, then gave me a tremendously sensual massage, starting with my feet, digging his thumbs into my soles, heels and ankles. He made me absolutely totally relaxed until I was crying out for him and waiting for him. He was the best lover I'd ever had; I was so relieved to put another body between me and Michael. I slept like a baby, then woke up to find him fully dressed, sitting on the end of the bed, putting on his shoes. He apologised, saying he had to sign some papers at his office but that he would then be able to spend the day with me.

"Well, that's great. Try not to be too long."

But I really wanted to be on my own for a while to think about what had happened. He was gone for most of the morning. I dressed, had breakfast, then tidied up my room. I also managed to write up my diary, which had been badly neglected. Just in case I might some day lose my diary, I didn't mention Carlo by name, didn't put down the details of our love-making the previous night; I believed I didn't need to, they were so engraved in my brain that it would be impossible ever to forget what had taken place. How could I? It had been an agonisingly sensuous experience, the kind of experience that is so enlightening because it opens your eyes to how a commonplace event can be transformed through its performance by a genius in the art of loving, as I came to regard Carlo.

Even though he might regard me as a summer fling, I really didn't care all that much. I enjoyed being with him any time of the day or night, most of all I enjoyed being in bed with him, making love, enjoying his enjoyment of me, his praise, his adulation.

He taught me about wine and about food. I had always considered Italian wine to be inferior to the French, but he ordered some that surpassed in flavour anything I had ever tasted. I loved the pine nuts, the melons, the cheeses, the bread, the lasagne, the baked egg-plant and the sunburnt dried tomatoes. The fresh grilled fish was wonderful, all from the sea; I have no idea what it was called, but Carlo knew, that was enough for me.

I was curious about his ancestry, when they had got their title, that sort of thing. It came out in bits and pieces. Carlo didn't seem to like talking about it, but it appeared that the family had been prominent since the Middle Ages, with enormous estates in Tuscany and Sicily, members of the family had been cardinals and there was even one pope, ambassadors galore, in more recent centuries he was related to the royalty of Italy, France and Spain, he spoke the languages of these countries fluently, as well as English. Most of the upper-class English have an elegant life, but this was different. This civilisation was older and more artistic. Every nation that had intruded into Italy had left permanent traces of its occupation, Greek, French, Spanish, even Arabic remnants overlay the original Roman and Italian cultures, reflected in the food, the wine, and the language. One could spend a lifetime studying the history of Italy without plumbing its depth.

Later we went into Positano and he took me up a road past Zeffirelli's house to a lovely hotel perched high on a cliff with an elevator going down to the beach, way below. We ate dinner on the terrace watching the sunset. The old feeling of contentment had been a stranger to me for such a long time; it was a joy to have it back. I wanted to hear music, classical music which would fit in to this magnificent setting to complete the euphoria I was feeling. Of course it would have to be Italian music, Vivaldi, Verdi, dramatic, sensual and passionate. Carlo was a kind of dream.

"I feel like Persephone returning from the underworld. This is a fantasy, you know that, don't you?"

"Fantasy? In that case I should be Orpheus, though I can't play the lyre."

"Every woman dreams of this kind of life."

"No, they don't. Ask me, I've dated many women."

It turned out that Carlo had been hurt just as I had been. His wife had dumped him for another man. I really didn't want to hear about it, especially the thought of another woman in his arms. So I changed the subject. I didn't want to talk about Michael either. Just us. The world he lived in was one that I would probably never experience again. First of all, it was a world of beauty. The country itself was beautiful, but also the culture, the food, the wine and the way Italians had so many customs that were special. The sea was always around us, but I knew that even in Tuscany it would be classic landscape. But here there was the sight and the sound of the sea as well, the orange groves, flowers everywhere, islands in the glittering sea, perfection.

Carlo was from Tuscany although he had a house here. I had yet to see it. His grandmother had just arrived with six servants and his sister was coming with three children in two days time. I felt lost, not speaking Italian and they didn't speak English. I wondered how long it would take me to learn the language, I wished I had not wasted so much time reading pointless books and novels, still, I am what I am and Carlo seems to like me as I am.

For the next two weeks we met every day. We went swimming, walking, drinking and sometimes made love twice a day, after lunch and after dinner. He bought me flowers and little presents—all too sentimental for words. I couldn't believe I was there. I felt out of my depth. I was dealing with rich, sophisticated people. They were no fools. He needed an Italian woman who could hold the reins, he was too spirited to be left running around with his tastes, desires, creativity, energy. I wouldn't know how to do that. I spoke my thoughts to him.

"Nonsense. I need someone like you who is not Italian, who has some freshness and still appreciates the things we both like in Italy. Besides, I'm in love with you."

"That's the first time you've said anything about love."

"Yes, I told you."

"No you didn't. I would have remembered."

The whole affair had been so sudden. Did I really want to settle in Italy with Carlo? He had, in fact, swept me off my feet but I still had to be reasonable and try to be realistic. This time it would really mean giving up the theatre and acting. There was no way I could act in Italian, unless I started an English-speaking theatre of my own, it just wouldn't be possible.

The romance was so overwhelming I wanted some space to think things through. I decided to go back to London. Carlo was returning to Milan anyway, so I would have time to consider his proposal. The idea was so seductive, but was it realistic? Too many unknowns. Peter had left me some books including a volume of Chekhov's plays. I was amused flipping through the book to come across this speech which somehow seemed so appropriate.

> "He wants me to give up the theatre. He could make love to an actress, but marry one—never! All of a sudden my eyes were opened! I realised then there was no holy art of acting, it was all lies and pretending, and I was just a toy, a slave to other people's pleasure, a clown! Just a cheap clown! That's when I realised what the audience was after, what they wanted from me! And after that I never believed the applause, the bouquets of flowers, the glowing reviews. It's true. They applaud me, they buy my photographs, but we are strangers to one another, and they think of me as trash, as a whore! They want to get to know me because I'm a celebrity—it flatters them—but they wouldn't lower themselves to let me marry one of them. And I don't believe their applause! I just don't believe them any more!
>
> "You're scaring me . . ."
>
> "That's when I finally found out what it was all about. I understood what they were like, and that knowledge has cost me dear! After that I rushed off without any direction, didn't care what my life was like, never thought ahead. I played cheap parts, cynical parts, I played the joker, I seduced anyone I could get my hands on . . . but what an actor I was, what an artist! And then I let my art go, I got vulgar and commercial, I lost the divine spark . . . that black hole out there swallowed me up!"

When you have the opportunity laid out before you like a magic carpet, to move into a more sophisticated lifestyle, a more moneyed lifestyle, are you an idiot not to do it or at least give it a try? What should you do? I guess you have to think about the consequences. Can you just enter into a new life and not miss the old one? The life Carlo was offering was certainly luxurious and sophisticated, except it would all be in a different language.

"You'll easily learn Italian," Carlo smiled as he stroked my arm.

"I'm terrible at languages."

"You'll pick it up very quickly."

"But when you're not there to translate I won't even be able to go shopping for groceries."

"You won't have to, my darling."

It didn't feel right somehow. I wish it did. You admire the beautiful lifestyle, the elegance, the polish of their manners and speech, but there was something wrong. You need to be able to see six months ahead, how things would be then, but I couldn't. Carlo had to go back to Tuscany on business, so I would have time to think things over.

"You'll be so popular with my family, they'll love you."

"Why? Especially as I can't speak Italian."

"What does that matter? You can speak French, and nowadays most people speak English. What language you speak is of no importance, who you are, what kind of person you are is all that counts."

It's not that I didn't trust Carlo, I just didn't really know him. His face was open and he looked honest, but there was no doubt that he was different from anyone else I had dated. Admittedly I had gone out with Anglo-Saxons only, had even married one. Some of them had the old Anglo-Saxon prejudices against Latins, Spanish, Italian, Portuguese and so on, but none of that had ever bothered me.

The beach boys who each day put out our sun mattresses were little replicas of him. They smiled, trying out their English on me. However, I knew that they were sort of making fun of me; I felt this about the grown-ups too in the cafes. Perhaps I was imagining things.

Carlo said I was, that everyone would treat me well in Tuscany. I loved the idea of the old palaces, he said he'd show me Venice, Florence and Sienna as well. I couldn't imagine why he liked me so much. Perhaps because he wanted to show me off or something. He had seen the film I was in as it was playing in Naples with subtitles. I had yet to see me dubbed into Italian. I couldn't wait.

Next day I explained to Carlo that I had some unresolved business to attend to in London which I had to do. Besides, I wanted to have time to reflect on our relationship, find out if I felt the same attraction to him once I'd left the island to be transported back to reality.

It's odd, but where you meet a person has such an influence on how you might perceive them. If I had met Carlo in England he might have seemed to me just a foreigner, all very well, but a little bit out of place in spite of his good English; while I might have seemed to him a little exotic in Italy with my white skin and blond hair, whereas in England I was just another Englishwoman, one of millions. It would be a good idea to find out, perhaps Carlo could be persuaded to come to England, to meet my friends, say, or see me work on stage. Anyway, it would be useful for me to see him out of his element, also good for him to see me in mine. Maybe the scales would fall from our eyes, we would see one another as we really are. Or perhaps I was more truly myself in Italy, more honest, more open than I am at home. Maybe Carlo, without the support of his environment and the deference he was accorded, would seem an ordinary man, nothing more.

Carlo had given me one of his favourite plays to read, which had been translated. He had seen it in Rome last year and thought I would like it. It was a comedy of sorts; it gave me time to think through what I was going to do next. I put down the play after reading it through and gazed out the window. It was a glorious morning. So it was that simple. Could I really give it all up, just like that? Well at least I could try. I thought of Grace Kelly. Well, that was slightly different, as she had married a prince after all. However, close sources said she did miss her work terribly, and it was painful for her especially as everyone was begging her to act in another film. I knew that if I were offered a good script it would be difficult to turn it down. But I would have to promise Carlo I would. The initial pleasure had worn off a bit, I suppose, but it was still very tempting to stay. The real test would come if Carlo became too busy with work and left me to get on with Italian lessons and housekeeping all day. They had servants of course, but I knew it would be entirely different from a theatre job.

I decided to go back to London while Carlo was in Milan, to think things over; there was always the possibility that I would find Michael.

Chapter Twelve

THERE WAS A BOMB SCARE at Naples airport, which delayed the flight for over two hours. Watching all the people at the phone booths and on their mobiles tempted me to call Carlo, but I was afraid he would tell me not to fly, which would entail going back to him and not having the chance to think it all over. The Naples airport was packed with tourists and locals; no doubt about it, the Italians are a noisy race. They love children, obviously, and I watched a family force-feed three little girls with lots of hysterical, animated gestures, also a wedding party which must have had every relative saying goodbye to the couple, shouting as they did so. Finally, bomb scare notwithstanding, the plane took off with me on it.

On board I sat next to a woman about my age. After we'd both had two gin and tonics we just started talking. What that woman said to me just seemed to be exactly what I had thought about for the past few years. It was uncanny, I couldn't believe I was hearing her story. I could have finished most of her sentences for her, as I knew the story so well. It was almost a cliché, I smiled with recognition as her voice registered increasing emotion. She'd studied at a drama school about the same time I had. The decisions she made were very similar to mine, mostly domestic ones, which all actors have to confront. She had fallen deeply in love, just after she had found her first professional job, but her boyfriend was leaving to settle in Canada. His job paid well and he wanted her to go with him. Her story was just riveting to me, because she had actually given up her career for love.

After twenty years of marriage, when her husband died of a heart attack, she decided she wanted to "find herself" now that the children were grown up. But rather than finding herself she found that she no longer stood a chance of getting work in the theatre. She went back to London, but couldn't find an agent who would represent her—no experience, no track record. All her contemporaries had résumés as long as your arm! The National, the West End, TV and film. It was no go from the beginning.

"So what on earth did you do?"

"I was spinning wheels, writing letters, auditioning so diligently, until one day I was standing at the kitchen sink, when I suddenly realised I would never be paid to act again."

"Paid?"

"Well, you know you can get fringe work if you are desperate. No pay, of course. There was no possibility of any other work, except of course being a film extra, which is very depressing—all the waiting around for one thing."

"But surely you had some old friends who had stayed in the theatre?"

"Unfortunately no, I hadn't kept in touch, twenty years is a long time. The awful thing is, I know it is the same way for many actors. They go off to do something else, then they find they are forgotten."

She turned to look at me and of course recognised who she had been speaking all these thoughts to.

"But you are Nicole Bennett, aren't you?"

"Yes, I am."

"Well you must know all about what I've been saying."

"Of course, but it is fascinating."

We decided to have a glass of wine with lunch.

"We're getting high in the sky," she laughed. Our conversation continued for the next hour. I realised as she was talking that I would have to get a job very quickly or else I would be in the same boat. I tried to give her some encouragement but knew that what she was depressed about was total reality. It woke me up with a jolt, so I couldn't wait to get back in harness. She said she had been on Capri for a two-week holiday, but I'd never bumped into her at all, which was a pity because we had so much in common.

My flat was dark and cold, but at least it was clean. I had phoned Patricia from Capri, and she had come over to clean up the place before I arrived. She left the mail on the kitchen table for me. I phoned her to tell her I was home as she was about to go to Scotland with the family. Next I phoned Peggy and left a message for her. The apartment was small, it had one bedroom and a sitting room overlooking a small park. I had chosen light furniture, beige carpets and pale beige curtains. I had moved into it during my first job in London before going to New York, then rented it out when I left for Chicago. I wanted still to have a place to hang my hat in London. The kitchen was tiny but at least I had a window with room enough for a table and chairs. Most of my books were in a large bookcase beside the television.

I looked through the pile of mail. There were two letters from Chicago. One was from Tom telling me our divorce had gone through, the other from the lawyers saying Tom would give me a monthly allowance until I married again. Oh, that's useful, I said to myself. Even though I knew it was going to happen it was still a shock. My heart turned over and I caught my breath as I stared at the letters, trying not to weep, remembering immediately all the good times we'd had. It was still a huge turning point, one that I had expected but seeing it all written down on paper suddenly brought it all home. I opened the rest of the mail. There was nothing else very important, mostly bills. I had asked Carlo not to phone or contact me after I left Capri and not to try to persuade me by telephone calls, which might influence my decision, as I wanted to think things out for myself. He could be very persuasive, I felt slightly overwhelmed by his demands. It could be so totally different after a few years, I must think rationally about our relationship. He was charming; it was an almost irresistible charm, he was passionate, interesting and could offer me a new way of life, but not as an actress. I called Peter but he was out. Leaving a message, I then went to bed.

Next morning dear Tony called. He took me for lunch at The Ivy. It was good to see him again after such a long break. We chatted on for at least an hour, he kept waving to people across the room, then over coffee he reached out for my hand.

"Remember when you once told me who inspired you to go into the theatre, Shakespeare, Chekhov and Coward?"

"Yes, and they still do."

"Well, you've done your Shakespeare, and I can't offer you Chekhov at the present time, but I do believe I can get you a Coward play."

"Brilliant," I said. The thought of Coward himself always gave me a terrific lift. He inspires you to get out and live your life, to get on with it, to rise above it. He stays with you, he's with you when you book your passage on a Cunard ship, he's there when you realise you have to stop being so bored with your life and dive into something different, something you can feel passionate about again. He comes along when you go to a brilliant play and the acting is great. He pushes you to get out, go to parties, check out art exhibits, accept invitations, and strike up conversations with strangers.

"It is a play of Coward's that has never been produced."

"That sounds interesting."

"You will have the script in a few days. It is a four-week tour, then into the West End."

"Sounds like I will be working again."

"I hope so. It's about time."

As I walked home, it was a perfect day, a shaft of sunlight went straight through the clouds, almost like the proverbial "ray of sunshine". I felt light-hearted. I am going to stop talking about Michael and worrying about him. I'm going to be just fine. Most of the time I believed that.

Peter came over that night, I told him about the divorce. He too knew it was in the process so we opened a bottle of wine to cheer me up. The wonderful side of Peter is that he is always cheerful and energetic, I love that about him. It is unusual in a writer, I expect, as the work is so difficult. That evening we went to bed together for the first time, I guess because we both needed each other desperately and he really had been expecting us to arrive at that point before then. I was amazed that he was so gentle and sexy. However, he wasn't as passionate as Carlo. It was really quite different, more comforting in a way, as we knew each other so well by then.

"We should have met years ago," he said.

"I know. It's just lucky we did meet at all."

Carlo kept his word and didn't phone. Day by day I slowly came to the decision that although he was definitely serious I knew it would never work. I couldn't speak Italian, his culture was so different from mine and I'd be out of place, besides, I was scared of becoming an Italian housewife. The time came when I had to sit down and write a letter to him. I didn't want to talk to him on the phone because he would interrupt me all the time. I needed to be very tactful, to explain why I wouldn't be returning, I didn't want him flying over to London to prolong the relationship. It was difficult to explain without being hurtful, but it was something that must be done. He was such a nice man. How many of us fall in love, or have a fling, to be more honest, with a foreigner? Hundreds. It's a break while on holiday, then when we go back home, we find the affair is really very impractical. The poetry is what's lost in the translation. I wondered if I would bitterly regret my decision—after all, it was a great invitation to change my life completely—but in the long run I knew I would miss my work too much.

"Peter, you seem to be so much more mature than I am. Why is that, do you think?"

"Well, for one thing, I'm older than you, and secondly, perhaps it's because you're an actress."

"What's that got to do with it?"

"Actors are like children. Sorry I didn't mean to be unkind, don't get me wrong, I'm not being patronising."

"Oh yes you are!"

"No, I'm not. I mean actors must be like children. Always inquisitive, always curious about other people, with huge amounts of energy just like children have. I don't have that. You make up for us both, that's why we get along so well together. I love you for that. I love your energy and enthusiasm. I wonder if you know how much you mean to me."

I smiled at him as I poured another cup of coffee for him. We were sitting in my kitchen, watching the rain pelting down on the window. It was warm and cosy inside. It all seemed so natural, so comforting in a way, as I felt much calmer when he was around.

We used to play a game together, it certainly helped me to get to know him better. "Who would you like to share a meal with?" was the question. He answered by giving a different name every time. It made me wonder if my life was dreadfully narrow. The people I would like to share a meal with were all connected with the theatre—Shakespeare, of course, all the great playwrights, directors, actors and writers. But Peter's choices were far more eclectic. Perhaps because he was interested in so many different fields. How would you converse, for example, with Einstein? Or Freud? Actually I don't think a meal with Freud would be all that much fun.

My background was not too dissimilar to his. My parents were church-going people, but Dad reluctantly, to please mother. She was the one who instigated things. Sometimes we'd go to London just for the weekend, go to a matinee, shop in Oxford Street, then have dinner at a nice restaurant. Quite apart from anything else, she instilled in me the love of theatre. We'd go to all the plays that came to Manchester.

Peter said as he stirred his coffee, "I want you to understand that I'll be very upset if you go back to Capri."

Well, don't worry, I'm not going. Do you want to see the letter I wrote to Carlo?"

"I don't mind, if you want me to read it, but that's between you and him."

I went to find it in the living room, then decided not to show it to him in case my words seemed too juvenile to him or in bad taste. I went back into the kitchen.

"Sorry, I've changed my mind. I'm embarrassed to show you because you might hold it against me."

"OK, if that's what you want."

All that week I felt guilty about Tom and the divorce. I suppose it was my fault, I had not given any thought to what it would be like living in Chicago. I knew it was my actions that had made the marriage fail. Yes, I did feel guilty. "It's over, get on with life," I muttered, cleaning the bathroom floor the next morning. "Get busy, do something."

Michael was gone. Tom was gone. Don't mess up this time. Peter was right, but would he be able to teach me to grow up? Carlo is a fantasy. It was just the sex, in all honesty. Perhaps it was just the sex with Michael? No, he was my whole being. He was like a drug, I was high every time I was with him. He was so stimulating, his ideas, yes, his ideas. I wondered if Peter could keep me equally stimulated. We had decided not to live together, I wanted to keep my independence, and if I moved in with Peter it would be too similar to how I started off with Michael.

Chapter Thirteen

THERE'S NO BUSINESS LIKE SHOW business. Tony called several days later to say that the Coward play had been postponed, that he didn't know when the producers would actually be doing it. So what else is new? It sounded too good to be true anyway. I was feeling pretty worthless at this stage, not even being able to play the housewife or helpmate any more. I was desperate to find something to do.

To get out of the house, I volunteered to do some recorded books for the Library for the Blind. I'd been looking forward to it as I thought at least I would be doing something worthwhile, for at least a few hours each day. They showed me the tiny sound booth, showed me how to work the controls. If I wanted to stop at any time I could take a break.

The book I started reading was a love story. As I started recording it, so many memories came flooding back to me that I was completely overwhelmed. I tried to keep going but the emotion in the writing was just too much to bear. It was all too recent. I stopped the tape to compose myself but I knew I couldn't continue. How embarrassing—I sat there for about fifteen minutes, trying to think of what I'd say to cancel out all this. In the end I just got up, walked out to the desk and told them I was not feeling very well—I wasn't! Then I apologised saying I would phone them in a few days. I never went back. I felt so stupid. It was a great way to start.

That evening there was nothing on television We now have a hundred channels, still there's nothing worth watching. The phone rang. It was Peggy back in town from another tour of the provinces. "Come over for tea tomorrow, Nicole, I want to see you."

Peggy is a chubby, warm, bubbly brunette but has too many mannerisms, such as always playing with her hair, but she has a brilliant technique as an actor. It is inborn; even though she trained in drama school, what talent she had was instinctive. She is quick-witted and mischievous; however, she never seems to attract men, or at least not for long. Her relationships are soon over. I wondered if she makes fun of men in bed, but I never dared broach the subject. It was after staying with her that I realised she is a totally devoted actress. It never occurs to her to do anything else, she doesn't want to do anything else. I was curious as to why she didn't have the urge to paint, or to write a poem, or to learn another language; it never bothered her. Travel didn't interest her, neither did men except for her sexual needs. If I wasn't actually working in a play, I wanted to be working on something outside the theatre, travelling to me was an escape but for Peggy it was a waste of time.

"If you go away, you will miss out on something. It always happens." She turned off the kettle, made the tea and took down a cake-tin full of shortbread. "Have one. They're delicious."

That was another thing, she never worried about her weight. Occasionally she might say she should lose ten pounds but she never did. Whereas I was always on a diet—no ice-cream, no pizzas, no pie, it was always too easy to put on extra weight.

I put down my cup and looked at her. "The incredible thing is that you know someone intimately, you think you know exactly how they feel about you. You believe you know them completely, you believe what they say about loving you is true, the sincerity of their true feelings gives you confidence until one day it has all totally changed. Something is said or done, then you know you've lost them. How does this happen? It's like a small death, but what causes it?"

"Another woman, I guess." Good old Peggy.

"No, it wasn't that," I answered, "it was something else. I can't put my finger on it. I shouldn't have gone away."

"Why couldn't he have gone over to LA.?"

"Because he didn't want to, he was working on another book and he knew I would be at the studio every day at the crack of dawn, then learning lines every night."

"But you would have been together." She took a bit of shortbread dipping it in her tea.

"Don't you ever want to settle down, Peggy?"

"Of course I do, but I've never found the right man." She got up to turn off the radio. "I can't stand that music. Philip Glass is so repetitive. Give me Mozart every time."

"Come on, you're not going to sit around moaning about Michael. We've been over it so many times, it won't help to keep going on about him. You must put it behind you."

I envied her her stamina. She never seemed to let things bother her, except work. Because of her one-track mind, it was difficult to go on explaining how I felt. When we had been at drama school, she was far above the rest of us. She memorised lines quickly, she got the character quickly then worked on it. Most of us were way behind her. She made me feel like an emotional cripple.

Why is it that some women seem to be able to exist without men in their lives? Her work was everything. We started discussing the subject for a one-woman show. Peggy was enthusiastic. "There are so many great women you could do a show about. Why not look up some of the truly brilliant ones? All you have to do is find some of their letters, read their biographies and go from there. Why not Virginia Wolf?"

"It's been done," I answered.

"Well yes, so it has."

We went through a list from Sarah Siddons to Gertie Lawrence. An ambulance went by, its siren piercing the atmosphere. It was as if it was a sign of the dire emergency I felt to get connected with a project that would fill the huge void in my life. It seemed that urgent. Now I could easily understand why unemployed actors take to drink. You have to be working. The euphoria of performing Shakespeare, for example, when you begin to fly with the text after memorising it, is such a high, what can replace it?

Next evening there was still nothing on television. I threw the TV guide across the room switching off the set in disgust. I went to the bookcase and scanned the shelves. Finding the biography of Dame Ellen Terry, the famous London actress who worked with Sir Henry Irving, I read about half of it, then a few more pages in bed. Most theatre people know about her even if she is forgotten or unknown by others.

Waking up early I suddenly decided to write a one-woman show about her and spent the whole morning in my dressing gown and slippers, writing down a rough draft. The hours went quickly, it was almost as if someone was guiding my hand. The words just flowed, I looked at the clock; it was already noon. I quickly showered, dressed, grabbed a sandwich and went on with it. It was astonishing to find how much her family meant to her. During her long tours in America she missed her children desperately but persevered and kept on. So at least I had found a project. Each day I wrote another scene. Can we believe that a muse can be a departed person? Can they advise you? I felt as if Ellen was visiting me. She was smiling and encouraging me. I spoke to her once but then felt foolish. Why would she bother with me?

Peggy called several times suggesting lunch, but I said I was working on the play and couldn't go.

Ellen's life was extraordinary, her disappointments, her grief, her blindness in old age—it was a kind of balm to know that she had suffered far more than I ever had. She was almost a legend in British theatre, not only for her acting but her beauty, her kindness towards other people.

Peter called and I told him about my brainstorm.

"It would be good to read what you've done. Maybe I could help."

"Yes, please. It could be terrible, terrible!"

"Everybody loved Ellen Terry."

"Even though she was an actress."

Peter laughed and asked me out that night.

I looked in my wardrobe.

"What on earth will I wear?"

"The black," said Ellen.

I didn't take the outline with me because I wanted to finish it first.

We met in Charlotte Street in Soho at our favourite wine bar. He looked very loveable in his blue shirt, and my heart jumped a little, thinking about last night. He took me by the hand after kissing me and smiled lovingly.

"Let's have a real Italian meal tonight, some pasta perhaps to remind us of Capri," he said as we left the pub and went into a nearby Italian restaurant.

"Sounds great to me. How's the book going?" I turned to him affectionately.

"I'm on the re-writes now, I'm still not happy with it. Maybe I'd better drop it for a few days." He picked up the menu.

"Did you get things sorted out with the publisher today?"

"Well, at least they extended the deadline, but I'm not happy with the new editor they have given me, that's one of the reasons I had to come back from Capri. I didn't want to mention it before because it was upsetting me too much and you had enough to worry about, what with the divorce going through and the play being postponed."

The waiter came over and we chose our meal. First some antipasto, as I love the salami and olives in it, then we both ordered some pasta with a pesto sauce, grilled fish to follow accompanied by a chilled Soave Bolla. The owner came over to say hello to Peter who was a regular there, and he brought us two aperitifs. After he left, we started to talk about my play and Ellen Terry. During dinner Peter made the suggestion that we drive down on Sunday to see her cottage in the country.

"There is a theatre in her back garden, you'll like that."

"A theatre? Really?"

"An old barn was converted and made into a theatre. Every year there are one or two plays put on there."

"Imagine having a theatre in your own back garden!"

That Sunday was one of those perfect days—not a cloud in the sky, the countryside as green as could be, making it a joy to be in England. Peter has a great sense of direction, so we found the cottage quite easily, parking just down a country lane south of the house.

Fortunately there were no other people there, except the guardian with her large Labrador. We walked slowly through the house looking at Ellen's books and possessions. It almost seemed to be prying in a way; this was her own private place after all. Upstairs were her stage costumes on models in display cases, they all looked a little dilapidated, of course because they were so old. I tried to visualise Ellen in these rooms wondering what her daily schedule would have been. It was a small cottage, so it must have been very cramped and smoky from the fire in the downstairs sitting room. Everyone who's been there loves the theatre in the garden, and Peter suggested we should return to see a play when they produced the next one. I stood by the garden gate, still trying to go back in time and visualise her there. After an hour, we slowly walked to the car. The country lanes were quite deserted as we started driving back to London.

"The portrait of her which her first husband, G F Watts, had painted is still to be seen in the National Portrait Gallery," I told Peter.

"Yes, I know the one. With flowers in her hair."

"She was so beautiful, especially her eyes."

"Oh look, there's a winery!" I pointed out to Peter. "Let's stop to see what there is."

Peter pulled the car into the parking lot, we got out to inspect. It was a market garden as well as a vineyard. The wine was made on the premises.

"British white wine?" I asked the salesgirl.

"That's right. Do taste some."

It was a very dry wine, more fruity than bitter. The sun was setting, we sat under a tree, drinking the wine in the beautiful garden. We bought two bottles, a pot of gooseberry jam and some tomatoes. We drove back to London after having a pub meal in the next village. It was nice enough to sit outside as the evening was warm. I said to Peter, "I feel inspired after seeing her home and possessions. Thank you, darling Peter, for taking me."

During the next few weeks he encouraged me to keep writing after he had read the first draft of the play, so I knew he must have thought I had something there. It was vastly different from learning lines of the pretentious BBC play which I had turned down two weeks ago. I couldn't stop talking about her. I told Peter that "Ellen used to say it was all to do with the three 'I's—Intelligence Imagination and Industry, but above all, Imagination." She worked and wrote about her friendship with Irving. Some say that they were never lovers, but it's hard to imagine that they weren't when they were together day and night, running a very successful company at the Lyceum.

Ellen and Henry were brought together by their love of the theatre, and it was a combination of genius and chemistry. She all brains and sympathy, scattering them everywhere and on everybody, he, all self, and concentrating that self on his stage as on a pedestal. GBS fell in love with her, their letters are still in print. He wanted her to act in one of his plays, but she never did. The parts she played were the big Shakespearean roles, the energy and discipline were phenomenal. Embittered by her success, her children rebelled and almost ruined her financially.

At least that won't happen to me.

Acting the life of Ellen almost became an obsession. I wanted to show people what she was like. So many men adored her, which means she must have conquered them.

Her life force, her life energy was the theatre. Even though her performances were written on water, the magic for her was in creating the role every day. Each evening there would be magic in the theatre when she was on stage. The eight performances a week didn't seem to bother her, her lovers were all connected with the theatre, so they encouraged and inspired her. It was difficult to discover in the research whether she did indeed have an affair with Henry Irving, certainly Irving's wife was hostile to her. However Irving's wife, like many wives married to actors, felt neglected and lonely when he was at the theatre night after night. She was left every evening to amuse herself, never having an escort to take her out or to dinner with friends. It was a terrible life for her

"Still is," I muttered as I put the book down, going to examine the contents of my fridge. I thought about Trevor, wondering how he could survive eight performances a week now that he was married, leaving his wife at home every night at five o'clock.

Part of being an actress is that one can also want the life of a character one might play on stage, sometimes not. Chekhov plays were wonderful, but the poor women were usually miserable, or rather the world in which they lived was miserable. Same thing with Ibsen. I wanted to be Ellen Terry. Not only was she beautiful but she was the leading lady in Irving's theatre company and seemed universally loved.

Peter said to me, "The best thing is to get another agent who might be able to get a theatre so you could do the play. The only thing is, you must be prepared to wait at least a year, most of the theatres are booked up well in advance, and you need a producer of course."

"I'd rather try it out in a showcase somewhere."

"You still need a producer," Peter said. It turned out that Peter knew more people than I had imagined. He was a genius because he arranged everything. He knew enough people to be able to raise enough money, and he found me a producer.

"I can't believe you managed to do all this for me," I said.

"It's just a matter of knowing the right people, I guess."

"But you got it done so quickly," I laughed.

"Again, it's all who you know."

I thought back to the old network I'd heard about when living with Michael, the Oxbridge set. The men who had come down from Oxford and Cambridge really knew the ropes. It's hard to imagine that the old boy network still exists as strongly as it always did. It took me years to get anywhere before I met Michael, and then I saw at first hand how he worked within the cat's cradle of pulling strings, it's almost impossible for outsiders who are not part of the Oxbridge set to break in.

A month later the play opened at the Vaudeville Theatre.

"It is a terrific show," Peter kept telling me.

"Only because you kept me at it."

"The audience is so different every night, I think all of them enjoy it in their different ways."

Peter looked at me and smiled.

"You look like Ellen tonight, you know. I think it's that dress, it really suits you."

Every night, Peter would come by the theatre to take me home. We used to walk. Down the Strand, up Drury Lane and into Bloomsbury.

I was still reluctant to move in with him, it was too similar to the life I had with Michael, but I knew both of us needed each other for companionship. I felt it was the only way to forget Michael and Carlo. The closeness was based on warmth and sympathy, I guess. The most important thing was to forget Michael.

Chapter Fourteen

PETER WAS TAKING TIME OFF to visit his ailing mother who lived in Wales; as she was over eighty he felt he should see more of her. He was taking his work with him hoping he would have time to do some writing, but he knew he would have his hands full with a list of things that would need repair and his attention as soon as he arrived. I didn't really mind because I was busy with the show each night, even though I knew I would miss him especially during the day, however I needn't have worried. The next morning the phone rang, when I was half asleep, at seven o'clock in the morning. I wondered who would call at that hour.

"Hello Nicole, it's Patricia."

"Hi," I said sleepily. It was quite a surprise because I hadn't seen her for some time, and she didn't often get a chance to call me.

"I'm sorry to call you so early as I know you had a show last night but I wanted to be able to talk to you when I was free."

She was obviously very upset, I couldn't imagine what had happened. She explained it very quickly.

"Bruce called from Australia last night, Nicole, he is on his way over to London. He was leaving last night. I am so upset, he wants to see me and convince me to go back to Australia with him."

I was hardly awake, but I let her keep talking because I didn't know what to say to her. Finally, after she had explained that she was furious he hadn't asked her or told her he was planning to fly over to see her, I said I'd call her back in an hour. She wanted to know what to do, because she was so confused and angry at him, she needed advice.

After the call I was wide awake, so got up and made coffee, then tried to think of a way to help her. It seemed ironic that this man was flying half way across the world to claim her, to try to persuade her to go back home, when she obviously wasn't in love with him, whereas I, who would have flown half way around the world to claim Michael, had to talk some sense into both of them.

I called her back and she pleaded with me to meet Bruce at the airport, as she first and foremost didn't want to, and moreover was working in a job where she was expected to be present.

"I can't take off and go to Heathrow just like that, because he would insist I go back to his hotel and talk for hours and hours about everything."

Fortunately I didn't have a matinee that day, and I was flattered that she regarded me as a kind of surrogate Mum to help her through what could be a messy emotional confrontation, one that she didn't want or expect.

We talked for ages, trying to face the reality of this passionate man arriving at Heathrow after a two-day flight—who would be jet-lagged, confused and probably angry that she hadn't gone to the airport to meet him.

"Patricia, don't worry. I will go and meet him. You have to tell me what he looks like first of all." We laughed about his description, because no doubt over half the male passengers would look like him.

"He'll be wearing white socks, of course," she said. "What is it about Australian men and white socks?" She laughed, "Even in a pin stripe suit they still wear white socks."

"Who buys them, do you think?" I said.

"They do, of course." There must be some kind of etiquette book in Australia that said white is best. We decided I should hold up a sign with his name on it at the arrivals entrance.

It worked, I held up a big sign and suddenly there he was. Six feet tall, curly black hair, clear skin, rather ruddy complexion, a bit on the heavy side, but a no-nonsense air about him that rather intimidated me. He must have shaved in the plane because there was no beard or five-o'clock shadow. He had on a white shirt, blue jacket and jeans—I didn't dare look at his socks.

"Hello. Welcome to Britain," I said. "Are you Bruce Taylor?" Obviously he was, as he had come up to me.

"Yes I am. Who are you, may I ask?"

"I'm Nicole. Welcome again. I'm sorry Patricia couldn't come to meet you, but she just couldn't get away."

"Well it's nice of you to come, you must be a close friend of hers."

"Very much so, in fact, Patricia stayed with me before she started working here."

The next hour was difficult. He had nothing to collect at baggage claim as he had all his clothes in a large dress bag which he carried through the airport. I threw away my sign.

"Where are you staying?" I ventured to ask, hoping he wouldn't say, "With Patricia of course." But he had booked into the Strand Palace, and as we drove there I tried to keep the conversation going. Luckily, there wasn't much traffic, so the taxi didn't take too long. As we drove up to the hotel, I felt sorry for him, arriving alone after such a long flight and with such great expectations of seeing Patricia, I felt I had to be a kind of cheer-leader, or to let him down lightly because he looked quite forlorn and exhausted.

"I tell you what," I heard myself saying, "why don't you check in and sleep for a bit, than call me at this number and I'll see when we can get Patricia down here."

"That sounds good to me," he replied, I let him off at the hotel and went home. Patricia was on the phone as soon as I got in. "What did he say?" She was almost in panic.

"He's calmed down and he's sleeping." I reassured her that he wasn't too upset.

Several hours later he called me. It was then about three in the afternoon and I'd asked Patricia to come by to my flat so I could talk to her. Then he called again saying he was feeling fine and where were we?

When Patricia came in, she was totally hysterical.

"I really don't want to see him at all. He was so unfair to just come over here without even warning me, I dislike him for that already."

I calmed her down, saying she must placate him, charm him, just from a basic human instinct that she would be rewarded for one day, and for the first few days to try to imagine what emotion he had gone through in flying half way around the world for her. She couldn't just say, "Forget it." She had at least to be civilised to him.

"You never told me if you have slept with him or not."

"Of course I have," she said, looking at me as if I was something out of the Ark.

"Well then, at least you can sleep with him tonight, and reason it out later. Don't get him in a hostile mood, whatever you do."

"That is so old-fashioned, Nicole." she said, looking at me with just a little contempt.

"But you can't be too cruel," I said, reacting to the look she gave me. "It will calm him down, then after a few days he will be easier to talk to, to reason with." I knew the passion he was feeling, only too well, and I was thinking, if I'd made the same flight to find Michael, how could I have endured it if he had turned away from me after such an ordeal.

"All right," she said, "but please try to help me get out of this."

I phoned the hotel and told Bruce that Patricia was on her way to the hotel.

That night I hoped she had taken my advice. I thought about them. I thought about how the evening would go, that she would at least appreciate the motivation that had forced him to take some kind of action to get what his passion demanded. Later that night after the show I rolled over in bed, thinking of my own passion and wondering where he was and what he was doing.

The next morning I waited for the phone call. Finally it came. Patricia was on her way up here with Bruce.

"Is it all right, Nicole, if we come over to see you? We'd like to talk, and thank you for all your help yesterday."

I put on the kettle, then watched them walking up the street. Patricia had said it was her day off, but she really did want to keep her job even though he had arrived and she had to tell him the truth somehow, without upsetting the equilibrium of her new life.

They sat and had tea and the hot coffee cake I had warmed up. It was awkward for me as a third party, I felt like an outsider, not knowing but surmising how much they had discussed overnight. The tension was relieved by my TV aerial falling down just outside the window, which Bruce immediately offered to fix for me.

"Did you find it too terribly difficult?" I asked her as we watched him through the window.

"We haven't talked much about anything, I'm afraid," she said, smiling, and it was obvious that she had at least been receptive to his sexual needs.

"Nicole, you have to help me. You have to tell him. I don't know how to handle this kind of obsession."

"But is it obsession? Perhaps he just loves you and wants you to be with him for the rest of your life."

I knew that's what I'd wanted with Michael. Oh why didn't he want me for the rest of my life? I dreamt about him every night, sometimes they were good dreams, he'd come to me smiling, but most times it was some kind of rejection.

While Patricia was working, Bruce and I saw London together, we'd walk to see the changing of the Guards, we'd sit in Green Park, we'd window-shop and he would buy me lunch somewhere in Covent Garden or down by the river. I showed him the sights during the day, he came to see my play, and when Patricia was working, each night after the show we went to whatever place he wanted, mostly discos and the better bars in the West End. I wanted him to see the city because he had come so far; the atmosphere of the true British pub escaped him, so we went to Earls Court. I introduced him to a social scene which I organised, a jolly group who could always be found at the Green Room Club or Gerry's Bar. He was angry with Patricia, but I worked on him, and offered him the vision of him being married to someone who could be so much more interesting if he would let her fly a little. Wait a bit, what was I saying? This was rubbish, as if someone had said the same things to me about Michael: "Let him fly a little." But then, Bruce was an engineer, he didn't really understand what creative people were on about. Could we say to a strapping young engineer, "We wanted to find our own voice"? But we had to say something. Finally, he did see that he would feel guilty if he didn't let Patricia spread her wings.

"Tell him, Nicole. It's over! He doesn't care about my life, my painting—I want to see and go everywhere, not to become an Australian housewife and raise six kids."

I was amazed that she was so determined, but then, she was stressed out thinking how she could get rid of him and send him back to Australia.

"You don't love him at all, then?" I asked.

"No, I don't. I thought I did at one time, but I then knew what he had to offer in the long run was not what I wanted at all."

"Even though you know your parents approve?"

"No. No, they will never admit that I could perhaps do something with my life, besides looking after a husband and kids and being a dutiful daughter."

I knew then that I would have to talk to Bruce, about her painting. He wouldn't take it from her, and it was cruel, because I had the same affliction as he had. She stimulated him as Michael had stimulated me, she was his whole world, as Michael was mine, but I had to find the words to tell him.

Patricia went back to work and told Bruce not to phone her at the house, so I was left to pick up the pieces.

They spent the weekend together, and on the Sunday evening they came over for dinner at my place. It was obvious that he was very upset and she had been crying. I pretended not to notice, served up a barbecue chicken, and after a few glasses of wine they relaxed. Bruce had got only two weeks off from his job so he was getting rather impatient with Patricia. We had a three-way discussion on how they could resolve their differences. It seemed that Bruce had backed off slightly, as his love and attention were not being reciprocated, and I think he thought that Trish, as he called her, had changed considerably since he had last seen her. He no longer found the fun-loving simple girl he had fallen in love with, but a far more mature, almost business-like woman who had grown up quickly. In fact, she was more like the women he had been dating back home who were far more aggressive than he thought she was.

The conversation went on to wider issues. He filled us in on what was happening in Australia politically on the monarchy issue, whether Australia should continue having the Queen of England as the Australian head of state or become a republic, and he made it clear where he stood, on the republican side. Patricia and I went into the kitchen to do the dishes while he watched the news on television. She told me that he was going back on the date planned because he knew that he had to let her make her own decisions about what she wanted in life.

"I think he is disenchanted with me, because I don't want to marry him. It's a big blow to his self-esteem and it will be difficult to boost his ego without him getting the wrong idea."

Tell me about it! It's murder, I thought. We put the dishes away, and I asked her how the job was going.

"I'm really enjoying it, and it looks like they will take me to the States with them. They plan to leave as early as next month. They will help me find a good art school in New York."

Bruce came over to say goodbye the day before he left, before he saw Patricia probably for the last time. He was not looking well and I found it difficult to say anything to him as I knew what he must be feeling, especially with the long flight ahead of him. We talked about Tom, then about Michael for a while, but he had no idea that I had something of the same problem that he had, because Patricia fortunately hadn't told him. I wondered what he would have told me to do if he'd known. I felt rather hypocritical because I couldn't let go of my obsession either. How could I advise him? I couldn't, any more than anyone could advise me. Nothing I could say sounded natural. What an awful thing for him to go so far away from Patricia! At least I knew that Michael was on this side of the world, at least I thought he was. She called me later in the day to say that Bruce's flight had left on time, at least she'd gone to the airport to see him off, but I could detect in her voice that she was relieved because the decision had been made.

"I'll keep writing to him for a while anyway because it was decent of him to come so far, even though I hadn't asked him to." She said she'd let me know when she was going to the States.

I couldn't help thinking about Bruce sitting cramped up in the plane, knowing the pain he must be feeling. Love is cruel, it is full of pain and disappointment. From what Patricia had told me, he was resigned, even though he had been extremely hurt at first. What he had hoped to achieve in his trek across the world had turned to failure. His obsession probably would never be forgotten. The obvious thing would be for him to meet someone else as quickly as possible, someone who would perhaps have qualities like Peter had—of a different sort. Kind and loving. Peggy used to say, "There is the one who is loved and the one who loves." The balance will always be uneven. On one of our walks in Green Park he told me he couldn't listen to certain kinds of music any more, mostly favourite vocalists they both liked because they used to listen to them together in bed. Michael always played Beethoven sonatas when we were in bed, and now I couldn't bear to listen to them either. I flew to the radio to turn them off after the first few chords, it was too painful. A pity, because I used to love the sonatas. I decided I would write regularly to him if Patricia would agree. Kindred spirits holding a dream of what might have been if our dreams had come true. It reminded me of Keats's poem "Ode to a Grecian Urn".

> "Never, never canst thou kiss, though winning near the goal—yet, do not grieve; she cannot fade, though thou hast not thy bliss.
> For ever wilt thou love, and she be fair!"

When Peter returned I filled him in with the details of the whole story which I hadn't bothered to tell him on the phone, as he was calling on his mother's line. He said he was pleased he had been away and that he wouldn't have wanted to be around the two of them as he may have been called in to mediate and talk to Bruce, even though he had a lot of sympathy for him.

His mother was much improved, and Peter had managed to hire part-time help for her so that she wouldn't be on her own so much. "She bought a duck," he said, "and called it Daffy. It's a funny little thing, but quite aggressive; you must come down and visit her sometime." We kept up our living arrangements as before and he would stay over two or three times a week because I was usually too tired after doing the show during the week and needed lots of sleep.

Peggy came back from her tour and we had tea at Fortnum's and Mason's where we splurged on the cream cakes and scones. Peggy was trying to find a gift for her new boyfriend. Finally, she had found a nice man, who wasn't an actor.

"Thank God for that!" I laughed.

"I don't want to get him a tie or sweater, it's too personal, so let's go to Fortnum's for some pâté or chocolates."

We walked along Piccadilly and stopped in Hatchards on the way.

"This is my favourite bookshop by far," Peggy said as she pushed open the door.

There was Michael's new bestseller staring at me right on the table ahead of us.

"Oh my God, Nicole, I'm sorry. Come on, let's move on."

"Just got to look at his photo first." I flipped to the back flap. Yes, a new photo and lots more grey at the temples.

"Great, he looks old." Peggy picked up a copy.

"Yes, he looks much older. He's aged terribly."

I looked at her sharply.

"Should I buy it?"

"No way, put it down."

I hadn't seen any reviews about it, but I guessed they'd all come out last month when I was totally absorbed in Capri. I knew I would buy it of course, but not then. Did it matter that he had been such a bastard to me but could be such a good writer? Like actors who dump actresses, I thought, the women still go to see them act out of some kind of morbid curiosity.

We did buy several other books and then we were in hysterics over a sex manual we picked up.

"How could you possibly get your body into that position and enjoy doing so?"

"Put it down, people are looking at us."

We went outside and once again I checked the traffic for a red Volvo as we walked to Fortnum's."

"You must be absolutely nuts to buy him something very expensive. You've only just met him, remember."

The choice was a big box of chocolates, which she had gift-wrapped, and wrote out a card. I felt tempted to buy a box for Peter but he was on a diet and I'd end up eating all of them.

We went next door after tea and sat in the bar of the Cavendish Hotel.

"This used to be a brothel, you know," Peggy said.

"You know a lot about nothing," as I attacked the nuts.

I looked over the bar, and on the other side of the room was someone I knew. For minute I couldn't place her, then I realised it was Julia, the woman I'd met in Bellagio. She was sitting with a man.

"Excuse me, Peggy, I've just seen someone I know, I'll be right back."

I walked over to Julia and tapped her on the shoulder lightly.

"Hello Julia, what a nice surprise. Remember me, we met in Italy."

Julia smiled and said she did remember. She introduced me to David who was her husband, who got up and shook hands.

"Please don't get up. I just wanted to say hello. Are you in London for long?"

"Only two days. We're on our way back to Florida."

I suddenly noticed that she had Michael's book on the table beside her purse.

"Oh, are you reading that book?" I asked stupidly. (What an idiot, of course she is!)

"Yes, I am. As a matter of fact that's why we stopped over in London, to meet him. We are inviting him out to Florida to give two lectures for us, one in Palm Beach and one in Miami."

"Oh really?" I said like I was some kind of animated dummy. "And when will that be?"

"We're just discussing dates with him at present, probably in about a month."

"A month?" That would be when my play was finishing.

"Where is he now?" I asked, beginning to shake. I held my breath in case she wasn't going to tell me. Little did she know how I'd been searching for him and how much I needed to see him. I tried to act nonchalantly, as if it really didn't matter one way or the other. Why was my stomach turning over? I waited for her answer.

"Out of London till tomorrow. Why, do you know him?"

I smiled at her and thought, if only she knew. Then, trying not to show any feeling at all, I answered casually, "Yes, and I'd like to see him again." Shit, why not, I thought, would I like to see him again—would I like to see him again—

"Well, we will see him tomorrow and tell him. What's your number?"

I wrote it down and handed it to her. I got their number also.

"I read about your wonderful success in the play about Ellen Terry. We really want to come and see it, but our time has been so short in London this time, every evening we have some kind of function, it seems, but congratulations."

"Thank you, I'd love you to come." But I knew they wouldn't, somehow, as I didn't they'd have much interest in Ellen Terry.

"It's great that you have got back to work. Remember, you were thinking of giving it all up."

We chatted a little, then I said goodbye. "I'm here with a friend so I'd better get back to her."

"What was all that about?" Peggy was looking a bit exhausted really.

"You'll never guess."

"No, I won't, so you'd better tell me."

I repeated the whole conversation for her. We saw Julia and David get up to go; they walked over to us, and she touched me on the shoulder saying, "Remember my invitation, you are always welcome in Florida." She smiled at Peggy and they left.

I paid the bill. "I must go. I have a show to do tonight." We picked up our things and hailed a cab.

That evening the show went very well, all things considered. I was jumping out of my skin. Thoughts flew around my head, nerves jagged. Ever since the show had opened I'd wondered if Michael had come to see it. Just out of curiosity. He wouldn't come backstage afterwards, I knew that, but had he been? After all, he must have read the reviews. Bugger him, I thought. He was a real shit.

I phoned Julia at her hotel the next day, she was out, so I left a message. I'd hoped she'd call so I'd know if Michael had accepted her offer and if she'd tried to find out if he would be going alone. Most important! She called at four o'clock. Yes, she had seen him. She explained that he was now living in Brighton and had come up for the meeting.

Ah ha! Brighton! So that's it. Bloody cold place. Serves him right. No wonder he'll go to Florida for two lectures, I thought. However, my thoughts were not of him.

"Are you paying him a lot of money?" I laughed.

"Well, it's a fund-raiser and he will attract a big crowd."

Casually, I said, "Is his wife going?"

"I really don't know. She's invited of course, but it's a long journey for three days."

"Three days?"

"One lecture for us on Saturday and the other in Miami on Monday."

"Oh I see."

"Well, Nicole, I'm sorry I didn't see your show, but maybe next time. Please keep in touch. You have my number in Florida."

"Yes, maybe I will. Maybe I should come out and hear Michael speak."

"Yes, you can do that. Of course."

Chapter Fifteen

THE PHONE RANG. I WAS at the kitchen sink trying to clean the casserole dish, thinking about the new chicken recipe I had just tried. It needed more garlic.

"Hello." I picked up the phone with wet hands.

"Hello, Nicole."

It was Michael. I couldn't speak. I was totally caught offguard.

"Hello, are you there?" he said.

"Yes, I'm here." I was too shaken to say anything else. My stomach turned over, I held my breath—just keep calm, I said to myself. I stared at the tablemat in front of me. It had a bluebird on it.

"I hear you've been looking for me," he said.

"Well I wondered where you were." My voice was shaking.

"Yes, Julia told me."

I still couldn't speak, my throat was dry.

"Nicole?"

"Yes, I'm here."

"Look, I think we should meet and talk things over. Julia said that you wanted me to phone."

I thought to myself I wanted him to phone, I wanted him to be here, I wanted him.

"I see. That's all right with me."

"Shall we make it tomorrow, Sunday, Julia said you're in a play?"

"Yes, that's fine." My face was burning, my hands were shaking, my heart was beating violently.

"I just need to explain a few things to you. Where do you want to meet?"

"Well, I'm back in my apartment obviously, so why not here?"

"All right."

"About six o'clock?"

"OK I'll be there."

I put the phone down remembering when I had last spoken with him before I left for LA. How things had changed. Now I felt like a complete basket case with a tremendous sadness mixed with anger and all kinds of hostility towards him. I poured myself a large gin to stop the shaking and calm my nerves.

So Michael was going to give me an explanation of why he had abandoned me for someone else. Crazy thought raced through my head, I had invited him to my flat, would he think that my only interest in his explanation was to give me an opportunity to seduce him, that I really only wanted to get him into bed with me? I didn't really know how I was going to handle him.

He was only five minutes late, thank goodness, as I was already pacing the floor. I let him in, he followed me into the living room. He noticed my new paintings immediately.

"Are they yours?" he asked. "They look like scenes of Tuscany and the Lake District."

"Yes, I was in Bellagio for a while. Why don't you sit down, would you like a drink?"

"They're very good."

He looked much older, almost haggard, as if he'd been drinking too much. I was pleased. At least he wasn't thriving on his new relationship.

"These scenes almost look like Capri," he remarked.

"They are—I was there recently."

"Were you? When?"

I could have kicked myself, I didn't want to let on that I had been looking for him, he would be quick enough to realise why I might have been there. I went into the kitchen to get his drink so didn't answer him. I hoped he wouldn't follow me, and I made a lot of noise getting the drinks, banging the ice tray and cupboard doors looking for glasses. When I went back into the room my heart missed a beat to see him standing there. Did I really still love him, or was it just the shock of seeing him again? Then why was I so nervous? I felt as if he could devastate me with a word or even a glance, I was so vulnerable. It was nice of him to compliment me on my paintings. Little did he know how much pain I was in when I painted them. It seemed ironic that he was now looking at what I had done when I had been looking for him.

"I always thought you could be a successful artist if you ever gave up acting."

I wondered when he would get on to his explanation. I was still very apprehensive. Was he going to talk about paintings all evening? What about the explanation? He did give me one, not immediately and not at all with any thought of an intention on my part to seduce, I didn't know whether to be relieved or disappointed.

We talked at first about his writing, how hard it all was, writer's block and all that; he was as self-absorbed as any actor. He didn't have more than a couple of questions about my acting, and those only in relation to my interpretation of the character I had played in the movie version of his work. Finally, he opened up the subject of his leaving me, and why he did.

"Nicole, I know how hard it is for you to understand, you thought our relationship was perfect, and it was in the very beginning, but you can't keep that interest on the same high level unless there's some development, something new, a fresh idea. Like a book."

"I was happy, happier than I ever had been in my whole life, and I thought you were too."

"Yes, I was, in the very beginning, as I just said, but after a while, as I also just said, there was nothing new."

"You got bored with me, is that it?"

"No, I didn't, you're not a boring person, you get involved in interesting things, with interesting people, it's hard to keep up with you, a new idea almost every day, a new activity that excites you till it's overtaken by a new interest into which you throw yourself and carry me along with you."

"I'm confused, Michael, you said you need some development, fresh ideas, and now you're talking about my new interests, new ideas, being involved in interesting things and people, that I got you involved with too. I'm missing some point you're trying to make, you'll have to be more specific. I'm a literal sort of person, maybe I'm not clever enough to read between the lines of what you're talking about."

"No, you're clever, in many ways more intelligent than I am, but there are things you never talk about, don't think should be talked about, just taken for granted and never discuss, as if talking about them showed a lack of taste or good manners."

"Well, whatever these things may be, I'm willing to talk about them now, and I want you to talk about them too, or at least tell me what you're referring to."

"I'm referring to something you might like to take for granted, but can't always be taken for granted—I mean the physical aspect."

"I'm not pretty enough for you, too old or too fat or thin, or something's wrong with me."

"Jesus, Nicole, are you being deliberately dense?"

"Just making sure of what you didn't mean, you meant the sexual side of a relationship, of our relationship in particular. What was wrong with it?"

"In the beginning, nothing, as I said."

"But you got bored with me in bed, you wanted another woman to adore you, to make you feel whatever you want to feel, you wanted more than I had given you. Well, did you get it? Is she better in bed than I am? Tell me, I'd really like to know."

"I didn't come here to discuss Maria with you."

"Well, she's part of the explanation, why you prefer her to me must have to do at least in part with how she is in bed, with me being not as good as her."

"Believe me, Maria had nothing to do with my leaving you, I had decided to leave you long before I ever went to bed with her."

That was a bit of a shock; I'd always thought she had everything to do with it. He had decided to leave me even while we were still together, sleeping together. Did the idea of leaving me occur to him in the course of one of our episodes of passionate sexual intercourse, or just after or when?

"All right then, leave her out of it, what was wrong with me? Were there things I didn't do, or didn't do right, did I not react in a certain way that you wanted me to? It's too late to make any difference now, except I need to understand, not that so that you'll want any future with me, but to stop tormenting myself with questions I can't find an answer to. I'd rather know the answer even if it's depressing or humiliating—anything is better that the obsessive ruminating that I can't stop my mind doing."

"There's nothing humiliating about it, depressing maybe, and it's probably my fault. I said or implied that you never would talk about the sexual side of our relationship, but this is where I should have forced you to, then the depressing part of all this discussion might have been avoided—what might have been, why didn't you or I do this or that, all that sort of useless, repetitive going around in a circle. It's what I said, our sex together got to be boring—I admit that's how I felt, because it was always the same, so predictable, the time of day, the little signals that you were in the mood for sex, never speaking about it. We never said anything even slightly indecent when we were in bed together, a bishop wouldn't have been shocked at our pillow talk, nothing explicit, nothing even implied.

"I'm beginning to understand, please go on."

"For example, when I was twenty, I had a girlfriend, she was more than that; we lived together, slept together, had sex any time of the day or night, but we talked about it, not seriously but to have fun, we'd speculate about which girls we knew were still virgins, those who probably weren't, even girls we didn't know, just saw on the street or on a beach. She'd kid me about looking at other girls, saying I was sizing them up as possible bedmates, did I think so-and-so would be good at it, would I like to seduce her, that kind of thing, and I'd accuse her of doing the same thing with men. It was just in fun, we laughed a lot talking this way."

"But you do look at other women, younger women especially, you did even when we were sleeping together."

"All men do, it's automatic, it doesn't mean anything, it doesn't mean I want to sleep with them. Girls do the same thing, I imagine."

"Perhaps, but not when they're in love with someone, sleeping with him."

"I'll have to take your word for it, it doesn't really matter to me."

"Was she your first wife, this sexy girl?"

"No, she dumped me for someone who had more to offer her at the time."

"In bed, or generally?"

"I don't know about bed, he had a hell of a lot of money; that was his main attraction, he wasn't handsome."

All this talk about sex, bedmates and sleeping around seemed to interest him, he was much more animated. He got up and said, "Would you mind if I had another drink?"

"No, go ahead, there's all kinds of wine in the kitchen, some white wine in the fridge, gin, take what you like, fix me a gin and tonic, equal parts, with ice."

I sat, looking at my paintings of Capri, thinking about Carlo, wondering if Michael would be surprised to hear about my passionate couplings with the Italian. I smiled to myself and said, "Continue what you were saying—your nice sexy bedmate twenty years ago, was she pretty too?"

"Very, but that wasn't the point, it was her personality."

"I thought girls were complimented on that only when they weren't sexually appealing."

"I know, but she had both. I spoke about her just to illustrate a point, actually you have both too, that's why I was attracted to you in the first place, I still am."

Good, we're getting somewhere, I thought to myself.

"It's an excellent illustration of what you found wrong with me, why you got bored with me, I took the sex for granted, I never tried to spice it up, suggest anything new or different, but neither did you. What would you have suggested, or wanted me to suggest? Let's be perfectly frank, as explicit as we need be, please. Should my conversation have been more sexually suggestive, referred to sexual topics now and then, not with disapproval, perhaps with enjoyment, curiosity or outright approval?"

"Yes, occasionally, just enough to communicate that you weren't inhibited, that I could say or do whatever came into my head without the risk of being met with a disapproving frown."

"But I was truly inhibited, at least verbally, it was the way I was brought up. I didn't see anything wrong with it, but you're telling me I was mistaken."

"Yes, mistaken, not wrong."

"Isn't it the same thing in the end?"

"The effect is the same all right."

"When would you have liked me to talk like that? In bed, I suppose."

"Yes, mostly, sometimes not."

"I really wish now I hadn't been brought up in such an old-fashioned way."

"It wasn't your fault, but it is, was, a disadvantage."

"Was, not is, I intend to be better in future."

"Good, I'm glad to hear it."

"You know, I went to Capri trying to find you."

"That was a bit silly, wasn't it?"

"I thought you'd be there."

"I was, for a couple of days."

"And what about Maria? Where is she now? Back in your apartment?"

"That's what I've come to talk to you about. I asked her to leave. She moved out last week."

"Oh yes?" Did I really want to believe him?

"It just didn't work out. I missed you too much, if only you hadn't gone away for so long."

"How does Maria feel about this?"

"She's very upset, of course."

"Of course." I was delighted.

"In fact, I just met her for a drink. She knows it's definitely over. She was furious, like a mad woman. I finished my drink and came straight to you."

"It's a wonder she didn't hit you."

I got up to pour myself another drink. It was going to be very difficult to tell him that it was over for me too. It was the rejection that finished me, and this feeling of apprehension was deep-seated rage. I was shaking, but it wasn't because I wanted him, it was because I was trying to control my anger and disgust at him.

"Nicole, I'm feeling very sleepy. Do you mind if I lie down for a while? Don't pour me another drink."

Oh, that's brilliant. He's just going to crash on me.

"Go ahead, I'll wake you up in half an hour."

He went into the bedroom and I switched on the television. There was no way I was going to go into the bedroom with him.

An hour later I banged on the door. He didn't answer. I went in and found I couldn't wake him up. I panicked, I shook him, he didn't move.

The phone rang. I was startled and began to shake in sheer terror. I stumbled over to the phone and picked it up.

"Nicole, are you there?"

It was Patricia. Thank God it was only her.

"Nicole, answer me, I know you're there, answer me."

"Patricia, something awful has happened, awful."

"Are you all right? You sound terrible, what is it?"

"It's Michael, he's asleep on the bed and I can't wake him up, I'm so scared."

"Michael? He's there with you now?" she asked.

"Yes, he came round because he wanted to see me."

Maybe he's had a stroke or something. You'd better call an ambulance and get him taken to a hospital. Hang up and then dial 911, or is it 999?

Dial one and if that's not right dial the other, but get an ambulance quick. Call me back when the ambulance-men come, let me know what hospital they're taking him to and I'll meet you there."

I called the emergency number in the front of the telephone book, they took my address and said to stay there, they'd send over an ambulance right away, no more than ten minutes. I started to scream over the phone, then slammed the phone down.

I dimly remember what happened. I don't remember opening the door, but I must have done, the men came in with a stretcher, rolled Michael onto it and carried him out. I followed them and luckily didn't forget to ask them which hospital they were taking him too. I dashed back inside to phone Patricia, I was so distraught I couldn't remember her number, I had to look it up.

"Patricia, they've taken him, I'll get a taxi and go there?"

"Go where? Which hospital?"

I told her, then put the phone down, but couldn't decide whether to call a taxi or hope to pick one up on the street. I couldn't wait in the flat for a taxi to come, I'd get one on the street, I'd stop a police car if I had to and make them take me. It's all a blur after that, I arrived at the hospital's emergency admission, found Michael still lying on the stretcher on top of some kind of a trolley, still unconscious, with tubes of various kinds attached to his body, bottles hanging upside down dripping something into one of the tubes which had a needle at the end of it strapped to his arm. He looked ghastly, sick, but at least he was breathing.

A young man in a white coat with a stethoscope round his neck approached me, a doctor obviously, an intern or registrar I suppose.

"Are you Mrs Rodham?"

"How do you know his name?"

"He had a wallet, a driving licence. Are you his wife?"

"Yes, yes, I am." What the hell, who cares at this stage? "Has he had a stroke?"

"No evidence of that, nor of a coronary thrombosis either. Do you know if he was depressed?"

"No, why?"

"It looks at the moment more like an overdose, the lab results haven't come back yet, we'll know more then."

"An overdose of what?"

"Hard to say without the lab results, barbiturates, or benzodiazepines more likely, his breathing is normal. Possibly diazepam, valium."

Just then Patricia walked in, I left the doctor and ran over to her.

"Thank you for being here."

"What happened to Michael?"

I told her what the doctor had said to me.

"But what happened at your place? Why was he there anyway?"

I told her about Michael phoning me, saying he felt he owed me an explanation, how I had invited him to my place, what had happened there—well, not all that had happened there—and that he had fallen asleep and I couldn't wake him and I had called her.

"But the overdose, did he take it in your place or before he came over? Could they be wrong, you never said he was depressed or in any way suicidal?"

"He never was, I can't explain it. Do you mind if we don't talk about it now?"

"No, but it's weird all the same."

"Let's get out of here, Patricia, there's nothing we can do, hospitals give me the creeps."

We walked back. I told Patricia that he had met his former girlfriend before he came to the apartment and I thought that she must have drugged him, put something in his drink.

Patricia believed that's what happened, she kept insisting that it was the wife who must have done it. I phoned the hospital after we got home and they verified that it was an overdose. I knew Michael well enough to know that he would never think of suicide and he hated taking drugs of any kind. He used to lecture me when I would take half a valium if I couldn't sleep, so it must have been her. The newspapers were full of reports about date rapes and warnings about the drugs that were used. The drugs were obviously very quick-acting, especially with alcohol. I wondered if she'd tried to kill him or just to detain him.

The next morning Michael telephoned me. He was furious, in a rage, I was glad he hadn't come over, he was frightening and threatening.

"You've gone too far this time. I could have you thrown in jail, it's what you deserve, I could have been killed! I don't know if that's what you intended to do and I don't care now. I never want to see you or talk to you ever again, if you contact me I'll report all this to the police and I'll see to it that you're put in jail for a very long time. I'm warning you, I won't warn you again."

"But Michael, I didn't do anything at all," I said softly.

"Of course you did, you're an actress after all, you don't know the difference between truth and make-believe. Your never stop acting, it's second nature to you."

I couldn't believe he was accusing me of such a thing, it winded me. Why did he feel so hostile about my acting all of a sudden, as if that had anything to do with it? I knew he meant it, there was real hatred in his voice. What would come next I didn't know, but it couldn't be any worse.

I put the phone down slowly as if my soul was being disconnected from my body. I knew that he would always have a part of my soul, it was deep down in my being, and it was a day I will never forget. The silence was deafening. If he hadn't been so cruel in the first place and had told me in the beginning about our problems it wouldn't have been such a shock. But now he thought he had a real reason to be cruel. I couldn't believe that he would think I had drugged him. I knew it was time to move on and I hoped that it wasn't going to be too late to pick up my career.

I sat down at the kitchen table and stared straight ahead. A blackbird landed on the windowsill and we looked at each other. My father used to love feeding the blackbirds in our garden when I was a child and I suddenly thought that maybe this blackbird was my father's spirit coming to visit me and saying, "It's all right, Nicole, I am here for you, keep your chin up." It was just an eerie feeling. The tears started to come but luckily Patricia came into the room and the bird flew off the sill.

"Hi, Nicole, how are you feeling? Not so good, I guess."

"Michael just phoned from the hospital. He's OK."

"Well, that's a relief. Look here, I'm really sorry if I sounded unsympathetic last night, it's just that I have never been in love as much as that, I guess."

"And I hope you never are. Passion is destructive, jealous, obsessive and painful, I hope I never feel passion again."

Chapter Sixteen

I PICKED UP THE PHONE, the first time I had used it since Michael had shouted at me, I called Trevor. He was home, thank goodness.

"Trevor, you're back. That's great. How are you?"

"Much better, thanks. I've tried to reach you several times. Sorry I didn't come round to see you after the show, we had to get home, but congratulations. Of course we were overjoyed when you got the Oscar."

"Thanks a lot. I need to see you, Trevor, can we meet?"

"Of course."

We arranged to meet at the coffee shop at the National Film Theatre on the Embankment at four o'clock. Sitting on a bench overlooking the Thames we sipped our tea. He was wearing the same old green windbreaker he used to wear in Ipswich. He looked better, he said he was just getting back to his normal self. The wind was blowing papers all around us, we watched the boys on their skateboards, twisting and turning around the concourse.

He looked at me, fondly I thought, and took my hand.

"And how about you, Nicole?"

"I'm rather lost, I'm afraid. It's hard to know what to do next. I feel as if I've been hit over the head with a cricket bat. Why is our personal life so difficult to handle?" I told him the whole story about Michael, what had happened, the accusations, the agony over winning the Oscar.

"The only thing is work, honey."

"Yes, I know that, Trevor, but it's not that easy. Why do women always seem to suffer the most in a broken love affair? You don't hear or read very much about a man breaking down or staring into blankness because he's been rejected by the woman he loves."

"You may not hear or read about it, but I'm sure it happens. In general, men don't like to admit to being rejected, Nicole, they are less inclined to talk about their feelings. If they're hurt by someone their reaction is usually one of anger—they might swear and sound off, abuse the woman who hurt them but don't let on that they've been badly hurt."

"But women don't cut off a relationship in an abusive way like men do, and I doubt that men desperately pick up the phone only to put it down immediately in despair. And I don't imagine men agonise over the woman being in bed with someone else."

"Oh come on, Nicole, remember your Shakespeare, how about Othello when Iago excites his jealousy. Men are just as liable to become jealous as women are."

"Actually, Trevor, I don't believe that. Men don't dream of scenes where their former lover makes fun of them when in bed with another man."

"Who knows what men dream about?"

"They don't write novels about it, Trevor, they write about espionage, spies and murderers, adventure, danger of a physical kind, not about the fear of losing love, of not being loved, they are more resilient, less romantic, far more objective."

"What does Michael write about, Nicole, or did you never read anything he wrote?"

"I tried to, but it was a bit beyond me, mostly about the financial world, Wall Street, insider trading, scams, dishonesty, never about women, their sexual and romantic disappointments and anguish."

"Did you ever talk to him along those lines about his writing?"

"Yes, I asked him to explain it all to me, where he got his ideas from, who was he writing for, why he chose the plots he did. It became obvious to him that I wasn't interested in the stuff he wrote about, not romantic enough, I suppose. I told him he wouldn't want to read any novel I wrote because he wouldn't understand it, wouldn't feel it, wouldn't even be interested in it."

"You don't know that, men read books written by women, I imagine."

"Women's books are mostly read by women. Now there's a thought, novels about women, about love and romance written by men would certainly be read by women. But I'm beginning to bore you, I see. What are you going to do next, Trevor?"

"I'm going back to work next month, I'm doing a play at Stratford." He picked up a stone and threw it at the pigeons who were bothering us.

"That's brilliant," I said. "I couldn't be more happy for you. What is it?"

"We are doing *Love's Labour's Lost*, I play Ferdinand."

"Who's directing?"

"Andrew, of course. He is so much in demand, Nicole, he wants to stay in Stratford."

"I don't blame him, he keeps that company going."

"Tell you what. Would you like me to see if there's anything for you?"

"Why, would you?"

"Yes, of course, I should have thought of it before. I'll call him tonight."

"But surely he will have cast it by now?"

"Not necessarily."

"I worked with him when he was just starting out, so he knows my work."

"Well, that's good to know."

We got up, then walked across the bridge and stopped to say goodbye at the bus stop. The following morning he phoned saying he had talked to Andrew who had said he was surprised to hear I would be interested. "I gave him your phone number, I think you'll hear from him."

It all happened very quickly. Some people might have called it serendipity, but that's really how it was, a matter of being in the right place at the right time, as every actor will tell you, or knowing the right people, Trevor for example. First the phone call, then the interview. It was good to see Andrew again after such a long time. He was absolutely wonderful, and I was hired. He said he was surprised that I wasn't back in Hollywood. "Anthony Hopkins seems to love it." He laughed.

Peter and I drove up to Stratford together. We had a picnic on the way. I'd brought some fresh French bread, some ham and cheese, boiled eggs, tomatoes, cucumbers and a bottle of wine. Warwickshire is the closest to a picture postcard of pastoral England. It is Shakespeare country with all the old oak trees overhanging the road. As we pulled into Stratford the white swans were drifting down the River Avon, the weeping willow trees at the water's edge casting shadows across the water, the bulrushes swaying lazily in the breeze. The scene was the same as it was when I first went there as a student.

I was exuberant with the thought of being able to work there in such a stimulating environment with all the people who were my contemporaries and some old friends. I am never happier than when I'm in a theatre. Peter made plans to stay in Stratford with me, saying that he could write here while I was at rehearsals just as well as in London. I knew that all along Michael hadn't really understood my love of acting, whereas Peter did, and didn't feel threatened by it.

I had to realise that men conceal their thoughts. I believe that without love there is no jealousy, or if there's no jealousy there is no love. When I went to LA Michael let me think he would miss me but he wasn't jealous—well, he wasn't jealous in a sexual way but maybe he resented my leaving for a part in a movie. All that was past, Peter was the centre of my life now. His books interested me, they were mostly biographies of men and women who achieved great things. He wrote about their marriages and affairs too, but said their inner anguish could never be explained by a biographer unless it was relevant to what he was achieving.

Peter was so much better for me than anyone else. He was like a rock and it was what I needed. His wisdom was almost like that of a clergyman—the village variety. Except that he was urbane and witty with it. His quick wit was equal to Michael's and we were both now more appreciative of each other. I had been abused by Michael, and I had only just realised it. He would have found out from the doctor's report—for it would have confirmed the time that he'd been given the drugs, which was much earlier in the afternoon—that I couldn't have drugged him, so my concern that he would bad-mouth me to his friends was over. He never even called to apologise.

The lines I had to learn for the play were easy to memorise, I knew most of the play anyway, as I had played it before. Each evening Peter would hear my lines, then often suggest we eat down by the river. We took bread for the swans and walked along the riverbank. I began to feel normal again. The massive old trees were friendly companions standing like guardsmen, especially the ones leading up to the church where Shakespeare is supposed to be buried. The timelessness of the river running by the theatre was comforting. It would still be there two hundred years from now. Shakespeare will still be being played, the young theatre-goers will see their first Hamlet or Romeo and Juliet, which they might remember for the rest of their lives.

Peter was an angel. He can never stir up the same emotional madness in me that Michael did, but it's better this way. He loves me very much, I know that, perhaps because he had been through so many heart-breaks himself he doesn't want to be exposed to any more. He has settled for me. Perhaps I'm not any different, I've resigned myself to having lost the love of my life, Michael, and I need someone, so I too have settled for Peter. But I do love him, we can make one another happy, maybe not ecstatically happy, but as happy as we deserve to be. In the end that's possibly all that one can hope for, because the other kind of love doesn't last.

Life is all a matter of chance and where chance takes you. I remember flicking stones across a nearby lake once, and I thought that life was like one of those stones; you flick some across the water and they keep the momentum going and one jump leads to another and then another which leads to great opportunities, but some of the stones just sink to the bottom. And so it is in life, if you're lucky you get one that makes it across, then you can use these little jumps to go on to inspire people to dream. I was ready to try. Peter convinced me you have to take every little jump, that is, every break that comes along, not knowing the consequences. It's up to the person you love to stand by you even if you can never tell if they will or not, and if they won't you're better off without them.

OTHER BOOKS BY ELIZABETH SHARLAND

Passionate Pilgrimages . . . from Chopin to Coward
Love From Shakespeare to Coward
From Shakespeare to Coward
The British on Broadway
A Theatrical Feast of London
A Theatrical Feast of New York
A Theatrical Feast of Paris
The Best Actress (Novel)
Blue Harbour Revisited . . . A Gift from Noel Coward (Novel)
Behind the Doors of Notorious Covent Garden
On the Riviera
The Private Life of George Bernard Shaw

www.sharland.com